Herm's Secret

by

Kate O'Hearn

Circaidy

Herm's Secret

by Kate O'Hearn

Copyright Information

Printed in the UK
by Berforts Group Ltd

ISBN 978-1-906451-31-8

Published by Circaidy Gregory Press
Creative Media Centre,
45 Robertson St, Hastings,
Sussex TN34 1HL

www.circaidygregory.co.uk
Independent Books for Independent Readers

Joy Chan ~ Illustrator

Joy Chan gained a Pass with Distinction for her MA and 1st Class BA (Hons) Degree in Illustration. Since then she has been working as a designer at The Royal Wolverhampton School. She has experience in producing a wide range of work, including traditional painting, drawing, textile, illustration for both fashion and children's books, posters, magazines and leaflets.

She was born in Hong Kong, moved to the UK when she was 14 and has lived here ever since. Working at the school and seeing the children every day inspired her to illustrate a children's book based on a Merry-Go-Round story she created herself. This is still a work in progress, which she hopes to get published in the near future.

If you are interested in her work, please visit her websites:
www.joychan.net
www.joychan.co.uk
email contact@joychan.net

Author's Note

Whales are the very heart of the ocean. Please end the senseless
slaughter and ask whaling countries to stop!
Remember, whales are people too...

~~~

They say the sea is cold, but the sea contains
the hottest blood of all, and the wildest, the most urgent.

All the whales in the wider deeps, hot are they, as they urge
on and on, and dive beneath the icebergs.
The right whales, the sperm-whales, the hammer-heads, the killers
there they blow, there they blow, hot wild white breath out of
the sea!

from
'Whales Weep Not' by D. H. Lawrence

Herm's Secret

Chapter 1

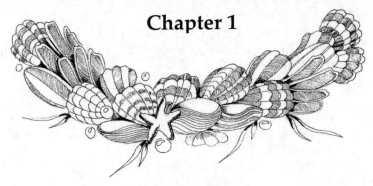

3 years ago

As dawn started to break on the eastern horizon, Caspian floated peacefully at the ocean's calm surface. Sandwiched between his mother and father, he waited patiently for his grandfather to rise and call them forward to begin the day.

When Andori arrived, he took a deep, cleansing breath and turned towards the rising sun. He raised his head in the air and started to sing.

Lost in the sweet, haunting melody, Caspian felt the same peace he felt every morning as he sang along with the fourteen other members of his family. He looked over to his grandfather where he saw the elderly mermaid, Undine, seated contently on his back. Her eyes were closed and she was trying to sing along with the family's song as best she could.

Suddenly the peace was shattered by a warning cry from Caspian's uncle.

"Whalers!" Zenith shouted. "Everyone get beneath the surface!"

Before diving, Caspian stole a quick look at the swiftly approaching hunters. At the bow of the factory whaling ship he saw a man standing before the large harpoon gun. It was pointed right at them. An instant later, he heard the whooshing sound of the gun as the whaler opened fire.

Caspian felt the first deadly harpoon sail directly over his back. It missed him by a breath. But then he heard an agonized scream and realised he hadn't been the target.

"Father!" He cried. Caspian swam closer and saw the end of the deadly harpoon sticking out of his father's side as the tow line

1

connecting it to the whaling ship was pulled taut. While the water around him turned red with blood, Caspian heard his father calling out to the elderly mermaid's daughter, Colleen.

A heartbeat later, another harpoon struck Caspian's mother. Her howls of pain and terror mixed with his father's as both his parents fought to survive.

"Mother, no!" Caspian shouted. He didn't know what to do; he was crippled with fear. Beside him, his father continued to howl in pain and thrash in the water. But on his other side, his mother became silent and still.

He swam over to her. But even before he touched her side, he knew it was too late. His mother was dead.

"Caspian, dive!" ordered his uncle Zenith. "Everyone, get down beneath the surface!"

Unable to think, Caspian followed his uncle's orders and dove beneath the waves. Above him he could still hear his father's screams as he thrashed and twisted against the tow line that connected him to the ship.

Before the rest of Caspian's family could submerge themselves, the whaler's murderous gun fired again and again. Three more members were struck by deadly harpoons. Their howls filled the air as their blood poured into the ocean.

"Father, no!" Zenith suddenly cried.

"Andori and Undine have been hit!" shouted another.

Caspian and two of his cousins rose to the surface. They were met by a sight more horrible than anything they had ever imagined. Their grandfather had been shot by a harpoon, but before it entered Andori, it had passed through Undine's tail and impaled the elderly mermaid to his back. In his dying agony, Andori rolled in the water. As the harpoon line coiled cruelly around his massive body, Undine was caught in the line and crushed to his side.

Struck silent by the sight, Caspian and the others watched the terrible scene playing out before their eyes as one by one their family was slaughtered by whalers.

"Boys, get over here," cried Zenith. "Help me with Zephyr!"

Caspian watched his uncle struggling to support his father's head at the surface to keep him breathing. But as he arrived to help, there was a loud whine and then grinding sound coming from the whaling ship.

"They're lowering the collection ramp!" Zenith panicked. "We must hurry. If they get everyone on board, we'll lose them forever!"

Caspian couldn't turn away from the murderous whaling ship. The blood-streaked ramp coming down into the water looked like a terrible, yawning mouth preparing to eat.

"Caspian," his cousin Coral shouted. "Come on! Help us before they haul your father on board. He's still alive and needs you!"

Tearing his gaze from the awful ship, Caspian concentrated on his unconscious father. Zenith was still at his head, while the other survivors were gathering around his wound.

"All of you," Zenith ordered, "use all your weight. Push down on Zephyr's tail. The tow line is still connected. If we push hard enough, it will tear the harpoon out of his side and we can free him."

As if in a dream, Caspian joined the others pressing their massive heads against Zephyr's side, forcing him deeper into the water. With the ship's tow line drawing tighter, they watched the shaft of the harpoon slowly cutting its way out of his wound. In one final, tearing pop, the deadly, three-pronged point was torn free of Caspian's father.

Once it was gone, two members of the family remained with the stricken whale to keep his head above the surface. The seven other survivors moved to free the remaining wounded members of the family: those who were still alive, but tethered to the whaling ship.

Caspian went over to help free a younger cousin. But as he worked, he caught sight of his mother's body being drawn out of the water and hauled up the ship's tall ramp.

"No!" he cried. Leaving his cousin, he swam over to the ramp and leaped onto the end, trying to catch hold of her. He couldn't let them take her. Not his mother. But he was too late; she was beyond his reach.

Sliding back into the water, Caspian howled in unbearable grief as he watched the faces of the men at the top of the ramp. Holding their vicious cutting blades, waiting to receive his mother's body...

Chapter 2

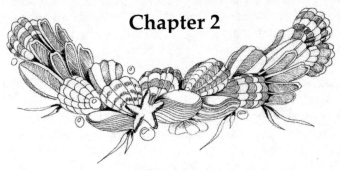

Present

Come to Herm now or you'll die...

The memory of her uncle's warning haunted Lori as she lay curled against the cold window of the Boeing 757 on its transatlantic flight from Toronto to London. She couldn't sleep. There were just too many disturbing questions spinning around in her head. Sitting up, she angrily punched her pillow, adjusted her blanket and struggled to find a comfortable position.

"You all right, kiddo?"

Lori turned to the concerned face of her father. His eyes betrayed what the rest of him was trying very hard to conceal. He was frightened for her.

"I'm fine thanks," she said, a little too eagerly.

He nodded, but wasn't convinced. "Then settle down and try to relax. We've got a long flight ahead of us."

When he looked away, Lori studied him a moment longer. He was trying desperately to believe in her, to convince himself that his thirteen-year-old daughter wasn't going insane. But it was difficult. Even Lori was finding it hard to believe she wasn't crazy. And she hadn't told him everything that was happening.

Letting her eyes drift away from her father, she looked across the aisle to her aunt Anne, who was seated between her two older brothers. Her seat was reclined and she was asleep. Danny was curled against his window and snoring. Lori's oldest brother, Eddie, was awake. Feeling her eyes on him, he turned to her and smiled brightly. "Hey, Bug, won't be long now."

5

Lori offered a weak smile back and nodded. Her brothers and aunt had no idea what was happening or why they were suddenly flying to England. Back when it all started, her father had thought it best not to tell them too much until they got to the bottom of the mystery. All they knew was that their mother's brother had been in touch and sent them free tickets to come to Herm, a small island in the Channel Isles.

They were blissfully ignorant of the strange voice that had suddenly arrived in Lori's head; with its dire warning that if she didn't contact her mysterious uncle on Herm she would soon die.

She turned back to the small window and gazed out at the night sky. *Are you there*? She silently called with her mind. *Can you hear me?*

There was only silence. The mysterious presence was there; somehow she could feel it. She just couldn't reach it with words at the moment. But even when she could hear it, it was never very clear.

Shivering from nerves and not the cold window, she pulled the airline blanket tighter around herself, lay her head down and tried to sleep.

Lor-lie, wake up!

Lori woke with a jolt; she hadn't been aware that she'd drifted off. Sitting up, she suddenly felt a sharp cramp cutting through her lower abdomen. She glanced over to her father. His seat was reclined and he was snoring softly.

Lor-lie, can you hear me?

The voice was back, booming in her head – louder and clearer than ever before. "Yes – yes, I can," she answered.

Thank heavens!

"Who are you?"

I'm Caspian.

Lori was terrified. The strange voice now had a name. This confirmed her worst fears. She was well and truly insane. "Caspian?" She looked around the small cabin to see if anyone was watching her. "Where are you?"

I'm here. But I am there with you too. We are connected.

"I don't understand," she whispered back. "You're just a voice in my head. You're not real!"

6

Lor-lie, I promise, I am as real as you are. In time you'll see for yourself. But right now there's no time to explain. Just listen to me. It's starting. You must be extra careful now. You are in such terrible danger. You mustn't let yourself get wet. Do you hear me? You can drink, but for heaven's sake, don't get wet! As soon as you arrive at the airport, tell your uncle Jeremy that I told you it's starting. He'll know what to do. The time of your Trial has arrived. Tell him Lor-lie. Your Trial has arrived.

"What's arrived? What trial?" Lori pleaded as fear rose in her voice. "I haven't done anything wrong, why am I on trial?"

It's not that kind of trial. It's more like an ordeal. We just call it the Trial.

"But what is it?"

The change. You are changing Lor-lie.

"Into what?"

Before Caspian could answer, another fierce cramp tore through her lower abdomen and down her legs. Lori also became aware of the terrible ache in her feet and rising nausea in her stomach.

"Lori? What's going on?"

Her father was awake and staring intently at her.

Every time Lori had spoken to her father about the strange voice, he'd become upset and angry. In the tight confines of the aeroplane, and feeling as she did, she couldn't bear it.

Instead she rubbed at her legs and said, "I really don't feel well. The pain starts in my stomach but then shoots all the way down to my feet." Suddenly she felt she was about to be violently ill. "Dad, let me out, I'm going to be sick!"

Her father stood and let her out of her seat. Lori raced down the long aisle to the toilet. Falling to her knees, she started to throw up. Before she'd finished, she felt her father's reassuring presence behind her.

"It's all right, I'm here," he gently offered, as he held back her long auburn hair. "Get it all out of your system."

When she'd emptied her stomach, Lori struggled to stand again. "Dad, I don't know what's wrong. I feel awful. I'm aching everywhere. Even my feet are killing me."

Her father reached past her and turned on the cold tap. "Here, throw some water on your face."

Don't do it Lor-lie! For heaven's sake, don't do it!

7

A deep frown cut across her brow. "Why?"

"Because it'll help," her father offered.

Lori looked up to him. "I wasn't talking to you. I was speaking to Caspian."

"Who's Caspian?"

Lori shrugged apologetically. "I'm sorry Dad, but the voice is back. He said his name is Caspian and that I shouldn't get wet."

"He?" her father said fearfully. "The voice in your head is a man?"

"I–I don't know," Lori answered, feeling she was about to be sick again. "I think so." She concentrated on the voice. "Caspian, why can't I get wet?"

If you do you will change. And there on the aeroplane, the change will kill you.

Lori looked desperately up to her father and shut off the tap. "He says if I get wet, I'll die."

Her father's concern turned to anger. Shaking his head, he looked at her reflection in the mirror. "What is going on here, Lori? Who is this Caspian? Why can you hear him when no one else can?"

"I don't know. I don't know anything any more. There's this weird voice in my head that says I'm going to die. Uncle Jeremy won't tell us anything but sends us plane tickets. I'm so sorry I called him." Tears rushed to her eyes. "We shouldn't be here, Dad. You should be at home in bed and I should be in an asylum with all the other crazy people."

He pulled her into a tight embrace. "Oh baby, it's not your fault and you don't belong in an asylum. I'm so sorry. I shouldn't have raised my voice. I'm just frustrated by what's going on."

"Me too," Lori agreed. "I keep getting the feeling that something really awful is about to happen. But I don't know what, and no one will tell me –"

"Brian, what's wrong?"

Lori's aunt Anne was standing at the door.

"Our girl's got a bit of a bug," her father explained. "She's not feeling well."

"Let me take a look," Anne said. "You go back to the boys and let them know everything is all right."

Backing out of the toilet, Lori's father said, "Just in case, don't turn on the water again. Not until we get to the bottom of this."

"I won't," Lori promised. When she was alone with her aunt, she sat down on the edge of the toilet.

"What's all this about water?" aunt Anne asked as she put her hand on Lori's forehead.

"Nothing – "

In that instant, Lori ached to tell her aunt everything. But her father had warned her not to. Anne was a surgeon. She only believed in things that could be seen, touched or analysed. If they told her about the strange voice, Anne would insist it was puberty playing tricks on her and refuse to come. But her father wanted a doctor along just in case something really was happening.

"Well," Anne said, as she finished her brief examination, "Your temperature is a bit high. I'd say you've got yourself a fever."

"But I never get sick."

"I know," Anne agreed. "But it's probably the excitement of the trip. Stay here for a moment. I'm going to see if I can scrounge up some Paracetamol from the flight attendant."

Left alone sitting on the toilet, Lori felt fresh waves of cramps starting in her stomach and flowing down her legs. "What's wrong with me?"

It's the Trial, Caspian softly called. *I'm sorry it hurts so much. If I could take the pain away, I would. But I can't. All I can do is say I'm here for you.*

Lori heard the caring in his deep gentle voice, but it didn't help. Caspian and his cryptic warnings of death terrified her. "Who are you?"

The one who loves you, Caspian responded. *Lor-lie I know this is hard for you to believe and that you're very frightened of me right now. But you don't have to be. You and I are joined. We have been connected all our lives. And I know you've only just started to hear me, but I've always heard you. We've grown up together. I've heard you like my father hears your mother, or like my cousin Coral hears your cousin Miranda. One day my sons will hear your daughters.*

"Daughters?" Lori repeated. "What are you talking about? I don't have any daughters. I'm only thirteen. I'm just a kid."

Caspian chuckled lightly; *I don't have any sons either. I'm just a kid too.*

Lori shook her head. "I still don't understand. What's happening to me? Why can we hear each other?"

Because, Lor-lie, you are unique. I wish I could tell you more, but your mother says I should wait until after the Trial.

"Wait a minute," Lori said. "That's the second time you've mentioned my mother. What's she got to do with this? She's gone. She ran away from us years ago and hasn't been back."

Lori heard a sound that might have been a long, deep sigh. *Lor-lie, you've been angry with your mother for so long, but you've been wrong. She didn't abandon you and your family. Your mother is trapped in a terrible, dark place. She's been living a life of misery in unbearable loneliness, praying for the time of your Trial when I could finally reach you and tell you what happened to her.*

Lori's head was starting to spin. Everything was happening too fast. She frowned. "No, you're lying. She ran away. She told us she was going on a work conference. But there was no conference. When Dad called the police, they tracked down her flight to Africa. She left us alone and didn't come back. So don't tell me you can talk to her because I know you can't!"

Lor-Lie, please believe me. What you thought happened to your mother was wrong. She is trapped and has been waiting for the day when you can finally free her.

"Free her from what? Where is she trapped?"

I know you are anxious, Caspian said gently, *we all are. But this isn't the time to tell you. Concentrate on yourself first. Just get to Herm and complete the Trial. Then we will tell you everything.*

This was getting her nowhere. "Well, if you won't tell me where she is, will you at least tell me what the Trial is?"

The Trial is when you will become your true self.

"What's that supposed to mean?" Lori winced as a fresh wave of cramps ran down her legs.

Please Lor-lie, forget everything else and try to relax. Tomorrow is going to be a very special day.

Lori crossed her arms over her chest. "You know, for a mysterious voice, you're not very helpful!"

In response, she heard Caspian chuckling lightly.

The return of her aunt cut off further conversation. "Here you go, sweetheart." She held out two tablets. "These should help with the pain and bring your temperature back down."

Lori took the pills and followed her aunt back to her seat.

"You all right, Bug?" her brother, Eddie, quietly asked.

"She's fine," her aunt answered. "Just a small case of airsickness."

When she was seated, her father leaned closer to her. "Really, how are you?"

"Truth?" Lori asked. When he nodded, she said, "I feel rotten."

"I'm so sorry. Hopefully you'll feel better by the time we arrive."

Lori nodded and settled back down to rest. Caspian said she would understand everything tomorrow. All she could do now was wait.

Several hours later, Lori woke. The pain in her stomach and legs was greatly diminished. Activity in the cabin was picking up and breakfast was being served.

She yawned, and gazed out the window. The sun was well up above the aeroplane, but beneath them dark thunderheads blocked their view of the sea.

"Looks like there's a big storm beneath us," she said to her father.

He leaned over and peered out the window. "The news did say London would be rainy all week."

Lor-lie, you must be very careful! Caspian suddenly warned. *Don't let yourself get wet. It will kill you if you do!*

Lori's expression darkened and she felt herself shivering. It was starting again.

"What is it?" her father asked.

"It's Caspian. He keeps saying I'll die if I get wet."

"What is it with him, you and water?" her father demanded. "What's so dangerous about it?"

"He won't tell me," Lori said. "He said we'll find out when we get to Herm. But that I shouldn't get wet before then."

"I don't like this, Lori. What's all the mystery about? Why can't he just come out and say what's going on?"

She shook her head. "I don't know. He just says that we've got to talk to Jeremy."

"Oh don't you worry about that," her father said darkly, "we'll talk to your uncle all right. Then maybe we'll find out what is going on."

Above them, the seatbelt sign burst to life as the captain's voice came over the speaker and announced that they were approaching Gatwick Airport.

"We're starting our descent," her father offered, as he reached out and took her hand. "It won't be long now."

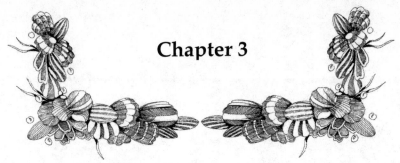

Chapter 3

"Come on, I won't hurt you."

Luc Robichaud held up a piece of apple to the nervous parrot. "Please, come and see; it's very sweet and good."

Slowly, hesitantly, the powdery-blue bird crept down its perch toward the treat.

"That's right, good boy; this is all for you."

Luc smiled as the bird moved closer. It stopped just short of his outstretched hand and cautiously took hold of the apple in its large, sharp beak.

"Luc, stop!"

The sudden noise caused the parrot to drop the apple and screech in terror as it flew wildly across the large aviary.

"Get out of there this instant!"

Luc looked at his father's furious face as he quietly left the walk-in cage.

Andre Robichaud stormed forward and caught hold of Luc's arm. He squeezed it painfully and shouted, "How many times must I tell you to stay out of there? Do you have any idea how dangerous that was?"

"He wouldn't hurt me, Papa," Luc said. "You saw, he took the apple from me."

"I'm not concerned about you," his father said furiously. "Do you have any idea how precious that bird is to me and what you could be exposing him to? Luc, that parrot is the very last of its kind from the wild. It cost me a fortune to get him. I won't have you contaminating his cage. If you can't agree to that, I'll send you back to school right now and you can finish your term break there. Do you understand me?"

To stress his point, Luc's father tightened his grip on his arm and shook him violently. "Do you understand me?" he demanded.

"Yes, Papa, I understand," Luc said. "The bird is precious. I will stay away from him."

Luc's father held on to his arm a moment longer. He shook his head and sighed tiredly. "Why must you always make my life so

14

difficult? Tell me, Luc, what should I do to make you understand the importance of this collection?"

"I do understand," Luc mumbled. "Your collection is the most precious thing in the world to you."

"Yes, it is," his father agreed. "I have spent half my life gathering these rare species together. Don't you realise what you are seeing in here?"

"Yes Papa," Luc replied. "It's your collection."

"It is more than that," his father responded. "The true importance of any collection lies in possessing the only one of a kind." He pointed at the terrified parrot. "Like this blue bird here. The Spix macaw. It is now completely extinct in the wild. This bird was the very last wild specimen and I don't want him touched, tamed or infected."

Drawing Luc away from the huge cage, his father took him into another room of the private zoo. "And here is another specimen that is officially extinct; the Tasmanian wolf. It was last seen in the 1930s. There have been reports of other sightings, and I have my men out searching, but until they find more, this one too is the last of its kind, making it all the more precious to me."

Luc looked at the sad, strange animal endlessly pacing the confines of its cage. It looked like something nature couldn't decide on – whether to make it a wolf or a tiger. Instead, it ended up looking a bit like both and a lot like neither.

"Papa, I don't understand," he said hesitantly. "Why must you always own the last of a kind? Wouldn't it be better to let others know these exist? Maybe they could do something to bring them back from extinction?"

Andre Robichaud turned dark, piercing eyes on his son. "You have disappointed me yet again. After all these years, you still do not understand. What value would all of these animals have for me if they could be brought back from extinction?"

Luc said nothing, but shrugged.

"None. I would no longer have the very last. Believe me; I will not share my precious collection with anyone. They are mine and mine alone. Possession is power. I possess these things; therefore I hold the power over them. The life and death of entire species rests with me. It is my privilege and my right."

15

Luc listened to his father and felt a shiver start down his spine. "But Papa, what kind of life is this for these animals? They're always locked in cages, never smelling fresh air or going outside. It's just not fair."

"Fair?" his father shot. "Luc, these animals have never had it so good. They get the best food, clean conditions and protection from predators, hunting and diseases. What more do they need?"

"They need their freedom, Papa. They should be out in the wild. Not locked away."

A dark expression rose on his father's face. "You sound more like your mother every day."

That was meant as an insult. Finally his father calmed down and rested a hand on his shoulder. "Luc, I must be your role model, not your mother. Look around you. I have attained everything I have ever dreamed of. Your mother had nothing until the day I found her. And one day, all of this will be yours. You must be prepared for when that time comes."

His father started to direct him away. "Now, come along, I have just had a special delivery and I want you to see it."

As they passed through another section of the private zoo, Luc stopped. This area had remained empty all of Luc's fifteen years. It held the biggest aquarium he had ever seen: larger even than the ones in marine parks that held killer whales. The glass and steel-framed walls climbed high into the air, and also went deep underground to where there was a private viewing area built into a chamber far beneath the estate. The aquarium was filled with sea water and decorated with exotic sea plants, rocks and coral, but held nothing else.

"Papa," Luc cautiously asked, "What goes in here?"

Throughout the years, Luc had asked his father that very same question countless times and never received an answer.

At first his father said nothing. Then he looked at the tank and sighed. "There are things in the sea, more precious than can ever be imagined on land. When that tank finally holds its intended occupants then, and only then, will my collection be complete. Now come along."

Luc knew better than to press further. Instead he silently followed his father away from the zoo and back into the main complex of the huge estate. When they reached the spacious front foyer, he saw several of his father's men surrounding a pair of delivery men. They were all gathered before a large packing crate.

At their approach, his father's men bowed their heads and nodded respectfully.

"This is it?" Andre Robichaud demanded.

"Yes, Monsieur," one of the delivery men said. "It is delivered as you ordered."

"Very good, open it up."

Luc stood beside his father as the crate was carefully opened. Soon the men were pulling out a package and peeling back the covers to reveal a beautiful Van Gogh painting.

"I bought this at auction in Paris last week," his father explained. "I won't tell you how much it cost but as I have already explained, nothing worth having comes cheaply."

Luc looked at the painting and saw its beauty but he still couldn't understand his father's obsession with collecting unusual pieces of art or animals.

"I have the perfect spot for you, my friend," his father said as he received the painting. Without a backward glance, he rudely called to his men, "Pay those men and get them out of here."

Luc trailed behind his father as they made their way though the huge mansion. "Where are you going to hang it," he finally asked.

"In my study," his father answered.

Luc felt a flutter of excitement. He'd not been allowed in the study since he was young. He kept close to his father and hoped he would finally see what was kept in the mysterious room.

When they approached the heavy oak double doors, his father handed over the painting. "Don't drop it," he warned, as he fished the keys from his pocket.

As the double doors opened, Luc anxiously peered in. The room was richly decorated and furnished with beautiful, dark antiques. A large grandfather clock was ticking softly in the corner. A thick, Oriental rug lay across most of the hardwood floor. The walls were covered in tall bookshelves that were filled with first editions. But as far as he could see, the study didn't hold anything unusual enough to explain why he was never allowed inside. Then his breath caught in his throat as his eyes settled on the large painting hanging behind his father's ornate, antique desk.

It was a portrait of a beautiful woman. She had rich, dark auburn hair hanging long and wavy down her bare shoulders, stunning, electric blue eyes in a smooth, alabaster face. But looking into those eyes, Luc could see heavy sadness resting there.

"Mother," he finally muttered.

Forgetting his father, Luc placed the Van Gogh down on a studded leather chair and walked over to the painting.

Until this moment, Luc hadn't been able to remember anything of his mother. She'd left when he was just a young boy. But as he studied the fine features in the beautiful face in the portrait, flashes of memories long buried came rushing back to the surface. Her smile and how she always smelled of flowers. Her sweet laughter, filling the air and making him feel safe and loved – but then memories of other sounds awoke: the sound of her crying late at night, and the terrible fights between his parents. And then the bruises on his mother's face that she would try so hard to conceal. Suddenly he remembered all the fear and violence of his early childhood.

"Papa, why didn't you tell me you had this portrait," Luc finally asked. "You've removed every other trace of mother from the house. I haven't seen her since I was young."

His father became greatly disturbed and tried to lead Luc away from the portrait. "Luc, your mother is gone," he said. "There was no point in keeping her pictures around. It would only have caused you pain."

"But I don't have anything to remember her by," Luc said, refusing to turn away from the portrait.

"What do you need to remember? She was here and then she left. Your mother never cared for you. I was the one who stayed. I am the one paying for your education, not her. She doesn't deserve your love and devotion."

"But –"

"No Luc," his father insisted, as he forcibly turned him from the portrait. "It is time you accepted the truth. Your mother was a weak woman. Believe me, we are both better off without her."

Luc studied his father's face as he looked at the painting. His expression contradicted his words. He still loved the woman in the portrait.

"But if she was so bad, why do you still have that."

18

Finally, his father drew his eyes from the portrait. "That is none of your business."

The sudden ringing of the telephone ended their conversation. When his father answered it, he looked up at Luc. "Close the door behind you when you leave."

Knowing how swiftly his father's mood could change, Luc decided it was safest to obey.

"Luc," his father called after him. "I don't want to catch you in here again. The past is gone, finished. There is nothing for you to find in here."

"Yes, Papa," Luc said softly, as he left the study.

As he closed the double doors behind him, Luc heard his father start shouting into the telephone, "I don't care what they want them for or who they kill with them. That's not our concern. If they have the money, we ship the merchandise. Do you understand me? If you can't do that, then we have a problem. And you know how I solve my problems –"

Luc didn't wait to hear more. It had taken him years to discover the truth about his father and what he did for a living. But once he had, Luc wished more than anything that he didn't know the truth.

Andre Robichaud was an illegal arms dealer. A criminal.

For so long, his father's brutal reputation had been the cause of countless fights at the private schools Luc attended. He'd struggled for years to defend his father, until he finally discovered the truth. That dreadful revelation was also what kept him from having friends. Every time he started to form a friendship, the other person would learn who his father was and stop talking to him. Everyone was frightened of Andre Robichaud, and frightened of knowing his son, too. So Luc lived his life in silent loneliness, never finding anyone he could talk to, or share his most private thoughts with.

As Luc moved through the large house, more lost memories of his mother rose to the surface. There was something about the study – something terrible. But the more he tried to catch hold of a solid memory, the faster it would slip away again like water through his fingers.

Chapter 4

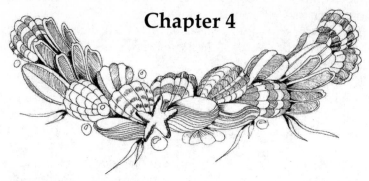

Gatwick Airport was huge.

Lori's family cleared customs, collected their luggage and headed towards the arrivals lounge.

"How are we ever going to find Jeremy in all of this?" Danny miserably complained, walking between Lori and Eddie. "This place is too big."

"Jeremy said he'll be carrying a sign with our name on it," Eddie explained as he pushed the trolley loaded with their luggage.

Scanning the crowd, Lori saw a man with a sign. Then another. And another. Finally she turned to her father. "Dad, they're all holding up signs."

Her father suddenly pointed. "Yes, but only one of them says Watson on it. Over there, look – "

Lori followed her father's finger. "Wow!" she cried. "He's huge!"

"Wouldn't want to get him mad, eh Bug," Eddie teased, as they watched their uncle waving his arms frantically in the air to catch their attention.

Jeremy Muldoon was a giant. Standing nearly seven feet tall, he had the body of a wrestler. Beside him, Lori saw a boy about Danny's age with fine, blonde hair. He was already very tall, but string-bean thin. Beside him was a girl. Lori realised she could have been her twin sister. They were almost the same height and had the same dark, reddish hair and freckles. But as Lori approached, she saw that the girl had bright green eyes, while hers were blue.

"My God, I'd know that face anywhere!" Jeremy cried as he ran forward and scooped Lori up in his tree-trunk arms. "Child, you're the spitting image of your mum! Lord, are we glad to see you." He put Lori down and opened his arms to embrace Eddie and Danny. "We're glad to see all of you."

"We didn't think we'd ever meet you," said the blonde boy, shyly stepping forward. "Hi, I'm Aaron."

"Lori, Eddie and Danny," Jeremy said, "these are your cousins. This is Aaron and here is Miranda."

Lori's father offered his hand. "Jeremy, I'm Brian Watson, it's nice to meet you."

As Jeremy accepted the outstretched hand, he pulled Lori's father into a warm embrace. "Glad to meet you too, Brian. Wish I could say we've heard all about you, but we haven't. All we knew was that you existed. Colleen would never tell us where you were or how we could get in touch. One thing we did know for certain was that she loved you and was very happy."

"Well, you know more than I did," Lori's father said. "She told me she didn't have any family and that she was an orphan."

"I'm sure she had her reasons," Jeremy said, cryptically. Then his eyes came to rest on Anne and he smiled again. "And who have we got here?"

"This is my sister, Anne," Lori's father explained. "She's a doctor. I wanted her to come along with us. You know, just in case."

"We've got a doctor in the family?" Jeremy said. "Thank heavens. It's about time."

Lori watched her aunt's face turn red with a blush as she was introduced to Jeremy. But then she turned to her brother. "Just in case what?"

"Nothing," Lori's father said.

As her family chatted, Lori could hear Caspian's excited voice in the distance. She could also feel his emotions. But there was a definite edge to them. Something was seriously wrong.

"Why are we all standing around here?" Jeremy finally said, laughing and slapping Eddie playfully on the back with a blow that nearly knocked him over. "You must be thirsty and hungry after your long flight. How about we find ourselves somewhere to grab a snack? Our flight to Guernsey doesn't leave for a couple of hours yet. From there, we'll take a ferry to Herm. So we've got some time to get to know each other better."

Lori stopped walking at Caspian's urgent call.

No, Lor-lie, you can't waste precious time. You've got to tell Jeremy that your Trial has already started. Tell him about the cramps in your legs.

"Lori?" her father stopped. "What's wrong?"

"I don't know," she answered, truthfully. Looking up to her uncle she frowned. "Um, Jeremy, please don't think I'm completely crazy, but it's about that voice I've been hearing. You know, the one I told you about on the phone –"

Jeremy smiled broadly at Lori. Going down on one knee, he was as tall as she was as he reached out and took both her hands. "Who is it then? Caspian or Coral?"

"It's Caspian!" Lori said excitedly. "You know about him?"

"Sure enough! He's a wonderful lad, full of beans and the pride of his father."

"Voice?" her aunt said, stepping forward. "What voice?"

"Yeah Bug," Eddie added. "What are you talking about? Who's Caspian?"

Jeremy looked up at Lori's father. "You didn't tell them?"

He shrugged. "Tell them what? I don't even understand what's been going on. That's why we're here. To finally get some answers."

Lori explained to her aunt and brothers about the strange voice in her head and its dire warning that she would die if she didn't get to Herm immediately.

When she finished, Anne gave an accusing look at her brother. "And you didn't bother to mention this to me or the boys? Brian, what were you thinking?"

"I was thinking of Lori's welfare," her father shot back.

"But Dad, if Lori is hearing voices, she should be in a hospital, not going on vacation," Eddie said.

"Lori doesn't need a hospital," Jeremy said, joining the argument. "What she needs is to get to Herm."

"Why?" Anne demanded. "What's wrong with her?"

"I can't tell you here," Jeremy said. "We must get to Herm first."

As the argument between her aunt, brothers, father and uncle intensified, Lori felt Caspian growing more agitated. Finally he called to her; *Stop them, Lor-lie. You don't have time for this. You've got to tell your uncle that the Trial has started. Tell him now!*

"Everyone shut up," Lori shouted. She could feel the pressure of fear building in her stomach as Caspian's warning rang in her ears.

She turned to Jeremy. "Caspian says we're almost out of time. He says the Trial has already started."

"What!" Jeremy cried in horror. "How long ago did it start?"

Stunned by his sudden change, she shrugged. "I'm not too sure – um –"

Jeremy grasped her by the arms, his face hovering inches from hers. "Lorelie, listen to me very carefully, this is very, very important. How long ago did it start? What are you feeling right now?"

Lori looked back up to her father, "I–I'm not sure when it started – a few hours, maybe. I had bad cramps in my stomach and legs. Anne gave me some pills and I fell asleep."

"What does all of this mean?" demanded her father. "What the hell is happening to my daughter?"

Jeremy ignored her father as he stared intently at Lori. "Lorelie, this is terribly important. How do you feel? Are your legs itchy? Do they sting or burn?"

"Brian, we should go," Anne said worriedly. "Voice or no voice, coming here was a mistake."

"Answer us, Lorelie," Aaron pleaded. "Please, tell us, how do you feel?"

"My name is Lori," Lori suddenly snapped. "Not Lorelie. And you want to know how I feel?" She turned to her cousin as tears filled her eyes. "I'm really scared! I don't understand what's happening to me and no one will tell me anything."

Jeremy's voice softened as he put his arms around her and hugged her tightly. "I'm so sorry, lass, I know you're scared. We all are. But you must tell us about your legs. Do they itch or sting?"

"No. I've just had some cramps, but they're fine now. Please tell me what's going on?"

Instead of answering, Jeremy looked back to Aaron. "You and Miranda take everyone upstairs. Find a quiet corner and wait for me. I'll arrange a flight directly to Herm."

Before Lori or her family could say another word, Jeremy was running away, and swallowed up by the crowd.

"What's going on here, kids?" Anne asked.

"We're really sorry to be frightening you like this," Aaron said, "but there's a lot going on here that you just don't understand."

"Then help us understand," Eddie demanded.

"Not here," Aaron said. "Let's do what Jeremy says and go upstairs." With that, he headed towards the escalator.

Lori held her aunt's hand as they rode the escalator up to Gatwick's second level. Shops and restaurants filled the entire floor and were crowded with travellers waiting for their flights. Lori didn't notice any of them. Shock and fear were overwhelming her every sense. As it was, she was barely aware of the return of her leg cramps and backache.

As Aaron led the group to a cluster of empty chairs, Eddie caught hold of his arm. "All right Aaron, now you've got us up here. What's going on? Tell me, what's happening to my sister?"

"This isn't easy," Aaron started. "We are a very small, very private family."

"And?" Eddie demanded.

"And if we tell you right now, you won't believe us," Miranda cut in, "but you must, because it's all true."

"What is?" Lori asked.

"Lori, you are facing a Trial –" Aaron continued.

"I know," she said, throwing up her arms in exasperation. "Caspian keeps telling me. But he won't say what it is!"

"He was probably waiting for Jeremy or Gran to tell you," Miranda offered.

"Why?" Lori's father demanded. "Why can't you tell us? What's the big secret?"

Aaron looked at his sister, then over to Lori. "Because it *is* a big secret and I know for sure you won't believe it, coming from us."

Lori's father shook his head and started pacing the small area. "This is getting us nowhere! What kind of games are you people playing here?"

Miranda suddenly pointed. "Here comes Jeremy! He'll tell you."

Everyone turned and saw Jeremy racing towards them. His mobile phone was pressed to his ear and they could hear him saying, "We're on our way. Get ready to move the moment we arrive."

Snapping shut his phone; he stood before the group. "I've just found out they don't fly helicopters out of Gatwick," Jeremy gulped air and tried to catch his breath. "But we caught some luck. They do fly out of South Nutfield Airport. That's just a few minutes down the road. I've called ahead and arranged for a large private helicopter to

24

get us all straight to Herm. The pilot is preparing for take off right now. We just have to get there."

"I'm sorry, Jeremy," Lori's father said grimly, "but we aren't flying anywhere until you give us some answers."

"You didn't tell them?" Jeremy turned to Aaron.

"We wanted to wait for you. They wouldn't have believed us if Miri and I told them."

"That's probably true," Jeremy agreed. Reaching into his pocket, he pulled out his wallet and handed it to Aaron. "Look, it's really raining out and we can't risk Lori getting wet. You and your sister go and try to find something for her to wear that will keep her completely dry. But be as quick as you can."

Jeremy turned his attention to Lori and her family. "I understand your frustrations. You want explanations and you'll get them." He looked at Lori and placed his hands lightly on her shoulders. "But before I start, I need you to answer a question for me."

"Go on," Lori said.

"For the past couple of weeks, even before you started to hear Caspian, have you been having trouble with water and getting wet?"

Lori gazed past her uncle to her father and aunt. She shrugged.

"Have you?" her father pressed.

Lori finally nodded.

"When you got wet, your legs started to itch, didn't they?" Jeremy continued. "And if you spent any time at all in water, they really started to burn. Right?"

Lori was stunned. Her uncle knew everything about her – things she hadn't dared tell her father or aunt. "Yes," she finally whispered.

"Lori, why didn't you say something?" her father asked.

"I didn't want to worry you. You got really upset when I told you about the voice. What would have happened if I told you this, too? I was just hoping it would go away."

"But it didn't go away, did it?" Jeremy pressed. "In fact, it got worse."

"Yes, and before long my throat really started to hurt."

"Your throat," Anne repeated. "Lori, I'm your doctor. Why didn't you come to me? How does it hurt?"

"It burns, doesn't it?" Jeremy agreed. He traced a line on either side of his neck, "just about here and here?"

"Yes," Lori cried. "But how did you know?"

25

"Because that is where your gills will form."

"Gills?" Anne repeated. "What the hell are you talking about?"

"Everyone, please listen to me very carefully. Lori is a mermaid."

"A what!" her father cried. "Jeremy you are completely insane!" Shaking his head, he started to pace. "Let me get this straight. You brought us five thousand miles over here, insisting that Lori's life is in terrible danger. You wouldn't tell us what's happening or anything about the voice. Now you expect us to believe a story like that?"

"This is simply ridiculous," Anne said. "Mermaids don't exist. They are a physical impossibility, nothing more than silly fairytales and lonely sailors' fantasies.

"You listen to me, Jeremy," Lori's father continued. "I don't know why you are doing this, but it stops now. This isn't funny."

"No Brian, it isn't," Jeremy agreed. Then he looked at Anne. "It's deadly serious. My sister, Colleen, is a mermaid. My mother is one too. The men of our family carry it in our blood, but it mainly shows up in the women. When they reach puberty, they become mermaids."

"That's crazy!" Lori's father cried. Reaching forward, he caught hold of Lori's arm. "We're not listening to any more lies. Anne, boys, grab your things, we're leaving."

No Lor-lie! Caspian cried. *It's true. I swear everything Jeremy is saying is true. You are a mermaid! So is your mother. You haven't changed yet, but it is coming. That's the Trial; when your body changes from legs to your tail. Tell your father, please. You must believe us!*

"It can't be true!" Lori cried, shouting at empty air. "Caspian, you're lying. Mermaids don't exist!"

"Lower your voice!" Jeremy hushed, catching Lori by the arm. "For heaven's sake, lower your voice. What's Caspian saying?"

Lori tore her arm away from her uncle and curled into her father. "Dad, Caspian says it's all true. He says I'm going to have a tail. But it can't be. They're lies, they've got to be."

"Lori, stop and think about it," Jeremy pleaded. "The pain you felt in your legs when you got wet, the sickening weakness when you tried to stand: You didn't mention your hands, but they hurt too when you're wet. Don't they?"

Lori buried her head in her father's chest. "Stop it!"

26

"Don't they?" Jeremy pressed.

"Lori?" her father asked, drawing her away from him. "Is he right? Do your hands hurt?"

Lori lifted her frightened eyes upward and nodded.

"Listen to me child," Jeremy said gently. "I wish to God you didn't have to hear it this way, but we're out of time. Your hands hurt when you got wet because the next time you get wet, there will be webbing between your fingers."

"No!" Lori cried, clinging to her father again.

Pulling her close, Lori's father said to Jeremy, "You keep insisting there is no time. What's that supposed to mean? No time for what?"

Jeremy turned away from Lori and lowered his head. His big shoulders slumped and he started to wring his hands. When he finally spoke, he was shaking.

"The Trial is when one of our girls first suffers the change. When it starts, the new mermaid must be in Herm waters for the change. If she is not, then –"

"Then what?" Anne demanded.

"Then within hours of the start of the Trial, the girl will change anyway. She will change – and she will die."

"No!" Danny cried. Suddenly breaking his long silence he stepped forward. "That's not true. You're lying."

"No I'm not," Jeremy said gently. He turned to Lori. "Ask Caspian, he'll tell you. My little sister died during the Trial. It started late in the night and came on so fast. By morning she was half-turned. We got her down to the water, but it was too late. Serena died in my father's arms. And we were on Herm!"

Lori looked back to her father and nodded. "Caspian says it's all true. He says we've got to get to Herm now to complete the Trial."

"Why does it have to be Herm water?" Lori's father demanded. "What about other water?"

"Any other water can trigger the change, but that is the danger. Once the very first change starts, it can't be stopped. And unless it's in Herm's water –"

"I'll die," Lori finished grimly.

"No. That's impossible," Anne argued. "This is all some kind of insane fantasy. You people are delusional. Do you forget I'm a doctor? Mermaids simply can't exist. They are physically and genetically impossible."

"But they do," Jeremy argued. "And if we don't get Lori to Herm soon, her death will prove it."

Chapter 5

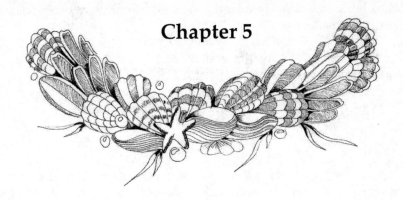

Aaron and Miranda raced back to the group, carrying several packages in their hands. "We didn't know what we could get that would be completely waterproof. So we bought lots." Aaron reached into the bags and pulled out two large men's raincoats. "We figured these might work. Miri tried them on and they both came down past her feet."

"And we got some tape," Miranda added, "so we can seal them closed."

"We also bought some umbrellas, scarves, hats and gloves," Aaron finished. "So hopefully she'll be kept dry."

"Very good," Jeremy agreed. "Everyone, gather your things together, we've got to get moving."

Passing back through the crowds at the airport, they headed down to the ground floor then towards the exit. Lori gazed at the thousands of people around her but couldn't focus on anything. Everything felt odd and surreal, as though she was walking around in a dream.

"I'll grab us a cab," Jeremy offered, as they reached the exit. "Brian and Anne, will you and Eddie, start to work on Lori. Make sure there isn't an inch of exposed skin – especially her legs. They are the most critical at the moment."

Lori was dressed in the men's coats. Long scarves covered her hair and were wrapped around her neck, and then a large rain hat was put on her head.

Aaron caught hold of the large roll of duct tape and started to tear off lengths. While Lori's father lifted her off the ground, Anne and

Eddie taped the coats closed at Lori's feet, hands and at every other opening on her body.

"But I can't walk now," Lori protested.

"You don't have to, I'm going to carry you," her father said. "Just like when you were a little girl."

"But Da–ad," Lori complained, "I'm not a little girl any more."

"Quiet, Bug," Eddie said. "We've got to be extra careful."

Lori was about to argue further when the worried look on Eddie's face stopped her. Shutting her mouth, she settled quietly in her father's arms.

"Do you guys think we could possibly draw any more attention to ourselves?" Danny said, without humour, as he looked at the curious expressions on the faces of some passers by.

"That's enough, Danny," his father warned. "We've got more than enough stress here without you adding to it."

"Yeah right, like we're going to believe their wacky story anyway," Danny grumbled, as he walked towards the doors to wait by himself.

From behind them, Jeremy appeared. "I've got two cabs waiting. You ready to go?"

"We are," her father said, as he carried Lori to the doors. Eddie and Aaron started to open the umbrellas. Eddie handed his to Anne while Aaron kept hold of the other.

Saying nothing, Danny held open the door. Miranda ran ahead to open the second set.

Lori felt a blast of cold wind as her father carried her outside. Anne and Aaron pressed the two umbrellas close to her head until all she could see was their metal spines and fabric. As she pressed herself against her father's chest, the fear of getting wet knotted her stomach.

"You okay under there?" he called.

"So far so good," Lori answered. "How far do we have to go?"

"Not far. The first cab is just a few feet ahead."

Lori saw daylight as the umbrellas were hastily pulled away. Her father lowered her into the cab's back seat and climbed in. Anne settled down beside her, while Jeremy took the fold-down seat opposite them.

"The boys and Miri are travelling in the second cab. It's not far so it shouldn't take us too long." He gave the driver a nod. "Let's get moving."

Traffic around the airport was heavy and their progress slow. Lori could feel the tension coming from everyone in the cab. Caspian was also giving off his share of nerves. Seated between her father and aunt, she could feel everyone's eyes watching her.

The ten-minute journey passed into half an hour as rain and traffic slowed their progress to a crawl. Lori started to feel something happening. Was it tingling? The sensation was so light, she wasn't sure.

Lor-lie, Caspian nervously warned, *I think something is starting–*

"I feel it too," she said aloud.

"Feel what?" her father demanded. "Lori what are you feeling?"

"I don't know. It's strange and kind of hard to describe."

"Your legs, are they starting to tingle?" Jeremy asked.

"I think so," Lori answered as she tried to concentrate on herself. "Yes," she said fearfully. Turning to her father, "Dad, they really are starting to tingle. It's kind of like they've been asleep and are now starting to wake up."

A worried expression rose on Jeremy's face. "We're okay for time," he said. "But still –" He turned to the driver. "My niece really isn't feeling very well. We've got to get to South Nutfield airport now. There's an extra hundred pounds in it for you if you can get us there as quickly as possible."

"A hundred pounds?" the driver repeated.

When Jeremy nodded, the driver smiled slyly. "That's a deal. Hold on everyone, we're going to take the fast lane."

The driver turned the wheel sharply, taking the cab onto the hard shoulder. He pressed his foot down on the accelerator and the car picked up speed. "If we get stopped by the police, we'll tell them it's a medical emergency."

"You won't be lying," Jeremy muttered darkly.

Chapter 6

"Monsieur Luc, are you all right!"

Luc opened his eyes and saw the frightened face of his father's butler hovering inches away from him. He was lying on his bed and must have dozed off.

"Jean Pierre?"

"You were crying in your sleep. Monsieur, you looked terrified."

Luc sat up and felt his face flushed and wet with tears. Angrily wiping them away, he looked at the butler. "I was dreaming. But I don't believe it was just a dream."

"Of course it was," the butler said gently. "What else could it be?"

Luc dropped his head. "A very bad memory." He patted the bed beside him and invited the old butler to sit down. "Jean Pierre, you've been working for my father for a long time."

The old man smiled. "Oui Monsieur, I started long before you were born."

"So you knew my mother?"

Fear rose in the old man's eyes and he started to stand up and walk away. "It is best that we do not discuss your mother."

Luc caught him by the arm and gently pulled him back. He knew Jean Pierre was very frightened. But after seeing his mother's portrait, the return of fragments of long lost memories and finally the dream, he had to know the truth. "Jean Pierre, please. I know my father did something to her. I can remember hearing them fighting in the night."

"You were very young," Jean Pierre said. "What you think you remember and what actually happened are two very different things."

"I do remember!" Luc insisted. "They were fighting about me. It was so loud it woke me up. I opened my bedroom door and heard my mother say she was taking me away. But my father said no. Then he hit her. She started to run and he chased her. I left my room and followed them down to the study –"

"Monsieur, stop," the butler insisted. "No good can come from this."

Luc looked into the old man's pale eyes. "He killed her, didn't he?" he asked. "My father murdered my mother in the study. That's why he never lets me in there. He was frightened I'd remember."

Jean Pierre shook his head and pleaded, "Please, Monsieur, if we discuss this, your father will make me disappear."

"Like he did my mother?" Luc pressed.

Finally the butler nodded. "He would kill me if he knew I told you."

Luc reached for the old man's hands. "I swear I'll never tell him. But please, I must know. I've lived my whole life wondering what happened to her and being angry because she didn't take me with her."

"She wanted to, but couldn't," Jean Pierre admitted. Finally he looked at Luc and squeezed his hands. "It was long ago. I remember when your father brought her home. She was so beautiful and alive. She was perhaps the most loving and generous woman I ever met. I think most of us in the house fell instantly in love with her."

"What happened?" Luc pressed.

The old butler sighed. "Almost from the beginning I could see something was very wrong. It was like your father wanted her to be something she couldn't. It caused a lot of fighting. And after you were born, the fighting became worse."

"Why?" Luc quietly asked.

"Because your mother wanted you kept here with her, but your father insisted you be sent away to school. When she'd finally had enough of his bullying, she packed her bags and wanted to take you with her. But your father became enraged. He said she could go if she wanted, but she couldn't take you. You were the price she had to pay for freedom."

Luc almost wanted Jean Pierre to stop. But instead, he nodded. "Keep going."

"There isn't much more to tell. They had a final, terrible fight on the night she tried to take you away –"

"And he killed her," Luc finished in a shocked whisper. "I remember. I was standing outside the study. One of the doors was opened slightly. I saw my father go to his desk to get something. Then there was the sound of thunder. But it wasn't thunder, was it? My father shot my mother."

The old man nodded. "When he discovered you outside the door, his fury was unstoppable. We thought he was going to kill you, too. Instead, he beat you into a coma. When you finally awoke a month later, you couldn't remember anything of the night and your father told you your mother had run away."

Tears streamed down Luc's face as he finally recalled the missing details of that awful night. "What happened to her? Where is she now?"

Jean Pierre lowered his head. "I'm so sorry, Monsieur, I swear I do not know. Your father had his men take her away. She may still be here, buried somewhere on the estate, but I can not be certain."

"You think she's buried here?" Luc asked.

The old man's fear increased. "Please, Monsieur, you must not start to search for her grave. If you do, your father will suspect. It will lead back to me."

Luc finally nodded. "I understand. I won't look for her. My father would have hidden her anyway."

Finally Jean Pierre stood and crossed to the cupboard. He pulled out a small suitcase. "The past is the past, Monsieur. Perhaps it should stay buried there."

Luc watched him open the suitcase and start to pack. "Is my father sending me back to school?"

The old butler shook his head. "The reason I came in here is your father has instructed me to pack some travel clothes for you. You are going on a trip with him."

It all seemed too much to take in. He'd finally learned the truth about his mother, and now was now being told he had to go on a trip with his father. The one who murdered his mother!

"A trip?" Luc said. "Where?"

"I do not know, Monsieur," the butler said gently. "All I know is your father instructed me to pack some warm clothes for you, and to tell you to be ready to go within the hour."

34

Luc shook his head. "I'm not going anywhere with him!"

Jean Pierre stopped packing. He came back to the bed and sat beside Luc. "Monsieur Luc, listen to me please. You are still too young to challenge your father. You are so much like your mother, gentle and caring. That is why your father treats you as he does. He desperately wanted you to be like him. But you are not. And because you are like her, it infuriates him. Please, I have always considered you my family. Do this for me. Humour him. Do as he commands until you are old enough to get away from him and perhaps make him pay for what he did to your beautiful mother."

"How can I?" Luc asked. "Knowing what he did to her. I can't imagine being in the same room with him. How can I possibly go on a trip?"

"Think of your dear mother. For all of her gentleness, she was perhaps the strongest woman I ever knew. Let her give you the strength. Let her memory lead you until you are old enough to stand against your father."

Luc sniffed back his tears. "For mother," he said softly.

Finally the old butler smiled gently, "Now, go get changed for the journey. I'll finish with your things."

Chapter 7

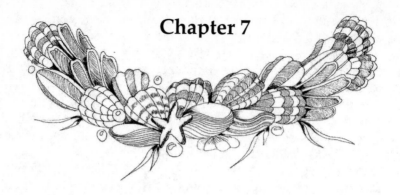

As the two cabs sped along the hard shoulder, Lori concentrated on her legs. It was just as Jeremy described. They were now definitely tingling and starting to itch.

"How long do I have?" she nervously asked her uncle.

"Quite a while, lass; it's not time to panic just yet."

"We'll make it," Anne promised as she put her arm around Lori. "Just hang on. We'll get you there in plenty of time."

Lori tried to ignore what was happening to her lower half by concentrating instead on the passing landscape. Around them were green fields with the occasional sheep and then some construction sites with no one working because of the weather. But there wasn't enough to keep her distracted for long. Looking forward again, she caught Jeremy watching her. His expression was grim.

When the two cabs pulled up outside the small terminal, Jeremy and Anne climbed out and opened the umbrellas. The wind had picked up and the rain became heavier as large drops pounded on the roof of the car. As her father lifted Lori out of the cab, the umbrellas were immediately shoved into place. Unable to see again, Lori leaned into her father and felt his breath coming in short, anxious gasps.

It wasn't long before they were inside the small terminal.

"Let's settle Lori over there," Jeremy suggested pointing to a cluster of empty chairs. "Then Brian, if you sort out the cabs and get everyone in here, I'll check on our flight. It shouldn't be long."

Sitting with her aunt, Lori tried to forget the growing problem with her lower half. Her legs were becoming terribly itchy. She tried to scratch them through the two coats, but with her hands also sealed in the long coat sleeves, she couldn't reach. She finally gave up and looked back at her aunt. "Do you believe all of this, about the mermaids and stuff?"

Anne shrugged and placed her hand on Lori's forehead. "I don't know what to believe any more. But I do know something is happening to you. I just can't explain it."

Before long, the rest of the family was gathered together waiting for Jeremy to return.

"This is going to drive me nuts!" Lori complained, as she squirmed in the chair and tried desperately not to tear at her legs. "What's causing it?"

Leaning down, Aaron spoke very softly. His voice became a worried whisper, "I think your scales are trying to push though."

Lori stopped. "Scales?"

Aaron nodded. When Lori looked over to Miranda, she nodded too.

Hearing this, Lori's father urgently scanned the small terminal. "Where's Jeremy? We've got to get moving!"

At last, they saw Jeremy waving his arms in the air, beckoning them.

"Come on everyone, let's get going," Lori's father said, as he lifted her into his arms. Giving her a reassuring squeeze, he said quietly to her, "Hold on tight, honey, we'll get you there."

Lori nodded but said nothing. Inside the coats, where she knew he couldn't see, she balled her hands into tight fists. They were really beginning to sting. Her throat was starting to hurt too. She would have liked to believe the pain was from where the duct tape sealed the coat collars closed at her neck. But she knew the truth. It wasn't the tape at all. Jeremy had said she would have gills on either side of her neck. They were starting to grow.

Jeremy led them through a set of double doors. Ahead of them stood a second set of doors. "Grab the umbrellas," he told Anne.

Once again Lori was covered up, and her father carried her through the outer double doors. A sudden blast of wind caught hold of Anne's umbrella and tore it violently away.

"Leave it!" Jeremy ordered as they raced forward.

The rain was blowing in every direction and started prickles wherever touched the exposed skin of Lori's face. "Hurry Dad!" she cried.

Above the sound of her father's heavy breathing and the whipping of the wind, Lori could hear the whine of high-pitched engines. Then Jeremy was moving the final umbrella away and her father was lifting her onto the large helicopter. Eddie was already on board and waiting to receive her. As she was passed into his arms, he looked down on her.

"How're you doing, Bug?"

"Not great," Lori answered. "My face is really burning where the rain hit it and I need to get out of these clothes before I go nuts!"

While her family loaded the luggage and settled in the helicopter, Eddie placed Lori down on the seat beside him at the window. He pulled out a tissue and started to wipe her face. "Sorry, but you need to keep them on. Jeremy says it's raining on Herm. I don't know what the heck is happening here, but until we know for sure, I don't want you getting wet."

When her face was dry, the pain subsided. She just wished it would stop everywhere else on her body. Forcing it out of her mind, she gazed out the window and watched them lifting off the ground.

"Are you all right?" her father asked, from the seat next to her.

"Guess so," she said. She tried to smile, but failed. Things were happening too fast and she was frightened.

"Well, it won't be long now."

Hurry, Caspian called urgently. *Please hurry.* Lori could feel the pain starting for him, too.

As the helicopter flew south and finally started across the English Channel towards Herm, things took a turn for the worse. The itching in Lori's legs turned to burning. Hidden under the layers of clothing, her fingers were swelling to the point where she could no longer make a fist.

Deep pain lines etched themselves across her brow as beads of sweat rose on her forehead. Lori could feel her face flushing and contorting from the effort of holding back the moans that ached to escape her mouth.

"What is it?" Anne asked from her seat across from her. "Lori, what's happening to you?"

"It hurts!" Lori finally burst out, as tears streamed down her cheeks. "It really, really hurts."

Seated beside Anne, Jeremy leaned forward "How does it hurt? Where?"

"Everywhere!" Lori cried. "My legs are on fire!"

Jeremy turned to Aaron. "Get on the radio. Tell the pilot to hurry. We've got an emergency here."

As Aaron reached for the headphones and speaker, the family huddled closer. Jeremy undid the tape on Lori's sleeves and pulled her hands free.

"Oh Lord," he cried, inspecting her damp swollen fingers. "She's sweating in all that clothing. The water is starting the change. Get her out of them. Now!"

Lori felt the cool air washing over her as her family helped her out of the layers of outer clothing. When she was down to her jeans and long sweatshirt, she started to feel better. But it didn't last long.

Anne reached forward to untie Lori's shoes. "Look at her legs. They're swelling up like balloons! We've got to get her out of those jeans."

Lori didn't fight her aunt as she removed her shoes and struggled to peel her jeans off. Sitting only in her underwear, she was in too much pain to feel embarrassed. But when she looked at the exposed flesh on her legs and saw her skin starting to pucker and bleed, she panicked.

"Dad, I'm bleeding!"

"It's all right!" Jeremy said reassuringly. "Lori, listen to me, it's all right. This is normal."

"How the hell can this be normal?" Anne demanded. "Look at her! She's going to bleed out through her legs!"

"It's normal for the Trial," Jeremy explained. "This is what the girls go through the first time they change."

"Oh, God," Lori's father cried. "What can I do? This is killing me!"

Jeremy shot a warning look at her father. "There's no need to panic, Brian. We'll just use some tissues to dry her off. Okay? Just take some and give me a hand. You can do that, can't you?"

Lori gazed up into her father's face. He was quaking with fear. His fear was making hers worse.

"Brian!" Jeremy called sharply. "Focus. Lori needs you."

Taking a handful of tissues, her father started to wipe her legs. "We'll get you cleaned up in no time," he said shakily. "Then you'll feel much better."

While they worked, Lori felt the burning increasing. Leaning her head back, she moaned, and squeezed her eyes tightly shut.

Aaron hung up the earphones and sat again. "The pilot said we're still a good fifteen minutes out. You can hold on for that long, can't you, Lori?"

Lori glanced down to her swollen legs at the red smears as Jeremy and Anne continued to wipe the blood away. "I guess so."

But as each agonizing minute ticked by, she felt the pain increasing. She could also feel the waves of fear and pain coming from Caspian.

"Caspian's hurting so bad," Lori uttered through gritted teeth, as she fought desperately to keep control. "He's in so much pain –"

Jeremy looked over to the family. "He's suffering right along with her. He's feeling what she feels."

"What can I do for you?" her father asked her, helplessly. "Tell me, Lori, what can I do?"

Unable to speak, Lori shook her head.

"You can pray we reach Herm in time," Jeremy answered grimly.

Several minutes passed before the next severe wave of pain struck. Crying out, Lori suddenly lunged forward to tear at her feet. "My feet! They're on fire! Daddy, help me. Please –"

"Brian, hold her still," ordered Jeremy. "Anne, help me get her socks off!"

Lori felt her father's arms wrapping tightly around her. Clinging to him, she watched Anne peel her socks off. Everyone gasped as her ankles flattened out and her feet started to extend and turn into a large fin.

"My God!" her father cried. "What's happening?"

"It's her fluke," Jeremy reported grimly. "Lori is dry changing. Without water, her tail is forcing its way out. The fluke will form where her feet are."

"This isn't happening," her father cried. Clinging to Lori, he rocked her in his arms. "My God, this just isn't happening!"

"Will Lori be okay?" Danny asked fearfully.

Jeremy turned to Danny and shrugged. "I honestly don't know. The change has started and we can't stop it. We've got to get her into the water soon."

Lori heard her family talking, but she could no longer join their conversation. Pain was overwhelming her every sense. It seemed her body was tearing itself inside out.

Anne reached forward and pressed her hand to Lori's throat. "Oh Lord," she cried. "Her pulse is racing off the chart. She's going to have a heart attack!"

Suddenly a violent convulsion struck and Lori started thrashing in her seat as though she'd been electrocuted. Starting at her upper thighs, her legs began to fuse together. Howling, she felt the sharp scales cutting through the soft skin of her legs.

"Lori!" her father cried. "Lori –"

"Jeremy, we're too far way," Aaron cried. He turned and looked desperately out the window. Herm lay dead ahead. But even as the helicopter was getting lower and nearing the surface of the water for its approach, they still had some way to go. "We're not going to make it!"

"No!" Jeremy angrily shouted. "I'm not losing another girl!"

As the first convulsion ended, Lori's head lolled to the side and fell weakly against her father's chest. She was barely conscious and only dimly aware of Jeremy standing and reaching for her. She heard him saying something to her father and Anne. Their voices were raised and angry but she couldn't understand what they were saying. Then she felt Jeremy lift her in his arms.

A moment later, Lori became aware of Aaron opening the side door of the helicopter. As a cold, wet wind blasted her face and exposed skin, rainwater touched her inflamed lower half. The pain of contact made her howl and start to convulse again.

"Hang on, lass," Jeremy grunted, moving towards the open door.

"Lori! No!" her father cried.

"Jeremy," Anne howled. "Don't do it! We're too high up –"

Then they were falling.

Lori didn't feel herself hitting the water. She didn't hear her uncle calling her name and cradling her in his arms. All she knew was pain.

Then finally, blessed darkness.

41

Chapter 8

Luc and Jean Pierre made their way down the grand staircase and towards the main foyer. Luc saw his father standing there impatiently waiting for him.

"Ah, you're finally here," Robichaud said. "Jean Pierre, have Phillip pull the car around. We're ready to go to the airport."

Jean Pierre gave a secret, slight nod to reassure Luc and then bowed to Robichaud and left the hall.

Standing alone with his father, Luc wanted to lash out at him – to scream, shout, do anything to let him know that he knew the truth. Despite his promise to the butler to bide his time, he couldn't wait. His father had murdered his mother and terrorised him all his life. He had to pay.

Luc made a decision. He would play along, behave himself and not challenge his father. But he would watch and he would listen. He would learn all his father's secrets. All the arms deals and deadly contracts he made. Then when he had enough evidence, he would go to the police to make sure his father paid for his crimes.

"Where are we going, Papa?" Luc asked, trying desperately to sound normal.

Robichaud turned to him. "You are now old enough to share in a project I have been working on for almost twenty five years. It has been my one true obsession. This trip may be nothing. There have been false alarms before. Or it may be the fulfilment of my dream. I won't know until we get there."

Luc felt the familiar fear rising again, but now it was mixed with excitement. This was the start of his evidence gathering. "What kind of project? What wish?" he asked.

"You'll see," Robichaud said mysteriously.

Luc saw something new in his father's dark eyes. There was a hard brightness that he'd never seen before; a kind of terrifying excitement shining from his whole face. Something was up. Only this time, Luc was going to be right there with him, quietly gathering all the proof he needed to condemn his father.

Chapter 9

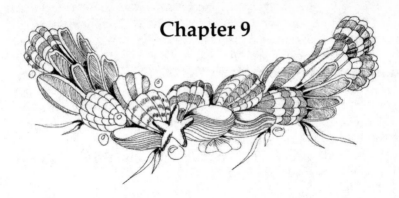

Lori wasn't conscious, but she wasn't unconscious either. She drifted somewhere between life and death. It felt as if she was floating on a cloud, bobbing peacefully across a midnight sky.

"Caspian?" she softly called into the darkness.

I'm – here – Lor-lie, he moaned.

"Are you all right?" She was aware of his great suffering, but could no longer feel his pain.

It hurts –

"I know. But I don't understand. How can I know what you are feeling?"

We – we are connected. Forever bound to – together. I feel everything you feel. You feel as I – do.

"How? What's happened to us? Caspian, I still don't understand."

You have changed in every way. You have suffered the Trial and been reborn. You are a mermaid now. But – Lor-lie, listen to me. You – you must not linger where you are. It – it's very dangerous.

Lori sighed contentedly. "But I like it here. It doesn't hurt any more. Can't I stay a while?"

No! You must leave now. Lor-lie, de – death is waiting for you there. You must drag yourself away. Rise back to the surface of life. Do it Lor-lie! Please. Do it now for the both of us before it's too late. There's no time left!

Caspian's voice was pain-filled and desperate. But Lori couldn't understand why. All the pain was gone and she felt an ever-increasing sense of peace.

Please Lor-lie, listen to me. Your mother des – desperately needs you. I need you. You can't stay or you'll die. We'll both die.

"But this is a very nice place. It couldn't possibly be dangerous."

It is! Please hurry. You are lingering in the realms between life and death. The longer you stay, the harder it will be to go back. Please Lor-lie. Remember what Jeremy said about his younger sister? You aunt Serena chose to stay. And because of it, my uncle Argo died with her. If you stay, I'll die too. I beg you. Choose life for the both of us. Please leave there now!

"Life and death –" Lori repeated absently, starting to giggle. "Death and life. Life and death."

Drifting along.

Floating.

In the distance, she heard her uncle's agonised cries. They seemed to be growing fainter. His voice was so strange, so frightened. He was begging her to come back. But come back from where?

Listen to him Lor-lie! Go back to your life!

A part of her wanted to stay. She felt so peaceful. Nothing mattered any more. Nothing hurt. But an even stronger part of her instinctively realised the danger and caught hold of her uncle's terrified voice, following it away from the peaceful place. It drew her back to the world of pain.

"Come on Lori, that's it! Come back to us."

Lori moaned loudly. Her body hurt all over.

"Oh my beautiful child –"

Was that a woman's voice? As Lori finished clawing her way back to consciousness, she became aware of arms supporting her at the surface of the water. Weakly opening her eyes, she saw the sky above was dark grey and stormy. Huge waves were rising and falling around her. A steady rain fell on her hot face.

Her arms were sluggish and too heavy to lift. She couldn't move her legs.

"Dad?" she weakly moaned.

"He'll be with you soon. The Trial is over."

"Jeremy?"

"Yes, lass, I'm right here. Your Gran's here too."

"Gran?" Lori's eyes slowly focused. Beside her, she saw the smiling face of an older woman. Her wet hair was back against her head. It still retained some of its colour, but was mostly streaked grey and white.

"Where are we?" Lori weakly asked.

"We'll be in Belvoir Bay soon. Just relax."

"Belvoir Bay? Is that near Herm?"

"That is Herm," her grandmother answered sweetly.

"I don't understand –"

Jeremy lowered his head and kissed Lori lightly on the forehead. "Don't try to move, lass. Rest now. We've got you and you're safe."

Lori's head was filled with questions, but already she could feel the welcome draw of sleep. "Caspian?" she weakly called.

I'm here, he tiredly answered. *Sleep now Lor-lie. Sleep and heal.*

Closing her eyes, Lori was lulled to sleep by the rocking of the sea as her grandmother and uncle slowly drew her towards Herm.

Chapter 10

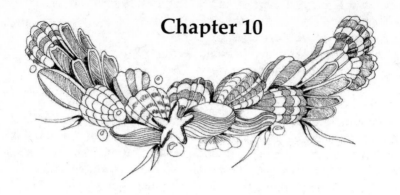

"Lori? Come on, wake up now."

Lori woke to the sound of her father's pleading voice. It sounded strange, as if it had an echo.

"That's it Lori, wake up," Anne called.

Lori slowly opened her eyes and saw the faces of her family gathered closely around her in the water. Her grandmother was still at her side. Rising behind her grandmother, she saw wet rocky walls climbing high to the ceiling far overhead. She heard the sound of waves and rushing water. But gazing around, she saw no exit leading to daylight – just a huge, underground cavern.

With each splash, she felt her body rising and moving as the water washed over her. Frowning, she looked at her grandmother. "Where are we?"

"You're in my cavern," her grandmother answered. "Under the cottage."

Beside her grandmother, Lori saw Eddie and Danny's worried faces. On the other side, she saw Jeremy, Aaron and Miranda. But straining her eyes, she couldn't see her father or Anne.

"Dad?"

"I'm up here."

Lori looked up and saw father and aunt laying on a stone outcropping above the water. Her father reached down and lightly stroked her wet cheek. His face was pale and streaked with tears. "I thought I was going to lose you –"

"How do you feel?" Anne asked.

"Rotten," Lori answered weakly. "I hurt all over."

"That will pass," her grandmother said, lovingly brushing away hair from Lori's face. "In a day or two, this will all be a distant memory."

"What happened?" Lori asked, frowning. "I can't remember anything but pain."

"Jeremy decided to play action hero," Aaron explained. "He jumped out of the helicopter with you. Miles from Herm, we were all sure he would drown."

"As if I'd ever let that happen," her grandmother snapped. "No dear, what Aaron means is that Jeremy saved your life. He brought you to Herm's waters to finish the Trial."

"You did?" Lori asked, trying to lift her head. "Does that mean we're on Herm now?"

"Under it, more like," Jeremy answered, smiling broadly. "Welcome home, lass."

Lori tried to sit up in the water, but found things weren't working right. Lifting her head further she looked down the length of her body. She saw a large green fin rising out of the water where her feet should be. Her eyes flew open wide at the sight of the long tail poking out of the end of her sweatshirt.

"Dad!" she howled, starting to thrash in the water.

"Lori, stop," Jeremy ordered. "You're too weak for this. Calm down!"

"But my feet? Where are my legs?"

Close beside her there was a large splash. A moment later, her father was at her side and taking her in his arms."

"Ssshhhh –" he softly said, holding her tightly. "It's all right, baby. You're all right."

"But my legs are gone!" Lori started. "Dad –"

"Your legs have turned into a tail," he said softly. "Jeremy was right. Lori, I can hardly believe it, but you are a mermaid."

"No!" Lori shouted, "I can't be! I can't be a fish."

"It's all right." Her father held her tighter and started to rock her in the water. "You're alive, that's all that matters. We can deal with the rest later."

"But Da–ad…"

"Lori, listen to me." Her grandmother's voice rose sharply with authority. Lori's protests were hushed when she saw her stern expression.

"We are not fish. Never call yourself that."

"But –"

"But nothing," her grandmother finished. "We are not fish. We are not human either. We are our own species. Special to this world."

Lori's cries turned into sobs as she clung to her father. Holding her, he continued to gently rock her.

"I'm sorry, Brian," Jeremy warned, tapping him lightly on the shoulder. "You've got to get out of the water now. It's too cold for you. If you stay any longer you'll go into shock."

"Cold?" Eddie frowned. "It's not cold for me. Is it cold for you Danny?"

Danny shook his head. "Not at all."

"It's not for us. For our kind," Lori's grandmother explained, her voice softening. "The water is never cold for us. But your father is human and it's very dangerous for him." She turned to him. "Jeremy is right, Brian, you must get out now."

Lori sniffed again and looked at her father's face. His skin was becoming very pale. He was shivering all over and his teeth were chattering. "One more minute," he said.

"Brian, out of the water, now," Anne said, suddenly sounding like a doctor. "In another minute you'll be dead."

"Go on Dad," Eddie offered, moving forward. "We're here for the Bug."

Lori looked at her brothers and saw that neither of them showed any signs of being cold. But her father's lips were starting to turn a pale shade of blue.

"I'm okay, Dad," Lori said seriously. "Really, I am. Please get out of the water. I don't want anything to happen to you."

"All right, I'll – I'll g-g-go," he surrendered, releasing her back into Jeremy's arms. He pointed back to the stone outcropping, "but I'll b-b-be right up th-th-there."

Jeremy took Lori back into his arms. "Aaron," he said. "Will you please run upstairs and get some towels for Brian. Miranda, go to my room and grab my robe – the heavy one. Be as quick as you can."

Aaron swam over to the edge of the water and easily hoisted himself out. Miranda was right behind him.

50

Lori felt her own panic fading away as concern for her father grew. He was moving far too slowly. When he tried to lift himself onto the ledge, his arms gave way and he fell back into the water. "G-g-g-guess I am kind of c-c-cold," he chuckled, embarrassed. "Eddie, give me a h-h-hand, will you?"

It took Anne, Eddie and Danny to get him out of the freezing, salt water onto the ledge, where he stood shaking uncontrollably.

"Who-who'd of thought the s-s-sea could be so c-c-cold," he said through chattering teeth.

"It is February," Jeremy said. "These waters can kill a man in a few minutes."

Lori turned back to Jeremy. "But not you?"

"No, lass. You ladies have the tails, but we are almost as much a part of the sea as you. We come down here swimming all year round."

"Come on, boys," Anne said. "Help me get Brian out of those wet clothes. They'll be keeping him cold."

Lori was still lying on her back in the water, supported by Jeremy. Turning over in his arms, she felt him release her.

"I've still got you," he assured her as he moved closer and caught hold of her arms. "Just let your tail drift down to bottom."

"The water isn't deep," her grandmother offered. "Rest your fluke on the bottom and you can stay up at the surface."

Lori frowned as she felt her tail sliding through the water. It was like nothing she'd ever experienced before. When her fluke hit the rocky floor of the natural pool, she found she could actually stand on it to keep herself upright. Catching hold of the edge, she pulled herself closer to her father.

"Are you all right, Dad?" she worriedly asked.

"It's m-m-me that should b-b-be asking you that," he answered as he stepped shakily out of his wet jeans.

"I'm fine," Lori said. "It doesn't really hurt much any more."

"Th-th-thank heaven's f-f-for that."

The sounds of heavy footsteps echoed through the chamber as Aaron and Miranda reappeared and ran towards Lori's father with the towels and robe.

Miranda handed Anne the robe and ran back to the edge of the water. Lowering herself to the ground she patted Lori's hand. "So, how are you feeling?"

"Weird," Lori answered truthfully. "Really, really weird."

"Does the webbing hurt?"

"What webbing?" Lori asked.

"Your fingers, silly. Does the webbing on your hands hurt?"

Lori held up her hand and saw the thick webbing between her fingers. It went all the way down to the first knuckle. Gasping, she turned to her grandmother.

"That's normal," she said, holding up her own two hands to reveal webbed fingers. "You'll soon find it helps a great deal when you are swimming."

"You've got a lot of discoveries ahead of you," Jeremy said, moving closer to her and patting her on the back. With graceful ease he hauled himself out of the water. "And one of the first things to learn is how to breathe under water with your gills."

Lori's hands flew up to her neck. She'd forgotten all about them. As she touched her throat, she felt the hard fleshy flaps resting over the gill openings.

"Dad!" she cried. "Dad, I've really got gills."

Dressed only in his underwear, Brian was briskly rubbing down his legs with the towel. "Yes I know s-s-sweetheart and lovely g-g-gills they are."

"Says who?" Danny said sharply, stepping forward. "It looks like someone's slit her throat. Gross-O-ramma!"

"Danny, that's not helping," Anne warned.

"Look at it this way, Bug," Eddie suggested as he rubbed down his wet hair with a towel. "You can breathe under water. Right?" He looked over to his grandmother. When she nodded, he continued. "This means you can go exploring places that no one's ever been before. Bug, do you realise, you could visit the Titanic if you wanted to."

"Oh no she can't!" her grandmother said firmly. She moved slowly through the water to Lori's side. As she moved, Lori noticed that it seemed to be a great effort for her. "The Titanic and wrecks like her are very dangerous. Corrosion has made them unstable. Lori you must not try to explore shipwrecks."

Gills? Exploration? The Titanic? It all seemed too much. "I just want my legs back," she said miserably.

52

Don't say that Lor-lie, Caspian said softly, speaking for the first time since she awoke. *Soon you will love having your tail. That will mean that you can come and see me.*

"See you? Caspian, where are you?"

I'm in the sea.

"The sea?" Lori repeated. She then looked at her grandmother. "Is Caspian like us?"

"No dear," Her grandmother said. "Caspian is a whale."

"A whale?" Lori cried. "Really?"

"Humpback, to be precise," Jeremy explained. Then, "Well, that's not entirely true either. He's as much a humpback whale as we are human. Which means Caspian and the family may look like other humpbacks, but are as unique in the world as we are."

"How is Caspian?" her grandmother interrupted. "Ask him how the family is. How are little Zephyr and Zenith?"

"Zephyr and Zenith?" Lori repeated.

That's my dad and uncle, Caspian responded. *Tell Undine that we're all fine. Like you, I'm very sore and tired. But that will pass. We're hopeful that now you've completed the Trial we can free Colleen.*

"Does that mean you'll finally tell me what happened to Mom?" Lori asked.

Her father drew on the robe and stepped closer to her. "What's all this about your mother? What's he talking about?"

"Where is she?" her grandmother asked.

When Caspian answered, Lori sucked in her breath. "It's really true? She didn't run away but has been trapped there all this time?"

"Where?" Lori's father demanded. "Lori, tell me what's happened to your mother."

Lori looked at her father. "Caspian says Mom didn't run away from us like we always thought. He says she's been trapped in a cavern at the bottom of the sea."

"What the hell was she doing at the bottom of the sea?" her father demanded.

"That was my fault," Lori's grandmother said softly. "She came to the sea to help me after the whalers attacked us."

"Whalers?" Lori and her family repeated.

"Whalers," Jeremy repeated darkly. "They slaughtered half the family and wounded Mum." He looked at Lori, "ask Caspian to tell you what happened."

With everyone gathered near, Lori started to repeat everything Caspian said to her about the day the whalers came to hunt the family. But as she spoke, she suddenly felt the strangest sensation. Almost as if she were leaving her own body and being drawn in to Caspian – as if she *was* Caspian, looking though his eyes, swimming with his body and rising to the surface to greet the new day.

Helpless to close her eyes or look away, Lori watched the arrival of the whalers' ship. She witnessed the terrifying murder of the family. She was with Caspian as he joined the others in driving his father down in the water to free him from the harpoon. Her heart broke for him as she saw the body of his mother being drawn up the ramp and taken away from him forever…

"Mother! No! Please stop! Give her back! Give her back –" Lori howled as her voice joined in with Caspian's grief and pain.

"Lori," her father cried. "Lori, what's happening?"

Suddenly Lori returned to herself. She opened her eyes in confusion and saw the concerned faces of her family hovering closely. She was in the cavern under the cottage. He father was wearing Jeremy's robe and her mermaid grandmother was at her side.

"Wha – What?" she asked.

"Bug, are you all right?" Eddie asked. "You were screaming and looked terrified. What happened?"

Tears filled Lori's eyes as the memories of what she'd just witnessed came rushing back. "Dad," she cried, "I was there! I watched the whalers killing the family. I saw all of it. It was terrible! There was so much blood in the water and they were all crying and trying to get free. Zephyr was in so much pain."

Lori's eyes then shot across to her grandmother. "I saw what they did to you! How Andori was killed and you were hurt. I watched it all –"

"Lori, calm down," her father said. "Take a few deep breaths."

"No, Dad, you don't understand!" Lori fought. "I was there. I really was! I saw it all. I watched them dragging Caspian's mother up the ramp of the whaling ship. There were men with knives at the top waiting to cut her up!"

Her father reached down into the water and put his arms around her. "It's all right. I don't know what you saw, but it's over. It's all in the past."

Jeremy moved in closer and knelt on the stone floor beside her father. "The attack happened three years ago for us. But for Lori, it's only just happened. Her connection to Caspian is so strong, he drew her to him and she saw everything as it happened. Lori was in Caspian's memory, reliving the attack as clearly as if she'd been there."

He reached for her. "I'm so sorry, lass, that you had to witness that. But you must tell us everything that you just saw and have Caspian tell you what happened next. Mother was hurt and unconscious. When she finally came around, she discovered she'd lost her sea-speech and the whales couldn't tell her what happened."

"Sea speech?" Anne interrupted.

Undine lowered her head. "It enables us to speak with the whales and all the creatures of the sea. But when I was hurt, something happened and I could no longer hear them. Now, even the silence is deafening."

"Perhaps I can help," Anne gently offered. "I'm a surgeon. This might be a simple case of nerve damage that can be corrected. If you would let me, I'd like to try."

"Thank you, Anne. I would welcome that."

"But first," Jeremy continued, "we need to know where Colleen is. Lori, you are the only one who can tell us what really happened on that wretched day."

"No way!" Lori's father shot angrily to Jeremy. "I'm not going put her through that again. The stress is too much for her."

Lor-Lie, Caspian said softly, *what you saw happened three years ago. My father is alive, so is Undine. You must tell your family what happened to us for them to understand.*

Nodding her head, Lori sniffed as she looked up to her father. "It's all right, Dad. I've got to tell you everything. You've got to understand what happened to them."

"To all of us, Brian," Undine said softly. "They are your family too. You must know the truth."

Chapter 11

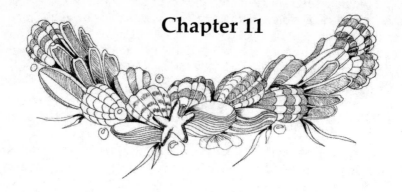

It was agreed that further conversation should be held in the cottage where they might be more comfortable.

"Come on everybody," Jeremy offered. "Let's get these ladies out of the water and then we can go upstairs."

"We brought the wheelchairs down for Gran and Lori. They're at the entrance," Aaron said. He then turned to Miranda. "Give us a hand, will you?"

They soon reappeared pushing two wheelchairs. Both had blankets on their seats. Reaching for a blanket, Aaron took it over to the water. Dipping it in, he soaked the fabric.

"All right, Lori," Jeremy said as he walked over to the edge of the water. "We're going to put you in the chair and keep you nice and wet with the blanket."

Lori looked pleadingly over to her father and Anne, then back to Jeremy. "But I want my legs back. You said the girls in the family didn't have their tails all the time, why can't I have my legs?"

"You will get them back," Jeremy explained gently, "when you are stronger. Right now, you are healthier in this form than any other. We'll see how you are doing tonight and then decide."

"But –"

"No complaints, kiddo," her father said. "You've had a rough time of it. We can't risk you having another bad turn."

Jeremy bent down and easily hoisted her out of the water. "Miranda, get the chair."

With her father's help, Lori was settled in the wheelchair. She tried not to look at her tail, but her eyes were constantly drawn to it.

It was long and green and covered with scales that lay neatly over each other. At the lower end, the wide fluke flapped as Jeremy and her father wrapped the wet blanket firmly around it. Finally, she couldn't watch any more and turned away feeling nauseous with fear and revulsion.

You won't always feel that way, Caspian called softly.

"Want to bet?" she muttered.

After she was settled, it was her grandmother's turn. Lori watched Jeremy jump back into the water. Taking her gently into his arms, he carried her to a ramp that fed smoothly into the water.

"We built the ramp to make things easier for Gran," Miranda explained.

When Jeremy carried his mother out of the water everyone saw the damage caused to Undine by the whaler's harpoon. Right where her upper thighs would be, a deep ugly gash ran almost six inches across and several inches down. No scales covered the folded and scarred flesh. Further up her body, they saw the deep and painful scars running from her waist all the way up the skin of her naked front to run off her shoulder from when the tow line had pinned her to Andori's body.

As Anne examined the elderly mermaid, Jeremy explained that since the attack, not only had she lost her sea-speech, but she had also been unable to return to legs. This was followed by Anne's diagnosis of broken femurs and neurological damage.

Lori listened to the details of her grandmother's injuries and saw her aunt's fascination with the theories and principles of being a mermaid and suddenly felt the life she had known, end. She was no longer the person she thought she was. She was an alien, a freak, something to be stared at and whispered about or studied and discussed. She was losing her identity as a person.

Lori was grateful when the conversation stopped and they started to move. Her father pushed her chair, falling in step behind Jeremy and her grandmother's. Passing through the spacious cavern, they followed a long tunnel that led further underground. The ceiling was very high and they could still hear the waves echoing through the rock hall as they travelled. Every few feet, electric lights were hung along the walls, removing any gloom that may have lingered in the deep tunnel.

"Did you build all of this?" Lori's father asked as they travelled along the smooth stone floor.

"Part of it was nature," Jeremy explained. "Part was our family from centuries ago, just in case we needed to make a quick exit to the sea. It actually runs right under our cottage and comes up through the wine cellar."

Before long, the tunnel started to climb. Further along, they approached a 'Y' junction. Danny turned to Aaron. "What's down there?" he motioned down to the right tunnel.

"That's the store room. It's where we keep all the weapons and treasure."

"Weapons?" Anne asked.

"Treasure?" Danny asked, a sparkle in his eyes.

"Weapons and treasure," Jeremy repeated. "Why don't we take a quick detour and show you."

Despite how she was feeling, Lori's eyes flew open with shock when they entered the treasure chamber. There were stacks and stacks of Spanish doubloons and other gold coins. Tables contained bowls overflowing with pearls. Lining the walls were crates of diamonds, rubies and sapphires. Some single stones, others set in beautiful gold necklaces, rings and broaches. Across the chamber an entire area had been devoted to gold bars.

"The mermaids of the family have been bringing up treasure from the seabed for generations," Jeremy explained. "There have been thousands of ships lost over the centuries. The ladies of the family simply go down and collect their spilt cargo and bring it back here." He turned to Lori's father. "If we were ever to declare it all, I'm sure we'd soon discover that we were the richest family on the planet."

Lori's father was left speechless. Finally, he started to nod. "Of course, it all makes sense now. Colleen always had loads of money with her. But she never did explain where it all came from. Her job certainly didn't pay well and she didn't keep it in a bank."

"She couldn't," Jeremy explained. "Neither can we. Banks want to know where money comes from. We couldn't exactly say we'd been wreck-diving. So we store the treasure here and only sell off little pieces when we need to or in emergencies."

"So we're rich?" Danny asked.

Aaron nodded. "Beyond rich!"

58

Jeremy turned his mother's wheelchair around again. "Tour's over for now. Let's get these ladies upstairs."

A few minutes later, they were approaching the cottage's hidden entrance to the tunnel. Jeremy explained that it led to a small wine cellar. Walking single file, they passed through the entrance and approached a narrow set of stairs.

With the practice of those who've done it many times before, without needing to speak, Aaron went up to Jeremy. Together they lifted Undine's wheelchair and started to climb the steps. When they reached the top, they came back down for Lori.

"Just hold on, lass," Jeremy said, taking a position at the side of her wheelchair. "We've got you and won't let you fall."

When Aaron was at the other side, Lori felt them lift her chair easily into the air. After a quick climb, her wheelchair was lowered to the floor beside her grandmother.

Belvoir cottage was spacious but somehow cosy. It had low, beamed ceilings, hardwood floors, and was comfortably furnished. It immediately offered guests the feeling of warmth and welcome.

With tea, biscuits and stronger drinks offered, everyone settled at the dining room table. Jeremy cleared his throat and asked Lori to finish the details of the whale hunt and to explain what had happened to her mother.

Stealing herself against the terror, Lori completed the story of the events of that terrible day.

Anne lowered her head and softly said, "Monsters. I've always hated whaling. But to hear it from this perspective, it's more than just hunting. It's murder."

"It is," Jeremy agreed. "But we've had to live under this shadow all our lives. The spectre of whale hunting isn't going away. Every day, we live in terror of the whalers coming back to kill the rest of the family."

"Maybe some day people will learn," Lori's father said. "We just can't go on destroying everything in the sea. Whaling countries must be made to stop!"

We can only pray, Caspian called.

From the head of the table, Undine finally spoke. "Lori, please ask Caspian what happened to Colleen."

Murmurs of agreement went around the table as everyone turned expectant eyes on Lori.

"Are you ready to go on, Caspian?" she softly called. Lori nodded to the group. "He's ready." Taking a deep breath, she started to repeat everything Caspian said.

The moment my father was hit, Caspian started, *Colleen felt it as sharply as if the harpoon had torn through her. Colleen also felt the deaths in the family. So she left you to come back to us. She had to help the survivors of the attack. But by the time she arrived, it was too late for my cousin. He bled to death from his wounds.*

After passing on the message, Lori had to stop again. She turned pain-filled eyes to her grandmother and asked, "I saw what they did with you and Andori. Why did the whalers cut you free when they took the others away?"

"I know why," Jeremy answered. "There is a seafaring legend that says if you see a mermaid, you respect her. You certainly don't try to kill her. To do so will bring the wrath of the sea upon you. When they saw Mum and realized what she was, they cut her and Andori free in the hopes that they would simply sink to the bottom of the sea without invoking the sea's fury against them."

"But it didn't stop them from taking the others away," Undine said bitterly. "They butchered our family like cattle." When she finished speaking, she lowered her head as tears trickled silently down her cheeks.

"Go on Caspian," Lori softly asked. "Tell us what happened to Mom."

"Indeed," Jeremy agreed. "This is where we lost track of her."

By the time Colleen found us, Caspian continued, *my cousin was dead. My aunt was recovering, but my father and Undine had raging infections. They were critically ill.*

Now, as Undine will tell you, scattered around the world are deep caverns, right at the very bottom of the sea. In some of these caverns special mosses grow that can heal almost any ill. All the creatures of the sea know about them and use them. It is where we get our medicine. So when Colleen arrived, she left us to gather the healing mosses. But in her grief and worry, she wasn't as careful as she should have been. Without realising the danger to herself, she entered a cavern not far from where humans were drilling the foundations for an oil rig –

When Lori repeated Caspian's words, Undine's hands shot up to her mouth. "She didn't!"

Yes, Caspian answered. *Those were the caverns closest to us. Colleen said she had no choice.*

"Colleen shouldn't have!" Undine cried aloud. "I taught her better than that!"

Caspian's voice grew soft and gentle. *Lor-lie, please tell Undine that Colleen's love for her and my father took over all her thoughts. She didn't care about the danger to herself. Her only concern was for them.*

When Lori finished, her grandmother nodded, saying no more.

"It's all right now, Caspian, please go on," Lori said. "What happened next?"

Colleen made countless trips to the caverns over the first few days and nights. She never ate or slept. She just kept going between the caverns and us. You see it took a lot of moss to help my father and my aunt. Not only did she have to pack it into their wounds, they had to eat it as well. And as you will soon see, we are not small.

"I had my fair share too, if I recall," Undine added. "But if I had known where she was getting the mosses from, I would have stopped her."

Lor-Lie, please tell Undine that my father says exactly the same thing. He feels so guilty for what has happened to Colleen. You see, on the fifth day after she arrived, there was a terrible cave-in at the cavern.

A hush filled the air after Lori repeated the story. Finally her father asked, "Was she hurt?"

Yes, she was, admitted Caspian. *She broke her arm and had many cuts and bruises on her back and tail. She lost a large part of her fluke, but that has since grown back. She also cracked a few ribs. You see she'd been pinned down by rubble and had to dig herself out.*

Lori could only stare in shock at her father.

"Well?" he demanded. "What happened to her?"

Lori repeated Caspian's message. Then she paused and held up her hand to silence the room when more questions started. "Wait there's more. Go on Caspian, we're listening."

The worst part was when she tried to leave the cavern. She found that the entire entrance area had been blocked. Desperate to get out, she explored every tunnel and crevasse in the cavern. Though she has flowing water for breathing, and the healing mosses for food, there is no way out. She's been trapped in there ever since.

When Lori finished the last message, a stunned silence filled the room.

She looked at her family in shock. "I can't believe it. Mom has been trapped all this time and we never knew."

She's been waiting for the time of your Trial when I could finally reach you to tell you what happened to her, Caspian finished.

Lori's father rose from the table and started to pace the room. "Oh my beautiful Colleen, I've been blaming you for leaving us and you were innocent." Finally he stopped at Lori's wheelchair. "Ask Caspian why the rest of the whales couldn't help her. They've got to be the strongest creatures in the sea. Surely they could have dug her out."

Lori heard Caspian make a sound that might have been a sigh or a groan. *Your father is right, we are the strongest.* Suddenly his voice broke, *and yes, we tried to free her. But, Lor-lie, we don't have hands! Every time we tried to shove the rocks and rubble away, we caused more damage and more rockslides. Our efforts only sealed Colleen in deeper.*

Lori shook her head sadly as she explained.

"I was there," Undine muttered weakly, "While my baby was trapped in that cavern, I was still with the pod. If I hadn't lost my sea-speech, we could have freed her long ago. Of all the things taken from me on that horrible day, this was the worst. I'm useless to this family now."

"Stop it, Mum," Jeremy said, with love. "We need you as much as we always have. Now that Lori is here, she can speak to the whales for us."

"He's right, Gran," Miranda said, touching her grandmother's arm. "The worst is over. Now that we know what happened to Aunt Colleen, we can go rescue her."

"Amen to that!" Jeremy said. Straightening, he reached for his glass. Raising it, he said, "Here's to healing old wounds and finally bringing this family back together!"

Chapter 12

It took the better part of two days to reach their destination. Throughout the long journey, Luc gently pressed his father for answers. Where were they going? What were they after? How long would they be there? As they travelled in Andre Robichaud's private jet, then onto his personal helicopter, his father said nothing other than, "You'll see."

Luc looked out of the helicopter window and saw only the open sea spreading out beneath them. The waves were high and angry, the sky filled with dark scudding clouds.

"Looks like we're heading into a storm," he said. "Do we have very far to go?"

"It is the time of year," Robichaud said casually. "And no, it will not be long now. We are almost there."

At that, Luc looked out of the window again, straining his eyes to see their destination. In the far distance, he saw a speck on the water. As they drew steadily closer, the spec grew larger until Luc realised it was an oil-drilling rig out in the middle of the sea.

"Is that where we're going?" he asked.

"It is," Robichaud answered. "I bought it from an oil company two years ago. It no longer drills the seabed and instead is doing research for me."

"What kind of research?" Luc asked curiously. His father wasn't the type to care about the environment or what lived in it – unless of course it was nearing extinction.

"A very special kind," his father said cryptically. "I've been working on this project over twenty five years. And only in the past two years have I had any hope of ever seeing my dream fulfilled."

Luc's eyes went back to the drilling platform. What could possibly hold his father's interest for so long, out here in the middle of nowhere? "And you think that platform is the answer to your dreams?"

"Not the platform," Robichaud said, "but the whales that live around it."

"Whales?" Luc repeated. Then he remembered the large sea tank at the estate. Suddenly everything started to make sense. "That's what the tank is for, isn't it?" He pressed. "You're going to try to keep a whale."

"You are half right," Robichaud said. "Now, no more questions. You will have all your answers soon enough. Just be silent and let me think for a while."

Luc knew better than to speak again. Once his father shut off a conversation, it stayed shut off. Instead he turned in his seat and watched the the oil rig drawing closer.

Chapter 13

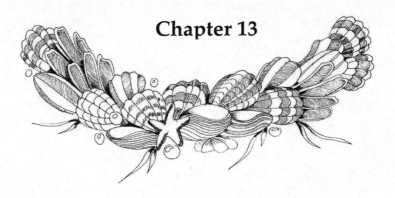

Lori sat back in her wheelchair and felt the mood in the dining room change as the family made plans for the rescue of her mother. They started to make a list of what items would be needed, and how long the rescue would take. Because the whales didn't measure distance the way humans did, they couldn't explain where the cavern was. So it was agreed that Caspian and Coral would come to Herm to lead the family back to where Colleen was trapped.

As the hours sped by, the family excitedly added to their growing list of supplies. When at last the conversation ebbed, and the long day drew to a close, Zephyr called the discussion to a halt. The pod of whales needed to eat and Lori needed to rest. Despite her protests, she knew he was right. She was mentally and physically exhausted and her body was aching badly. Lori and her grandmother were wheeled into the lounge.

"Well, lass," Jeremy said, kneeling beside her chair. "It's been a long and eventful day. How do you feel?"

"Kind of tired and my legs really hurt –" Lori paused to consider what she'd just said. "I mean my tail."

He patted her arm. "I know what you mean. So, what do you want to do? Stay as you are or change back to legs?"

"Lori, dear," Undine said. "You are better off in this form tonight. I don't think it's a good idea for you to change just yet."

"I agree with Undine," Anne said. "You did lose a lot of blood today."

"But I want my legs back," Lori protested. "And I've really got to go to the toilet."

"You don't need your legs for that," her grandmother chuckled.

"Oh, gross!" Danny cried, sitting beside Aaron on the sofa. "We really didn't need to hear that."

"I'm sorry, but I really want my legs back," Lori finished, ignoring Danny and the strange faces he was making at her.

Lori's father turned to Anne. "Do you think she's strong enough?"

Anne looked at Lori for a moment before turning back to her brother. "I think our girl is stronger than all of us," she said. "Aren't you?"

Lori nodded. "Does that mean I can change back?"

Finally her father nodded.

"If you grab Lori," said Jeremy, "I'll show you where she can change."

Lori put her arms around her father's neck as he lifted her out of the wheelchair.

"May I come too?" asked Miranda.

When Lori nodded, Aaron and Danny stood up to follow as well.

"Not this time," Jeremy said, as he stopped them. "I think it's best if you boys sat this one out. When Lori gets used to the change you can watch."

"But Dad –" Danny complained.

"Jeremy's right. Give your sister a break on this one."

Grumbling, Danny sat back down beside Aaron. "It's not fair."

"Nothing ever is," Aaron agreed.

Leaving the lounge, the small group climbed the stairs. Jeremy led them down a long hall to Miranda's bedroom. "Lori, you'll be sharing with Miri while you are here if that's all right?"

Lori smiled at her cousin. "I'd like that."

"Me too," Miranda agreed. Running ahead, she opened the door to her bedroom. "Come on in."

Her father carried her in and placed her down gently on the bed. Lori gazed around the bedroom in amazement. The walls were covered with photographs and posters of whales. On the dresser were glass and porcelain statues of breaching whales and dolphins. The windowsill had a large jar filled with various seashells. There wasn't one piece of free space that didn't have something from the sea in it.

Suddenly embarrassed, Miranda shrugged, "I like whales."

"Me too," Lori agreed. She turned to Jeremy. "What do I do now?"

"The first thing we are going to do is to remove that wet blanket," Jeremy said.

Working with her father and Anne, Lori unwrapped the blanket and pulled it away from her tail.

"Hey," her father said, as Lori leaned over to let them pull it out from beneath her. "I didn't notice it before. But you know what? You've got one heck of a dorsal fin back there."

"Where?" Lori asked, twisting to see the back of her tail. "Is it like a shark?"

"Right here." Her father directed her hand beneath her tail. "And no," he said, chuckling, "it's like a mermaid."

Lori felt the tall spiny fin. Pressing down, it folded neatly against her body. But when she released it, it popped back up again. "It feels really funny. I wonder what it's for?"

Jeremy started to explain that the fin was to help her glide through the water. When he finished, Lori's father smiled and shook his head. "Don't listen to a word he says," he teased as his smile grew. "We all know that's where you're hiding the zipper to that crazy outfit."

"Da–ad!" Lori complained. "That's not very funny." She gazed down on her new body. She'd had her tail for most of the day, but it still felt totally alien to her.

You'll get used to it, Caspian offered.

"I don't think I'll ever get used to turning into a fish whenever I get wet," she tightly muttered.

You're not a fish! Caspian protested.

"Close enough," she whispered back. Then she looked to Jeremy. "So what do I do now?"

"Miri and Anne will help you get out of that wet sweatshirt." Leaving the bed, he walked over to Miranda's desk. A towel was draped over the back of the chair. Coming back to the bed, he handed it to Lori. "Here, you'll need this. Miri, will you get a night shirt for Lori?"

Miranda crossed to her dresser and pulled out a long clean T-shirt and brought it back to the bed. While her father and uncle waited outside the room, Miranda and Anne helped Lori out of her wet sweatshirt. They helped her get into the long, dry nightshirt. When they'd finished, Anne invited the others back.

"Now dry your tail with the towel. It will speed things up a bit," said Jeremy.

Taking the towel, Lori started to rub her tail. Almost immediately she discovered that she could only wipe in a downward direction. Every time she tried to draw the towel up, it caught painfully on her scales.

"Do you feel anything happening?" Anne asked, sitting on the edge of the bed and closely studying her tail.

Lori looked at her tail and concentrated. Was she feeling anything? The answer was, yes. "It's starting to tingle. Will it hurt?"

Caspian answered before Jeremy could. *Your mother said the first time will sting, but it won't be anything like the change from legs to tail.*

"I sure hope not," Lori said, and then relayed to her family what Caspian had said. Moments later the tingling increased. Lying back on the bed, she shut her eyes and waited for the real pain to start.

It didn't; though it did pinch a lot. Lori could almost feel her scales retracting as the skin folded in on itself. It was like nothing she'd ever experienced before. But after a few minutes, it subsided. Leaving her lying on the bed with two very badly bruised, but very separate, legs.

"Well, thank God for that," her father said, kissing her on the top of the head. "Not that your tail wasn't lovely. It's just nice to have my girl back."

With the change complete and the excitement over, Lori's father asked if he could have a private moment with his daughter. Offering to make cocoa and crumpets for everybody, Jeremy directed Anne and Miranda out of the room.

When they were alone, her father sat on the edge of the bed and gave Lori a fierce hug. "You gave me quite a scare today."

"I'm sorry, I didn't mean to."

He hugged her again, "I know you didn't. You didn't know. None of us did." Releasing her, he sat back and took both of her hands. "It's been a really rough day but it's over now and, thank God, you're all right."

When Lori nodded, he continued, "I still can't believe it. You're actually a mermaid. How are you feeling about it all?"

Lori sighed. "I really don't know what I feel. So much has changed. It's kind of like my whole life before was a lie."

He became serious and squeezed her hands. "Yes, a lot has changed for you, and for all of us. But your life was never a lie. You are still you, the person you were two weeks ago, and the same person you'll be tomorrow. It's just developed further."

"But what happens now?" Lori asked. "Do we go back to Canada and pretend this never happened? What about school? How can I go back, knowing what I am? Do I tell Becky about it? Let her see my tail?"

Her father shook his head. "We've got a lot to figure out. And I know Becky is your best friend. But I don't think you should tell her or any of your friends. Jeremy is right. This is just too big a secret to risk sharing with anyone. I'm only now realising the kind of danger you and the boys could be in if the world ever found out about you."

"So what do we do?" Lori asked.

"I don't know," he answered truthfully. "We just take it one day at a time. But our first concern is getting your mother back."

Lori agreed and then yawned deeply.

Her father rose from the bed. "Now then, do you feel like you could eat something? Or do you want to rest?"

"Actually I'm really tired," Lori admitted. "I think I'll stay here and rest."

"Then climb under the covers and get comfortable. I'm sure the family will understand. Get some sleep, we've got a big day tomorrow."

Chapter 14

As the helicopter touched down on the landing pad, Luc felt his excitement growing. He's never been on a drilling rig before. And even though he didn't know what he was doing here, and despite his feelings towards his father, he was actually glad he'd come.

When the door to the helicopter opened, he followed his father out onto the platform. Luc watched a line of anxious looking men hesitantly approaching.

"Monsieur Robichaud," the oldest of the men said, coming forward and bowing slightly. "There has been a lot of excitement amongst the whales. But I must report something rather disturbing news as well. Come this way and we'll show you."

Falling in line behind his father, Luc followed them off the landing pad and onto the actual drilling platform. The oil rig wasn't as big as he'd expected, and despite the growing wind, it was strangely quiet. He could see all the equipment that would have been working if the rig was still drilling and pumping oil. Instead it was abandoned, and starting to suffer corrosion under the cruel, salty sea air.

The line of men left the exposed outer area and entered the covered complex. Luc was glad to be out of the chilling wind.

"This way, Monsieur," said the older man. "The cameras captured everything."

Walking beside one of the younger men, Luc said softly, "I'm Luc Robichaud. What did the cameras capture?"

"I'm Arthur McMillan," the young man said. "We thought one of the whales had died. He was having fits and rolling over in the water as though he'd been harpooned. The others stayed at his side and kept him at the surface. But we honestly believed he was dying. Then just as suddenly, he was fine."

"Really?" Luc said. "Is that normal for a whale?"

"Not at all. But then, nothing about this pod is normal."

"Pod?"

"That is the technical term for a family of whales," Arthur explained.

Luc nodded. "So what makes these whales so different?"

"These are humpbacks – of a sort, although their particular sub-species haven't been officially recognized. If you look at them, they are physically different from other humpbacks."

"How so?" Luc asked. "I never knew there was a difference."

"Neither did any of us," Arthur said. "But these whales are very different. The males are all white, whereas other humpbacks are black and grey with white on the undersides. Not to mention all other humpback species migrate. But not these ones; these guys haven't left this area since the rig was built. Which I assume is why your father bought it. So he could study them."

Luc frowned. "My father never mentioned this. Or that he had any interest in whales. How long have you been here?"

"Almost from the beginning," Arthur said. "After your father bought the rig, he gathered up some of the top marine biology students from several universities and brought us all here. I haven't been home in ages."

Luc's frown deepened. "I don't understand. You've been on the rig all this time? Why? What does my father have you doing?"

Arthur shrugged. "Not a lot. All we ever do is watch. We aren't allowed to approach the whales or do any underwater studies. We just watch them and report what we've seen."

"What does my father want?"

"I don't know," Arthur said. "I was kind of hoping you could tell me."

Luc studied his father's back as he charged through the complex. He realised he knew very little about the man, other than the fact that he had murdered his mother and sold weapons to anyone who had money – that and his obsession with his collection. As for the man himself, Luc knew nothing.

Robichaud was asking detailed questions about the pod and listening intently to the answers. But he didn't once mention capturing one and taking it back to the estate.

Luc's confusion grew as he followed the group of men into a darkened office. It contained a large, long control consul and a wall of large-screen monitors. They were on and appeared to be connected to multiple cameras that were placed around the drilling platform. All the cameras were pointed at the whales. Most of the screens were showing the surface of the water. But there was one that showed the seabed.

Luc stepped closer to the screens and saw the underwater images were not showing anything other than boulders lying in front of a tall rock face. The images had a greenish glow, which meant they were using an infrared camera. But the images at the surface clearly showed the spray of whale breath as the pod broke the surface to breathe. The sight of the large animals filled him with excitement.

"Show me the recording of the seizure," Robichaud demanded.

One of the technicians immediately went to the computer consul and pulled up the images.

"It started early in the day," the older man explained as he stood beside the large viewing screen. "We had noticed for a few days prior to the episode that the entire pod seemed very agitated. But on the day of the seizure, they remained at the surface for most of the morning and were encircling one of the younger males. That young male appeared to be in some distress. It got worse as the day progressed."

Both Luc and his father stepped closer to the screen showing all the whales huddled around one. As the images were speeded up, it revealed the sick whale obviously in pain. As the seizure progressed, the larger whales struggled to keep the young one at the surface to breathe.

The images on the screen disturbed Luc greatly as he watched the whale writhing in agony. Just when it appeared the poor creature couldn't take any more, it rolled over on its back and became still.

"We were all certain he was dead," the man was saying. "If you look, you can see the large scarred male nudging him, trying to get him to turn over again. Soon all the others started to push at the young male to get him back over. Now, if you look closely –" The older man pointed at a spot on the screen. "You can see the young male starting to stir. With the others' help, he was righted, and slowly recovered."

Luc's mouth hung open as he watched the older whales helping the younger one. They knew he needed their help and were giving it. For animals so big, he was amazed at the tenderness shown.

"You said there was bad news?" Robichaud said.

"Yes, Monsieur," the man said. "Yesterday, the sick whale and another youngster left the pod for no apparent reason. They haven't been back."

Luc studied his father. He was never good with bad news.

"Did your men follow them?" Robichaud softly demanded.

"Yes, of course, Monsieur," the man said nervously. "But with the bad weather and darkness, they lost them in the night. Wherever they were going, they were in a great hurry to get there."

Andre Robichaud inhaled deeply and turned to study the screens again. Finally he said, "The large scarred male? Is he still with the pod?"

"Yes Monsieur." The man stepped up to a different screen and seemed to study it for a while. Finally he pointed. "He is here."

Robichaud approached and gently touched the screen showing the scarred white whale at the surface of the water. "Just what are you up to, my old friend?" he asked softly. "What are you up to?"

Chapter 15

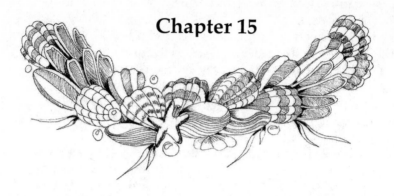

Lori woke to the strange sound of singing in her head. For a moment she felt disoriented and confused. Then the sound of light breathing brought everything back. Turning her head, she saw Miranda sleeping peacefully beside her. The bedroom window showed the first streaks of dawn rising on the horizon.

I'M A MERMAID!

Lori started to shake as the realization settled in. She wasn't human. She had a green tail with scales. She had gills and webbed fingers. Her mother wasn't human either. Neither were her brothers, cousins or uncle. They were all a bunch of freaks.

Trying to calm herself down, Lori took several deep breaths and listened to the sad, haunting melody that was playing softly in her head. When it finished, she quietly called out.

"Caspian?"

I'm here, he gently answered. *Good morning, are you feeling better?*

"Not really," she said softly. "Caspian, what kind of life can I have now? I'm a freak, a monster. I'm a fish."

No you're not! Caspian shot back. *Lor-lie, it is true that you are different. You are special. But you're not a freak, any more than I am. Look at Miranda, is she one?*

Lori glanced over at her sleeping cousin. "Is she a mermaid?"

Yes.

"Then she's a freak too."

Just what is a freak? Caspian asked. *Someone who is different from everyone else?*

"I guess so," Lori said hesitantly.

Then everyone in the world is a freak to everyone else. Some people have blue eyes, some brown, green or hazel. Some are right handed while others are left. Some people have different coloured skin or hair. Lori, if being different means 'Freak' then you could say the world is filled with them!

"But no one turns into a fish when they get wet," Lori argued.

And that is what makes you special, Caspian said cheerfully. *You should celebrate your difference, not despair over it!*

Lori realised she wasn't going to get anywhere with him. He just didn't understand how she was feeling. Finally she changed the subject. "Caspian, what was that sound? It was like music, but not. I've heard it a few times, but never very clearly."

It was music, he answered lightly.

"Music? From where?"

I told you in my memories that each morning we rise to the surface of the sea and wait for the dawn. Then when we see the first rays of sunlight, my father starts to sing. Then we all join in.

"But it sounds so sad and lonely. What are you singing about?"

It's very sad. We're singing about your mother and how she is suffering and lonely. We also sing about our dead family, and all the whales taken from the sea by the human hunters.

Lori thought back to the first time she heard the music when the voice appeared in her head. "The song you sang this morning sounds just like the one I've heard before."

It is the same song. And even though we are away from the family, Coral and I still sing it.

"Well, don't you know any other songs? Maybe sing something cheery for a change? I know a few I could teach you."

Caspian chuckled lightly. *I've heard your music. To tell you the truth, I prefer ours!* He then became serious. *You see, what we sing is more than simple music. Like you have books to record your history, we sing songs. It will be the same song all year long to remind us of our losses. Then next spring, my father will sing something new. Sometimes the other whales pick it up and carry it across the sea with them. As for us singing happy songs? Right now, what do we have to be happy about?*

Lori had to agree with him. After all the pain and suffering they'd gone through, why should they sing something happy? "But what about when we rescue Mom? Will Zephyr change it then?"

Oh yes. Dad's promised that the moment Colleen is free, no matter when it is he will sing a new song – a very joyous one.

"Then I hope he can sing it soon."

Lori settled back down in bed but sleep would not return. Lying on her side, she felt her legs throbbing badly, and her mind was spinning. Her life had changed completely. Watching the bright sunshine rising in the window, she wondered what kind of future lay ahead.

Lost deep in thought, she didn't hear Miranda waking.

"Good morning," her cousin said quietly, starting to yawn and stretch. "How are you feeling today?"

"Like I've been run over by a steam roller," Lori admitted. "My legs are killing me."

"Gran says that won't last." Miranda paused, something pressing on her mind. "Lori, can I ask you something?"

Lori nodded.

"What's it like having a tail?"

"Too weird. You think of moving your legs and feet and it sort of moves instead."

"I can't wait to change," Miranda sighed. "I'll finally be able to go exploring deep into the sea with the whales."

"I guess it's different for you," Lori said thoughtfully. "You've grown up knowing what you are. This kind of hit me like a ton of bricks. I had no idea until it was almost too late."

"But now that you know?" Miranda pressed.

"Now I'm not sure how I feel."

"Well, I'm glad you changed. Then when I do, we can go with Coral and Caspian and spend lots of time in the sea."

Lor-lie, Caspian called. *Tell Miranda that her Trial isn't far off. Her voice has been growing louder in Coral for some time. Just like it did for me with you.*

Lori passed on Caspian's message.

"Really?" Miranda exclaimed. "Would you please tell Caspian that I can't wait for them to get here!"

We can't wait either, Caspian agreed. *Coral and I will be there just as soon as we can.*

"What's he saying?" Miranda begged. When Lori passed on the message, she squealed with excitement. "What a time that will be!

76

Now, come on let's get dressed. I'm starving!" Springing from the bed, she started to get dressed.

Lori was much slower.

As she stood up, the throbbing in her legs worsened until she had to sit down again. "I don't think I'll be running any races today. I don't even think I can get dressed."

Deciding against jeans, Lori stayed in her long nightshirt and drew a robe over her stiff shoulders. "Gosh, I'm aching everywhere!" As she massaged her tender skin, she called out to Caspian. "Does your skin hurt too?"

Yes it does, Caspian admitted. *Right down to the tip of my tail. But at least we're alive"*

"Yes we are," Lori agreed, as she followed Miranda out of the bedroom. "Yes we are."

After breakfast, Jeremy suggested Miranda take Lori on a short tour of the island before they start to work on the rescue. Danny and Aaron had already planned to go exploring. With the weather clear, Lori excitedly agreed.

Jeremy also suggested they visit Belvoir Bay, but warned Lori to stay well away from the water's edge until she had recovered from the Trial.

"Oh, I won't go near the water!" Lori promised. "I don't want to change again for a long time."

Don't say that, Lor-lie, Caspian said sadly. *Please, don't hate what you are.*

"I don't hate what I am," Lori explained. "I just don't want to hurt again."

I don't want to hurt again either. But your mother told me to tell you that the next time you change, it won't. It will be easy.

"We'll see," Lori said uneasily.

After dressing in Miranda's loosest fitting tracksuit, Lori walked painfully to the front door. Miranda helped her on with her coat. "We'll be back in a while," she called to Jeremy as she held the door open for Lori.

Lori stepped out into the fresh, clear, February day and breathed deep the sea air. "This place smells wonderful."

"It is. I know you're going to love it here. Give me your hand; the trail can be a bit steep."

Lori held onto her cousin as they slowly walked away from the cottage and made their way down the winding track. Passing through trees and hedgerows, Lori could hear the waves breaking softly on the shore, but couldn't see the sea.

"How far is it?"

"Just ahead, round that bend," Miranda pointed. "Then we go down some stairs to the beach."

Rounding the bend, Lori's eyes were struck by her first view of Belvoir Bay. It formed a perfect half-circle with high, rocky walls rising on three sides. Ahead she saw the blue-green waters of the sea.

"It's beautiful!" Lori cried, "I don't think I've ever seen a place as perfect as this."

"Wait till you get down to the beach," Miranda offered, leading her forward.

A few steps ahead, Lori spied a platform that led to a set of wooden stairs. When she approached, she gazed down onto the beach over a hundred feet below. "I don't know about this," she said doubtfully. "That's a lot of stairs and my legs are killing me."

"I know, but you're going to love it. Don't worry, I'll help you down."

"It's coming back up that's got me worried."

"We'll manage," Miranda said, enthusiastically.

The stairs were steep and very slippery from the previous days' rain. Halfway down, they came across another platform opening up to reveal a small, hidden snack bar built into one of the rocky walls.

"It stays closed until the summer," Miranda offered. "This time of year, Belvoir Bay is ours. Very few tourists visit Herm in the winter."

"I'd never heard of Herm until Caspian told me about it," Lori admitted, as she started slowly down the second set of steps.

"I know. It's not very well known at all. But we like it that way."

"Does the family own the island?"

"Us? No. But there's something written somewhere about how we're allowed to stay as long as we want. Jeremy owns a pub on the other side of the island. It's run independently from the rest of the businesses here."

"Do the others know about us? I mean the family secret?"

78

"I don't think so. My friend Jenny has never asked. She lives here too. We both go to school on Guernsey."

Lori tried to compare her life and friends in Canada with the life Miranda had here. They were totally different. "It must be weird living on a small island."

"It's all I've ever known," Miranda admitted. "But I like it. I don't think I could ever live anywhere else except maybe in the sea."

"You should come and see Canada, it's really beautiful. Not like this," Lori admitted, finally reaching the bottom and stepping carefully onto the sand, "but beautiful. I'd like you to meet some of my friends. I know they'd love your accent!"

Miranda laughed, "I like yours, too."

When they stepped further onto the beach, Lori looked around. "Wow, this place is magic."

"It sure is," Miranda agreed as they walked towards the water's edge. She plonked down on the sand. Lori was much slower as she carefully sat down beside her cousin.

A comfortable silence settled as both girls looked out over the water. Light waves were teasing the shore and filling the air with their gentle hushing sound. Lori closed her eyes and inhaled deeply. A feeling of profound peace came to her.

Then the sound of laughter and heavy feet on the steps drew her from her reverie. Turning, she saw Aaron and Danny racing down the stairs. Jumping the last few steps, they bounded up to Lori and Miranda and plopped down in the sand beside them. Lori was surprised to see her moody brother actually smiling.

"Hi guys!" Danny punched Lori lightly on the shoulder. "How are you doing?"

Lori eyed her brother suspiciously. "Are you feeling all right?"

"Sure," he said. "Why? What's wrong?"

"Nothing," Lori quickly said. "It just that –" she paused again. "Nothing, everything is fine."

"Hey, you girls want to come exploring with Dan and me?" Aaron asked. "We're going to go see the ancient burial grounds at the end of the island."

"I'd really love to," Lori admitted, "but I'm not walking so well today. Maybe tomorrow?"

"Sure. There's always lots to see."

A moment later, the boys were off again and racing down the beach to explore a deep cave cutting into the sea wall.

"Dan?" Lori repeated. "Aaron called him Dan, not Danny. That's weird."

"How old are your brothers?" Miranda asked.

Lori watched the colour rising in her cousin's cheeks. "Well, Eddie just turned eighteen."

"And Danny?"

"He's fifteen." Laughing, Lori shoved Miranda, "and he's your cousin, so forget it!"

Miranda's blush deepened. "I didn't mean that!" she said shoving Lori back. "What I meant to say is that he always seems angry. Is he all right?"

Lori looked down the beach to her brother, running beside Aaron. "He is angry all the time. He doesn't have any friends and he's always getting into fights at school. Dad says it's a stage he going through but I think Mom leaving really bothered him. I mean it bothered all of us, but with Danny, it was much worse. They were very close. When she didn't come home, he became a different person. He was really moody and spending most of his time alone in his room on his computer."

"Maybe that will change when we rescue your mum."

"It seems to be changing already. I haven't seen him smile this much in years."

"Herm must be good for him," Miranda offered.

They watched the waves restlessly washing to the shore, each thinking her own thoughts. Picking up handfuls of cool sand, Lori watched it filter through her fingers. After a time, she turned to Miranda. "What happened to your parents? I saw pictures on the wall of all of you, but Jeremy never said."

Miranda took in a deep breath and Lori thought she wasn't going to answer.

"My mum died when I was little," she finally said. "She was going to have another baby, but there were complications – something about different blood types. It seemed the things that make us different from humans really showed up in the baby. So they kind of killed each other. The doctors wanted to do an investigation, but my dad said no."

"I'm so sorry," Lori said softly. "I guess I still don't understand that we're different. I mean I feel the same as I always felt. But now, to learn that I'm not even human and that my brothers are different too. It's kind of hard to take."

"I know," Miranda said. "But now that you know, Lori, you must be extra careful. My father was always telling Aaron and me that. He said our difference shows up in our blood. That we can't go to doctors, or ever let our blood be tested."

Lori was silent a long time. Finally she looked at Miranda, "And your dad? What happened to him?"

"He died two years ago," Miranda said softly. "It was after the attack on the family. When the whales carried Gran back here and she could finally speak again, she told my father and Jeremy the name of the ship that attacked them. So they went to Japan to sink the ship and punish the whalers. But the whalers fought back and shot them."

Lori's hands shot up to her mouth. "Jeremy was shot?"

Tears suddenly gathered on Miranda's lashes. "Lori, the whalers killed my father. I don't even know where he's buried or what happened to him –"

"I'm so sorry," Lori said as she put her arm around her cousin and held her until the tears finally slowed.

Sniffing loudly, Miranda hiccupped and said, "we're just glad that Jeremy managed to get away and come back to us. I don't know what would have happened to us if he'd died as well."

"I'm glad too," Lori admitted. "If he hadn't survived, then I'd be dead now. He saved my life. I don't think I can ever repay him for that."

Sitting together, both girls gazed at the water. Above them, dark storm clouds were swiftly blowing in, casting a patchwork of shadows on the cool beach sand.

"Looks like it might rain again," Lori offered, squinting up to the sky.

"It does that a lot here," Miranda said, sniffing back the last of her tears. "One moment it's bright sun, the next it's pouring."

"Hello ladies!"

Both girls jumped. Behind them, Jeremy, Anne and Lori's father started to laugh.

"Little bit jumpy there, kiddo?" Lori's father finally asked. He offered her his hand up.

"No. We're fine!" Lori climbed painfully to her feet. "We just didn't expect you to come creeping up on us like that."

"Who was creeping?" Jeremy innocently said.

"You were," Miranda said, suddenly brightening.

"We've come down to get you," Jeremy continued. "Brian and Anne here said they've never had pub grub. We thought we'd take our Canadian friends down to the pub for a meal. What do you say?"

Lori and Miranda looked at each other and nodded.

Walking stiffly back to the base of the wooden stairs, Lori gazed up and wondered how she'd managed to climb down all that way. There had to be at least a hundred steps, rising steeply up the cliff face.

When she hesitated, her father crouched down before her. "How about a piggy-back ride?"

Lori climbed carefully onto her father's back. "Just don't fall. Okay?"

At the top of the stairs, Jeremy looked up at the sky again. Above them, the dark clouds were moving in thick and fast as the wind picked up speed. "I think we'd better get you under cover before the skies open up on us."

Gazing up, Lori was amazed how fast the weather had changed. "How far is it to your pub?"

"It's on the other side of the island."

Lori checked the sky again. "We won't make it!"

"Sure we will, lass," Jeremy said. "This isn't that big an island. Ten minutes at most and you'll be safe and still dry."

It took them almost fifteen minutes to walk up the steep tree-lined path. At the crest of the hill, Miranda pointed to another island resting in the distance.

"That's Guernsey over there," she said in her best tour-guide voice.

Lori looked across the water to the larger island. She could see the ports and commercial buildings. The view was completely different on this side of Herm. It was not nearly as tranquil as the other side of the island, which offered only the sea.

"I prefer the other side," Lori finally decided. "This looks too built up."

"We all prefer Belvoir Bay," Jeremy put in. "Which is why we live there. That's our home. Not this side of Herm."

When they felt the first sporadic drops of rain, Jeremy moved them onward. "Tour's over for now. I think we'd best get Lori indoors before she transforms right here on the trail."

Jeremy's comment triggered a spark of fear in Lori. "How wet do I have to get before I change?"

Jeremy smiled and put his arm around her. "A lot more than these few drops of rain, lass, so don't worry. But if the skies open, we could be in a bit of trouble. So let's not tempt fate."

Lori nodded but still felt a deep sense of unease. This was just another thing to remind her of how much her life had suddenly changed. She'd never been bothered by rain before. Now it had become her mortal enemy.

Continuing on along a steep, paved road that went down the other side of Herm they reached an area that joined another small paved road. Just to the right, they passed several brightly painted tourist shops. Further along was a tall wall made of rough stone. Halfway along the wall was a large archway bearing a wooden sign. It showed a blue-tailed mermaid sitting on a rock, combing her long blonde hair. Beneath the painting were the words, 'The Mermaid'.

"The Mermaid?" asked Anne, raising her eyebrows.

"Don't tell me," Jeremy complained. "It was called that many years before our family bought it. But it's tradition for pubs to keep their names."

"Gran says the early mermaids weren't as careful as we are – they were always being seen," Miranda explained to Lori, as they passed under the arch and entered a neatly groomed stone courtyard.

Walking beside her father, Lori crossed over to the pub and went through the first set of doors. They then walked up to a second set. Passing through, she was immediately struck by the splendour of the old pub.

"This place is fantastic!" Lori breathed as she walked further in. Ahead of her she saw a magnificent old oak bar with several beer taps. She marvelled at the heavy wooden beams that crossed the ceiling. "How old is it?"

"Hundreds of years old," Miranda answered proudly. "You want a tour?"

Lori nodded.

"How about some drinks first?" Jeremy offered. Removing his coat, he stepped behind the bar and rubbed his hands eagerly together. "So now, what's it to be? Sodas or whiskey?"

"Sodas, please," Lori laughed.

As she waited for her drink, Lori's eyes continued to scan the old pub. Finally they came to rest on another painting of a green-tailed mermaid. Just like the one hanging outside the pub, this mermaid was sitting on a rock and combing her long hair.

"That's Gran," Miranda explained. "Granddad painted it years ago. The mermaid outside is her mother, Lorelie. I guess you're named after her."

"Lorelie," Lori repeated. "Was Gran's mother's tail really blue?"

"No, it was green, just like yours," Miranda, answered. "Gran says it was painted blue so it would be more unbelievable."

A gust of wet wind suddenly blew in and whipped their hair back. Turning to the doors, Lori saw Aaron and Danny enter. They were stomping their feet and shaking water out of their hair.

"That storm came out of nowhere!" Danny complained. "It's pouring out."

Passing over to the window, Lori peered out. "Looks like we just made it."

"Speak for yourself," Danny said. "I'm soaked to the skin!"

Outside the pub, the rain was coming down in sheets so heavy Lori couldn't see across the courtyard. Watching it, she knew there was no way she could have avoided transforming had they been caught in the downpour.

From his place at the bar, Jeremy called over to Danny and Aaron, "Stand over by the fire, lads. That'll warm you up."

In the centre of the pub was a huge hearth. Standing over the roaring fire, Danny studied the large ship's wheel mounted on the whitewashed chimney. "Is that real?"

"Yes. It's from a boat called The Mermaid," Aaron answered.

Lori joined them at the fire as Danny asked, "but I thought this pub was called The Mermaid?"

"Everything here seems to be called that," Lori lightly offered, noting that her brother still seemed to be in a good mood. She sighed. "Danny, isn't this place great?"

"This whole island is fantastic!" Danny said excitedly. "You should see the cliffs at the end. You can climb right to the top and watch the waves hitting the rocks at the bottom. There's even a pirates' cove down there. You can see the entrance right now, but Aaron says when the tide is in, it's completely hidden."

Miranda turned to Lori. "I'll take you there when the rain stops, if you like," she offered. "There's so much to see here."

Nodding her head, Lori saw Eddie emerging from the pub's kitchen.

"Lunch won't be long now. Jeremy, the soup is almost done," he said. "Everyone get washed and ready."

Seated before the roaring fireplace, they were served a huge lunch. Unlike the previous night, Lori was starving and attacked her food with enthusiasm. As the afternoon wore on, the tables were cleared and the kitchen cleaned. While Lori and Miranda did the dishes, Jeremy started making calls to arrange for supplies for the upcoming rescue.

Outside the pub, the rain turned into a gale. The wind was howling and the sky went black with scudding thunderheads while inside, Miranda gave Lori and her brothers a tour of the old pub.

When they returned to the bar, Lori went up to her father. "Dad, you should see this place, it's amazing."

"I will honey," he said. "But right now we need your help. We want you to contact Caspian and see if they can tell us when they'll arrive."

"Caspian?" Lori called.

I heard, Caspian answered. *Tell your dad we should be there in three or four days.*

"Caspian said they should be here in three or four days."

"Great, lad," Jeremy said. "You two be extra careful. Stay well clear of any ships. Whalers or tourists!"

We will, Caspian responded.

"Okay everyone," Jeremy said, as he walked back to the tables. "I want us to be ready to go the moment Caspian and Coral make it here. We can't waste a minute."

"And we don't want them seen here again," Miranda added. She looked over to Lori. "Herm isn't exactly on humpbacks' migratory route."

"Indeed," Jeremy agreed. "It always causes a bit of a sensation when the family come around."

"Maybe they shouldn't come all the way to Herm," Lori suggested. "We could meet them further out at sea."

Jeremy considered. "Good idea. With your connection to Caspian, you'll be able to lead us to them. They won't have to come all the way."

"But we still have to pick up the supplies," Danny put in.

"True," Jeremy agreed. "Aaron tells me you are a bit of a computer genius. Would you work with him to track down some of the items we need? You could order them online and we could pick them up in London."

Lori watched her brother blossom under the compliment.

"Sure! We could start looking today."

Chapter 16

The initial novelty of visiting the drilling rig soon wore off as Luc discovered there was nothing for him to do. He found himself spending more and more time with Arthur as the young marine biologist went about his daily routine. But even then, after the cameras had been checked, the whales counted and reports made, all there was to do was stand at the side of the rig and watch the whales through binoculars.

"You see over there," Arthur explained, over the biting cold wind. He pointed at the whales. "That big one with the deep scar running down his side? That's the leader of the pod. There's another really big one, but I think he's second in command."

Arthur lowered his binoculars and handed them to Luc. "It's strange really. They appeared to be such a close pod, especially when you saw them with the sick one. But watching them now, those guys don't seem to care about the two who have gone."

Luc pulled up his collar against the biting winds. He lifted the binoculars and looked over to whales on the swelling seas. "Maybe they drove them away," he suggested. "Maybe that one was really sick and they didn't want him to stay?"

"I just don't know," Arthur admitted. "But you may have a point. There really isn't a lot of food out here. Maybe they didn't want to share it with one who wasn't well. But that still doesn't explain why the other healthy one left with him. These whales spend all their time doing nothing. Why make a change now?" He paused and seemed to consider. "Mind you, there is an area at the bottom of the sea they spend a lot of time at. I have no clue why." He turned to Luc. "Want to see it?"

Luc nodded, grateful for the opportunity to get away from the freezing weather. He followed Arthur away from the side of the rig and back into the warmth of the monitor room. Apart from one technician doing his normal checks, the room was empty. Luc was glad to see his father wasn't there.

"Here, I'll pull up some old footage," Arthur said, as he took off his heavy coat and shook out his wet hair.

Moments later, Luc was watching a large screen that showed the sea bed and a bunch of boulders at the base of a wall. The colours seemed greenish and grainy and nothing was very clear at all. "What am I looking at?" he asked.

"Keep watching," Arthur said. "It takes time to get used to the distortion. There is no light down at the bottom, so we have to use special equipment. It cost your father a fortune to hook this up, but we've hidden an infrared red camera that can take the deep-sea pressure. It's disguised as a rock so we can move it slowly along the sea bed without disturbing the whales."

Luc continued to stare at the screen. Suddenly he saw movement as the large, white scarred whale came into view. Moments later, he settled on the sea bed facing the pile of rubble. Without moving, the whale just lay there.

"What's he doing?" Luc asked.

"We have no idea," Arthur admitted. "We've seen that same whale spend most of his days there. Not moving, and only leaving to surface for air. Then he goes right back down to the bottom again. Sometimes the others will join him and just lay there."

"Is that normal for whales?"

"Not at all," Arthur admitted. "But like I told you before, nothing about these whales is normal."

Chapter 17

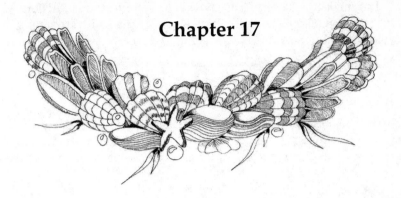

With the storm raging outside the pub, there wasn't a lot they could do for the moment. To fill their time, Lori and Miranda went into the pub's poolroom to play a few games. While they played, Lori told Miranda about her life in Canada and the way they lived, compared to life on Herm. Then they discussed the times to come when they would spend time in the sea with the whales.

When dinner arrived and everyone gathered together to eat, Lori noticed Jeremy and Anne's hair was soaking wet.

"What happened to you two?" she asked.

"We went back to the cottage to take some dinner down to the cavern to Mum, and to let her know we're stuck here for the night."

"We are?" Lori asked.

"The gale is increasing," Jeremy explained. "We've got plenty of room here and I don't want any of us to risk that muddy trail back to the cottage."

"Oh, one thing Undine said," Anne added, looking over to Lori. "She thinks you should go into the bathtub tonight and change. She wanted you to do it in the cave with her, but under the circumstances, she said the tub would have to do. She says in the beginning, you should do it quite often. Get your body used to itself again."

Lori dropped her fork. "I – I don't know about that," she said. "My legs still hurt a lot."

Jeremy started to laugh. "Mum said you would use any excuse to avoid it. Seriously, lass, you should try it. I remember when Colleen first changed she was just like you. She never wanted to do it again. But Mum said she had to. It's kind of like exercise. You've got to keep at it even though every muscle in your body hurts."

But this isn't exercise, Lori thought to herself. And it will hurt. A lot. Yet despite her fears, deep down inside, she knew she couldn't avoid water forever. If this was going to be her new life, she must face her fears.

Several hours later, Lori watched Jeremy prepare the bath. He was pouring salt into the water. "If you're anything like your mum and gran, you'll prefer cold baths to warm. The salt will help ease the soreness of your legs."

As she watched the tub filling with cold water, she felt nerves bunching up in her stomach. In the hall outside the bathroom, her two brothers and cousins were also anxiously waiting to see what would happen. Beside her, her father was clutching her hand.

"There you go, lass," Jeremy said. "Now, what your mum used to do is sit on the edge of the tub and swing both her feet into the water at the same time. The change will start from there."

Lori nodded. Removing her robe, she stood in her long nightshirt. For the first change, the family had asked to be with her. Stepping up to the tub, she looked down at the cold water in fear.

"Is all your jewellery off?" Jeremy asked.

Lori held up her hands and showed that she'd removed her rings.

"Very good. Now, sit down on the edge," he coached.

Following his orders, Lori sat down.

"Wait!" Eddie suddenly cried from the hall. "Can we come in and watch the change?"

Lori looked at her father and Anne and nodded. Soon Eddie, Miranda and Aaron were jammed into the small bathroom as well. Danny chose to remain in the hall.

"Now take your time," Jeremy said, taking hold of her other hand. "Only when you are ready."

Lori inhaled deeply. Her heart was pounding fiercely in her chest. She could feel shivers of fear coursing up and down her spine. Shutting her eyes, she released her father and uncle's hands. Not giving herself time to change her mind, she brought up her legs and passed them over the edge of the bathtub and slipped down into the cold water.

The change started immediately. Gritting her teeth she waited for the pain to follow. But it didn't. Instead, when she opened her eyes, she watched the skin on her legs swell and start to open. The scales slid easily out. There was no blood, no tearing of the skin. Instead, she felt a strange tingling sensation all over her body. Like before, it was as if her legs had been asleep and were coming suddenly awake. She was going through pins and needles, but no more than that. When it ended, her legs were gone. In their place was a silvery-green tail that ended in the wide fluke.

"Wow! That was amazing!" Eddie cried stepping up to the tub.

"Simply incredible!" Anne added. "Everything I've ever known about science says that's impossible. It can't happen. But it just did. How did it feel?"

Lori grinned. "It tingled a lot but there was no pain at all."

"Well, thank God for that!" her father said, smiling. "It really was a sight to see."

As she lay in the tub, Lori frowned and said to Jeremy, "I think you need a bigger bathtub." Looking down the length of her tail, she found that her fluke had jammed itself painfully under the taps.

Concentrating, she thought of moving her legs. Immediately her tail shifted. Lifting her 'feet', she watched the large fluke rise in the air. Higher and higher until it was clear of the taps. She tilted it to the left and then draped it over the side of the tub. Sighing again, she was finally able to stretch all the way out and lie back.

"It's amazing, I think of moving my legs and feet, then the tail really does move the same way."

And no pain! Caspian cheered. *No more pain!*

"No more pain!" Lori shouted. She slammed her hands down in the water and splashed the others in the room. "It's wonderful."

Soon everyone was laughing. There seemed to be a collective sigh of relief that the change had gone well.

"Okay guys," her father finally said, herding everyone towards the door. "Lori's all right. So let's get out of here and let her take her bath in peace."

When she was alone, Lori leaned forward and pulled off her wet nightshirt. She then lay back in the water and started to relax. Slowly scanning the length of her tail, she frowned lightly.

"Caspian?"

I'm here.

"Why green?

Why what green?

"My tail. Why is my tail green?"

What colour would you like it to be? He started to laugh.

"I don't know. But green seems such a strange colour."

What colour are your eyes?

"My eyes? They're blue."

Why blue?

"I don't know, they just are."

Exactly.

"Ha-ha, very funny," Lori said dryly.

Well, if you ask a silly question –

"You get a silly answer. I know." Lori paused and swept her hands under the water. She enjoyed feeling the water pressing against the thick webbing.

"You know something," she continued as she considered all the things they'd discussed since the first time he'd made contact with her. "You don't seem much like a whale to me."

What do I seem like? He was laughing harder.

Lori answered, "I don't know. Well, actually you seem like a really cool guy."

Thank you. I like you too.

"Thanks. But that's not what I meant. You talk normal. Like you've been speaking to people all your life."

I have.

"Who?"

You, you silly, he said. *Lor-lie. I told you, we are connected. But we're also very different. You could only hear me once you started the Trial. I have been able to hear you much longer. We've grown up together. I have been to school with you. I've played baseball and been to all the movies you've been to. I have shared everything with you.*

"Even the embarrassing stuff?" Lori asked.

Nothing you could do would be embarrassing to me.

"Well, I am a teenager, wait a bit and I bet I do something to embarrass us both!"

As they both laughed, Lori asked, "What's it like being a whale?"

Generally, I'm happy with my life. The seas and oceans are very beautiful. Right now, Coral and I are passing through a storm and it's very exciting. But – He suddenly paused.

"What is it?" Lori asked.

Well, sometimes a part of me desperately wishes I could be there with you. That I could walk in the park. I would love to ride a bicycle and actually play baseball. Visit shopping malls. Go ice-skating with you and meet all your friends.

Lori sighed, "The malls really aren't that great. You're not missing much."

That's because you can go there any time you want.

"But I bet the sea is amazing," she continued.

I'm not saying it's not. It is. You'll see for yourself when I get there. It's just that I'd like to be like you. Able to live in both worlds.

Lori hadn't considered that. She'd taken the things she did in her life for granted. She never once imagined that there might be someone else looking at her life with envy. Finally, she changed the subject. "So, how long before you get here?"

I'm not really sure. A few days. This storm is helping us along, so it might be faster.

"Well, get here as soon as you can, I can't wait to meet you."

Lori felt a strange warm sensation. She could almost feel his gratitude. *Thank you, Lor-lie, I can't wait to meet you either.*

After a while, when Lori was ready to leave the bath, she asked, "So, if I want to change back, I still just dry off. Right?"

That's right.

Lori pulled the plug on the tub. When the bathtub was empty she pulled a towel on top of herself. Drying off, she waited for the change.

Nothing happened.

She soon discovered that she had to dry the tub as well. Any trace of water in it kept her from changing. Finally she felt the change starting. Like the change of legs to tail, going tail to legs didn't hurt. But it did tingle.

When it was finished, Lori grasped the side of the tub and tried to stand up but fell back down again. Her legs were still tingling and very weak.

It takes a little longer to fully change back, Caspian offered. *You are a mermaid first. Your body would prefer to stay that way.*

"Yeah, but what about what I prefer?" she grunted, trying to stand again.

I would imagine in a short time, you'll prefer your sea self as well. It's only because it's so unfamiliar that you are uncertain.

No, it's because I'm a freak! Lori thought to herself.

I heard that, Caspian laughed.

Lori laughed too, "I told you I'd say something to embarrass myself!"

Chapter 18

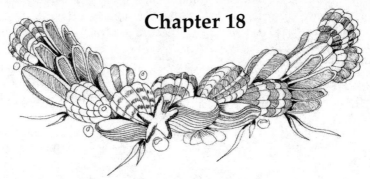

That night, ferocious winds and rain rocked the pub. With storms predicted for the next week, it was agreed that Lori and the others should remain in the pub while her father, Jeremy and Eddie travelled to London to start collecting the supplies that had been ordered.

Rising the next morning and remaining in the protection of the pub, Lori could only watch through the windows as everyone walked down to the ferry dock to see the travellers off.

"This really sucks," she loudly complained as she watched her family go through the pub's courtyard and under the arch.

I'm sorry the adjustment has been so hard for you, Caspian said softly.

"It's not your fault," she sighed. "Was it like this for Mom? Watching the weather and feeling trapped all the time?"

I think so, Caspian responded. *It's the price you have to pay for being different.*

"I bet there are a lot of prices to be paid."

There are, Caspian agreed. *But there are also benefits that far outweigh the disadvantages.*

"Such as?"

It's not for me to tell you, Caspian said cryptically. *You'll have to find those out for yourself.*

"Oh, gee, thanks Caspian, that's so helpful!"

All Lori heard in her head was his laughter. Finally she asked, "Do you ever wonder how this all works? Between you and me, I mean."

All the time. I don't know that we'll ever understand, but I do wonder.

"Me too. Maybe Anne can help. She's a bit of a genius and is into all kinds of science and stuff. She always says she loves genetics. Maybe one day she'll find that we're actually related."

We don't need a genius for that. We already know we're related. It's where we come from that's got me curious.

It was a question that stayed with Lori as she went into the pub's kitchen to make a cup of tea. Carrying it back into the seating area, she sat down by the hearth and stared into the open flames.

Before long, the doors to the pub opened and Anne, Danny and her cousins returned. "Well, they're off," Anne said, pulling off her wet raincoat.

"What do you guys want to do today?" Lori asked. "And Danny, please don't tell me that you're going to hide away with the computer again."

"What else would you suggest?" Danny replied.

"Well, I wouldn't mind getting home and back into my own room," Miranda put in.

"Me too," Aaron agreed. "They say it's going to rain all day, but if there's a break in the weather, how about we make a dash for the cottage?"

"I don't know about that, guys," Anne said hesitantly. "This island has the wackiest weather I've ever seen. We could get half way back and then the storm could start again."

Lori walked over to the window and peered out. "It's still raining pretty hard. With my luck, we're going to be stuck in this pub all week!"

Aaron joined Lori at the window. "Don't worry. We'd never do anything that could hurt you. I was just thinking there isn't a lot to do around here."

Lori looked back out of the window at the grey skies. "Well, if the rain does stop, I wouldn't mind trying."

While they waited, they spent their time playing pool and cards, keeping a close watch on the windows. As the afternoon approached they saw that while the skies were still very grey and threatening, the rain was starting to taper off.

"Well Lori, it's up to you," Anne said as they all stood before the open door. "Do you want to try running back to the cottage before it starts again? Or do you want to stay here?"

Lori looked at the scudding dark clouds. It was definitely going to rain again, but when? Around her, the air was full of water and made the skin on her legs prickle. But as she looked into the anxious faces of her family, she felt guilty for making them have to stay in the pub.

"You know how far it is," she said to Aaron. "Do you think we can make it back in time?"

He nodded enthusiastically. "I really do. There are lots of puddles out there, but we could carry you if we had to. I think we should try it."

Lori looked from him to Anne, Miranda and finally to Danny. They were all nodding. "Okay," she finally agreed. "But if it starts to rain again and I change, you're going to be the one to tell Dad, not me!"

They pulled on their coats. Just before they stepped into the courtyard, Aaron dashed back into the pub and ran upstairs. When he came back down again, he was carrying a large blanket.

"I'm sure we'll make it, but just in case we don't, we can always hide your tail with this."

Lori looked from the blanket to Aaron's smiling face and felt her doubt rising again. Taking a deep breath, she forced her fear down and stepped out into the open air of the courtyard.

As they approached the first big puddle, Lori hesitated. "I don't think I'm going to make it. You guys go back to the cottage. I'll wait in the pub until Dad gets back."

"Oh no you won't," Danny said. Much to her surprise, he turned and offered her his back. "Here, climb on and I'll carry you."

"You can't carry me! I'm way too heavy for you."

"We can take turns," Aaron suggested. "We can't leave you alone at the pub and we all want to get home."

Lori looked from Aaron back to the anxious face of her brother.

"Come on, Lori," he said. "We've got to go before it starts raining again."

"You're sure I won't be too heavy?"

"I'm sure!" he exclaimed. "Now will you hurry up and climb on."

Lori finally surrendered to the group and hopped onto her brother's back. She was surprised to find that he didn't seem to be straining at all.

You are all stronger than you think you are, Caspian said. *It's your sea-blood. It makes you much stronger than humans.*

As Danny carried her over the puddle and out of the pub's courtyard, Lori passed on Caspian's message.

"You should see how strong Jeremy is," Miranda said. "I don't think there is anyone stronger in the world."

When they hit the paved road leading up the steep hill, Danny was able to put Lori down to walk on her own, but just before they reached the top, they felt the first large drops of rain starting to fall.

"Oh, oh," Anne said looking up to the sky. "This can't be good."

"Come on, Lori, hop on!" Aaron offered his back. "We've come too far to go back, and the trail ahead is muddy and slippery. This way will be fastest."

Lori climbed on her cousin's back. Even before she was settled, he started running. "Everybody, let's go!" he shouted as he ran.

They ran as fast as they could. It wasn't fast enough. Suddenly the skies opened and heavy rain started to pour down. Clinging to Aaron, Lori felt her track-pants getting soaked. She immediately felt the tingling of change.

"Aaron, stop!" she cried. "We're too late. Put me down, I'm changing!" She already found it difficult to move her legs as they swelled and pressed against the fabric of her clothing.

Racing off the empty trail, Aaron carried Lori into a cluster of bushes. He put her down and reached for one of her shoes. "Dan, grab the other shoe, quick. Miri, help Anne get Lori's track pants off!"

"Hurry!" Lori cried as her webbed fingers struggled to untie the drawstring at her waist.

Working as fast as they could, they removed the track pants. As Aaron draped the blanket over her, Lori felt her underwear tearing away. Soon her legs grew together and the scales on her tail pushed out.

"Dad's going to kill me!" she panted as she lay back in the bushes fully changed.

"No, Lori," Anne corrected. "He's going to kill me. I'm supposed to be the adult here. I should have known better."

"Dad won't kill anyone if we don't tell him," Danny said, reaching to collect Lori's clothing. "Anne would you and Miri help

Lori get wrapped up in the blanket? I'll check to see if there is anyone coming along the trail."

Everyone kept their eyes and ears open. The rain was coming down in heavy sheets and making it difficult to work in the confines of the bushes but once Lori's tail was completely wrapped, Aaron bent down to lift her.

"Well, Dan?" he called as he swept her up in his arms. "Is the trail clear?"

A moment later, Danny dashed back. "Anyone would have to be crazy to be out in this. I think it's safe to move her."

"We're out in this," Miranda offered.

"Yes, and we're crazy!" Lori complained as she wrapped her arms around Aaron's neck.

They carefully picked their way along the muddy trail. Lori was terrified someone would come along and discover her secret. The blanket completely covered her tail and fluke but that didn't stop her quaking with fear. She felt as if everyone on Herm knew her secret and they were all out to get her.

"Would you relax," Aaron said, giving her tail a reassuring squeeze. "I can feel your tension all the way down to my feet. Herm is your home and you're safe here. We'd never let anyone hurt you."

"I don't think you'd be saying that if you were the one with the tail," Lori said nervously.

"I wish I did have one," Aaron said, seriously. "But I promise you, Dan and I would stop anyone who ever tried to hurt you or Miri."

Everyone was relieved to finally reach the sanctuary of Belvoir Cottage. Once they were safely inside, Aaron carried Lori up to the bedroom and lowered her down on the bed.

"There, see? Safe and sound. No one ever has to know about this."

Lori almost said, 'till next time,' but held her tongue. It wasn't Aaron's fault. This was her new life. Spending all her time living in fear of rain and getting wet.

"Thanks, Aaron," Anne said. "Miri and I will help Lori from here."

When he was gone, Anne and Miranda helped Lori get free of the soaking blanket. Anne sat on the edge of the bed and let out a nervous chuckle. "Well, that was exciting."

99

"Not the word I would have chosen," Lori complained. "What if someone had come along?"

"I don't want to even to even think about that," Anne said. "I guess we all have a lot of adjustments to make." She turned serious eyes to Lori. "I can't pretend to understand any of this, or how you must be feeling but I do know one thing. You have a good family who love you and will do anything to protect you."

"It's true," Miranda said confidently. "We all stick together, no matter what."

Lori looked at her cousin and wondered if Miranda would feel the same when the time of her Trial came and she had her tail. But watching her flitting around the room, she guessed she probably would. That was what separated them. Miranda didn't seem to have a care in the world, while Lori worried about everything.

Chapter 19

Luc spent more and more time in the monitor room watching the whales on camera. It was easier and warmer than standing out on the open platform in the freezing cold.

The technicians were used to him coming and going and no longer resented his presence. But when his father entered, the tension in the room became thick.

"I thought I might find you here," Robichaud said, as he joined his son at the monitors.

Luc felt as if he'd been caught doing something wrong. "I'm sorry, Papa. I just like watching them," he said. "They're so beautiful and graceful in the water."

"Yes they are," Robichaud agreed. "You have no need to apologise for appreciating true beauty."

Luc was shocked by the apparent change in his father. His face still contained the secret excitement and his demeanour seemed almost light. Hesitant at first, Luc decided to test his mood by asking him a question.

"Papa, Arthur has been teaching me a bit about whales. He has a theory that the two younger males have gone off to start their own pods. Do you think they left to start their own families?"

"You have been spending a lot of time with Arthur and learning about them. What do you think?"

Feeling the intensity of his father's probing stare, Luc shrugged. "I'm not sure."

"I am," Robichaud said mysteriously. "And to answer your question – no, those two have not gone off to form their own pod. That isn't the way of these whales. They stay together. Always. That large, scarred male rules his family. He wouldn't let the young ones go. Not without a good reason."

"How can you be so certain?" Luc asked.

When his father turned sharply to him, Luc immediately regretted the question. But instead of the pointed, cruel remarks that normally followed a question his father didn't like, this time he nodded.

"When I was a lad, like you, I went to the best boarding schools in Europe. But during the summer breaks, I would return home to work on my father's fishing fleet. One year, when I was just a bit older than you are now, we were out at sea when we came upon this strange-looking pod of humpback whales. No one had ever seen anything like them before. We followed them for as long as we could, but then they slipped away from us. I'll never forget that day."

"And you think these might be the same whales?"

"There is no mistaking. Believe me, I know them very well." Robichaud stepped closer to the monitor and touched the image of the large, scarred whale as it rested on the seabed. "Of course, he wasn't the head of the family the first time I saw him."

"How can you tell?" Luc asked, frowning at the images of the whales. "They all look the same to me."

Robichaud looked at his son for a moment. "If you'd been pursuing them for as long as I have, you'd learn to recognize each member. This one here was much younger when I first saw her –" Catching himself from saying more, Robichaud suddenly stopped speaking.

"What?" Luc asked. "Saw who?"

Robichaud's eyes trailed over to Luc and seemed to pass right through him. Finally he shook his head. "It was a long time ago and not important. What is important is that for some reason, they have stopped migrating and have chosen to remain here. I need to know why."

"So they used to migrate like normal whales?"

Robichaud nodded. "This is why in the past I have never been able to keep up with them for very long. They were always on the move, keeping one step ahead of me. But not now. For some reason, they have chosen to remain here. Something has happened with that pod and I intend to find out what."

102

Chapter 20

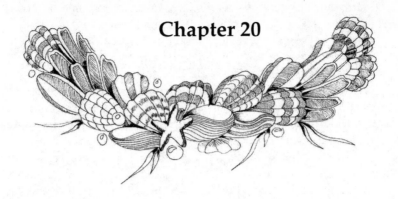

The next morning Lori awoke to the sounds of Caspian singing. Drifting along with the music, she wondered how she could have ever been frightened of his voice in her head.

When the song finished, she gazed past Miranda's sleeping form to the window. The wind had picked up again in the night and rain was lashing against the glass.

"Doesn't it ever stop raining here?" she sighed heavily.

It's early spring, Caspian said. *There are storms all over. There is a big one heading towards the family at that cavern. I just hope it doesn't interfere with the rescue.*

"Me too," Lori softly agreed. "How far out are you? When do you think you'll arrive?

With luck, Coral and I should be there tomorrow evening.

"Really? Lori cheered. "I can't wait!

Me neither, Caspian agreed.

As she'd expected, Lori was once again confined to the cottage. But with the foul weather, no one felt like going out. Instead they did what they could to fill the time, waiting for the return of her father, Jeremy and Eddie.

Late in the afternoon, the others returned from London. Everyone gathered in the dining room to discuss their purchases and the plans for digging Colleen out from the cavern.

"We've got hold of a great yacht," Eddie said. "It's being delivered here tomorrow.

"You bought a yacht?" Anne asked in surprise.

Jeremy nodded. "I told you, we have more money than we could ever use. We needed a large boat, so we bought a yacht."

"Of course," Anne chuckled. "Wouldn't anyone!"

"I could buy you one, if you wanted," Jeremy teased.

"No, one yacht per family should be fine," Anne finished.

Jeremy grinned and then looked at the others. "We also got some underwater drilling equipment. Brian and I figured we'll drill into the bigger rocks, mount hooks into them and, using the harnesses we bought, have the whales drag them away from the entrance."

"It sounds kind of dangerous," Anne said, becoming serious again.

"We'll be extra careful," Eddie responded. "Most of the time, we think it will just be digging and shifting rubble away."

"We won't need to make a big hole at the entrance," said Jeremy. "Just one large enough for Colleen to slip through."

We'll do all we can to help, Caspian offered.

When Lori passed along his message, everyone nodded.

"Of course you will, lad," Jeremy agreed, "and you can bet we'll need everyone in the family for this. Now, we don't have a lot of time left before the lads arrive, so let's head down into Mum's cavern and I can start to teach Eddie and Danny how to dive."

"You mean teach all of us to dive, right?" Lori's father corrected.

Jeremy shook his head. "I'm sorry Brian, not you or Anne. The water is just too cold and dangerous for you. When the rescue starts, we're going to need you on the boat overseeing the equipment. That's of equal importance, believe me."

Her father's expression dropped. "Jeremy is right, Dad," Lori offered. "I remember how you shivered when you jumped in the water for me a few days ago. I'd be worried sick about you if you tried to dive again."

After a moment, Lori's father combed his fingers through his hair and sighed, "I guess you're right. It just worries me, you boys going diving without me there to watch over you."

"We'll be all right, Dad," Eddie said. "It's for Mom. We've got to do this." He turned to Jeremy, "how long will it take us to learn?"

"More time than we've actually got," Jeremy answered darkly. "But I can show you as much as you need to be safe for this."

The sea family changed into their swimwear and gathered in the kitchen. Together they took the stairs down to the cellar and passed through the secret entrance that led to the cavern.

"Mum," Jeremy called. "Mum, are you in here?"

"I'm here," Undine's gentle voice answered. She arrived at the surface and slowly crossed over to the edge of the pool.

"We've come down to teach the boys how to use the scuba gear," Jeremy explained.

"Very good," Undine agreed. She then looked at Lori, "And I think it's about time you learned to breathe under water."

"Breathe?" Lori said. "Gran, I can't even swim with my tail. How can you expect me to breathe under water?"

"She's right, lass," Jeremy said. "A great deal of this rescue will depend on you. You'll be the one spending the most time in the water and we need you confident to do that."

Lori felt fear bunching up in her stomach. "But I've only just changed."

It's all right, Lor-Lie, Caspian called. *You come from the sea. Your body will know what to do even if you don't think it will.*

"I wish I had your confidence," Lori said back to him.

"You will, dear," Undine said gently from the water. "You'll soon find it's instinctive. Your body will know what to do. Trust me, child, I would never mislead you. You are a mermaid. The water is your home."

Standing at the edge of the water, Lori started to remove her clothes until she was wearing only a long nightshirt. She looked down at the dark water and hesitated.

"I'll jump in with you, if you want," Danny suggested.

"We'll all jump in," Miranda cheered. "Last one in is a rotten egg!"

Suddenly she was racing past Lori and jumping off the edge and making a big splash in the water. Aaron quickly followed.

Standing together, Lori and Danny both took deep breaths and then dove off. The moment Lori hit the water she felt her body changing. Before she made it back to the surface, the transformation was complete and she had her tail.

"Wow!" she cried, breaking the surface. "That was so fast."

105

"The colder the water, the faster the change," Undine said. "Now, without using your arms, kick with you tail and see if you can come over here."

Lori felt desperately awkward in the water. She wanted to kick as though she had two separate legs. Using her tail, nothing seemed to work.

"Stop thinking like a human," Undine scolded. "You have one limb, not two. If it helps, imagine someone has tied a rope around your feet. Tell yourself to move them both together."

"Come on Lori," Danny coached. "You can do it. Just move."

You can do it, Lor-lie, Caspian cheered. *Just swim like a fish.*

"A fish?" Lori cried. "Caspian, I'll show you I'm no fish!" Suddenly determined, Lori imagined her two legs moving as one. Instantly her tail reacted and she cut through the water to where her grandmother and cousins waited.

"Very good," Undine said receiving Lori's outstretched hand.

"You really slid through the water!" Her father called from the edge. "What did it feel like?"

"Weird," Lori said, frowning. "Really, really weird."

"It will soon be your first nature," Undine promised. "Now, I want you to practise for a while and then I'll start to teach you how to go under."

From the side of the outcropping, Jeremy clapped his hands loudly together. "And while Lori learns to swim, you boys will learn how to dive. Eddie, Aaron, come help me bring the equipment in here and we can get started."

The balance of the day was spent getting Danny and Eddie used to the diving equipment and swimming under the water. After Jeremy took them through the safety precautions, he had them taking their first dive.

While they worked, Lori's grandmother called her over and started to instruct her on breathing under water. After a few practice runs, Lori was ready to take her first full sea-breath.

"All right then," Undine said gently. "Now just remember when you are beneath the surface, keep your mouth open and inhale."

"What if she inhales through her nose?" Anne asked curiously, moving as close to the water as she dared.

"Nothing," Undine said. "Water won't flow through our noses, only our mouths." Undine smiled at Lori again. "Remember what I

106

told you and you'll be fine. Your instincts will soon take over and you'll wonder what you were fussing about. Are you ready?"

"Good luck, Lori!" Her father and Anne nervously called.

Yes, good luck, Caspian called.

Lori took a deep breath as she'd been taught. She held it and then with a flick of her tail, she rose out of the water. Letting her weight and the water pull her back down, she passed beneath the surface.

Following her grandmother's advice, Lori let out her breath. As the tiny bubbles floated to the surface, she suddenly felt the urgent need to take in more air. She could hear Caspian coaxing her to open her mouth and breath. But thirteen years of training to hold her breath under water was hard to break. Finally the need became too great. Clenching her eyes shut she opened her mouth and –

Inhaled.

Immediately, water rushed into her mouth. It flowed over her gills and then passed smoothly out again though the slits in her throat. The urgent need to breathe passed as her gills filtered oxygen from the water. Opening her eyes, she looked into the smiling face of her grandmother. The old mermaid nodded proudly.

In her mind, Lori could hear Caspian cheering and celebrating for her. *Now we can spend time together in the sea!*

I can't wait! Lori called back excitedly. Suddenly the world was full of wonder. She wanted to see everything. Do everything. Go everywhere.

I want to see it all! She cried joyfully, as she flicked her tail and started to swim around the cavern. She was amazed how fast she could go just by moving her tail. She was also shocked by how clearly she could see. While she was growing up, whenever she opened her eyes underwater, everything was blurry and her eyes would sting. But now, everything was sharp and clear with no pain at all. Passing to the seabed, she found a tiny, pretty shell and picked it up. She brought it back to her grandmother.

Undine pointed to the surface and mouthed the word, 'father'.

In that moment Lori wished more than anything her grandmother still had her sea-speech so she could share the joy she was feeling. Instead, all she could do was nod. Keeping hold of the shell, she gently helped her grandmother rise towards the surface. Lori took in a breath of air and was amazed to find it had been easier to breathe water than air. "Dad, it was fantastic!" she cried. "I can see so clearly underwater. Look what I found!"

Holding up the shell, Lori laughed at the surprised expression on her father's face.

"How was it?" Anne asked. "Could you breathe all right?"

"It's amazing. Just like Gran and Caspian said, you just open your mouth and inhale. You don't even have to breathe out, just in all of the time."

Anne shook her head in wonder. "If I hadn't seen it for myself, I'd never have believed it! You ladies are simply amazing."

Laughter filled the cavern as Lori made dive after dive. Without the need of bulky scuba equipment, she was able to swim circles around her brothers as they slowly learned how to dive.

Finally as the afternoon passed into evening and then night, Jeremy drew the training to a close. "I think it's time we all headed up," he said. "Mum, do you want to come up with us and have some dinner?"

"No thank you, I'm quite comfortable down here. But I wouldn't stop you from bringing down more tea later."

"Of course," Anne promised.

"Come on you lot, we don't have all night," Eddie said as he left the water and started to remove his scuba gear. "Out of the water."

Reluctantly, Miranda made her way to the edge and hoisted herself out of the water. Danny and Aaron followed right behind her. But when Lori tried to hoist herself out of the water, she couldn't. Manoeuvring her tail was becoming awkward again.

When her father offered to help, Undine held up her hand. "No, Brian, Lori must learn how to do this herself."

"I'm okay, Dad," Lori grunted as she struggled to get out of the water.

"Lori," Undine said, "Go back under the water. Then a light kick with your tail should give you the boost you need."

Taking her advice, Lori went back beneath the surface. Giving three forceful kicks with the full length of her tail, she was immediately propelled out of the water. Filling the air with her screams, she sailed across the cavern until she landed with a heavy wet splat on the stone floor several feet away.

"Too much kick," Undine softly chuckled.

Danny and Aaron fell about the floor crying with laughter as Lori sat up and shook her head. She could also hear Caspian's hysterical laughter, *Lor-lie, that was amazing, do it again!*

"Lori, are you all right?" Anne cried as she and her father raced over to her side. "You practically flew out of the water!"

Lori let out an embarrassed laugh. "I think so, but I've really got to learn to control that."

Danny and Aaron were still convulsing with laughter as Eddie came over to her. "You sure do. One more flight like that and you could break something."

Lori rubbed her bruised elbow, "Feels like I already did."

Please do it again! Caspian howled. *Please...*

"Would it make you happy?" Lori called out to him.

Yes.

"Then no!" she teased.

Chapter 21

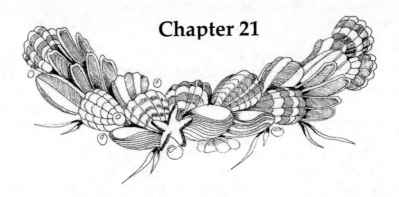

Activity in the house picked up as jobs were assigned and final preparations for departure made. The yacht arrived by midday and with the weather clearing, Lori was able to leave the cottage and join her family going down to the harbour to see their new purchase.

Not long after, Jeremy took the boys into the cavern for more water training. Everyone else spent the day stocking the yacht with the food and other supplies they needed for the rescue.

As the day progressed, Lori felt a growing flutter in her stomach. When she mentioned it to Caspian, he said he felt the same.

My father always says it's how he feels when he's around Colleen. This isn't just excitement, Lor-lie, it's our connection. Oh, it's so wonderful. We'll finally be together tonight!

"I can't wait!" Lori answered eagerly, as she packed up more food for the trip.

Finally, as the day ebbed and the night closed in, everyone anxiously climbed on board. Jeremy took the helm, directed the yacht out of Herm harbour and headed towards the sea.

Standing on the open deck, Lori gazed over the water and felt the fluttering in her stomach increasing. Caspian was calling her, compelling her to come to him. She realised that if they weren't already heading towards the whales, before long, she wouldn't be able to resist his call, and would have to swim to him.

It's the same for me, Caspian said softly. *I've got to find you, Lor-lie. The closer we get to Herm, the harder it is to ignore. Coral says I'm racing, but I can't help it.*

As Lori tried to explain her feelings to her family, her grandmother started to smile. Seated in her wheelchair on the deck of the large yacht, she nodded her head.

"It's your connection. I believe it is the strongest force in the world. We may love our husbands and be willing to die for our children, but I'm afraid this is still much stronger. You will understand when you leave the sea and have to say goodbye to Caspian. It will cause you a kind of physical pain the likes of which you've never known before."

"This is amazing," Anne said as she sat on the long cushioned bench encircling the open deck. "Not only is there an emotional connection between the mermaids and whales, but it seems to be physiological as well."

"Indeed it is," Undine responded. "And it will grow stronger the closer Lori gets to Caspian."

Lori turned in her seat and gazed over the side of the tall yacht. The sun had set some time ago and the moon was rising higher in the night sky, casting tiny diamond sparkles in the water. As she stared, she felt the sea calling to her, beckoning her to jump in and play amongst its welcoming waves.

"Lori, how are we doing for direction?" Jeremy called down from the uppermost deck where he was piloting the yacht. "Are we still on course?"

Lori instinctively closed her eyes. She could actually feel that Caspian was straight ahead of them and getting closer. "Keep going straight," she called up. "He's not far ahead."

Seated together on the deck of the boat, conversation was light and excited as they travelled deeper into the night. Before long, the flutters in Lori's stomach had spread throughout her whole body. Standing sharply, she started to pace the width of the open deck.

"He's very close now," Undine uttered softly. "Lori can feel him, can't you, dear?"

Suddenly a force much stronger than she had ever felt before gripped her. "Jeremy, stop the boat!" she frantically cried. "They're here! Caspian's here!"

Racing to the side of the boat, she couldn't stay on deck any longer. Peeling off her winter coat and jeans, Lori ignored the family's shocked comments as she climbed up onto the bench seat and leaped off the side of the boat.

112

Just before she struck the midnight water, Lori heard a sound she'd only ever heard on television before. It was the explosive whoosh of whales breaking the surface and letting out their breath.

Caspian! She cried joyfully. Directly ahead of her she saw the magnificent whale moving swiftly towards her in the deep water.

Lor-lie! He cried back.

With a powerful flick of her tail, Lori was cutting through the water to Caspian's head. She ached to reach out and put her arms fully around him, but he was just too big. Instead, she swam up to his huge eye and pressed her whole body against his warm side as she kissed his upper eyelid.

The moment their bodies touched, an electric current passed through them. It sealed their final, unbreakable bond. In that instant Lori realised that for the first time in her life, she felt complete. A part of her that she'd never known existed had been missing and, only now, was found.

I can't believe you're finally here, she said, trembling as tears rushed to her eyes, only to have them drawn instantly away by the salt water of the sea.

It's a dream come true! Caspian wept, with as much loving emotion as Lori felt. *My father told me it would be like this when we met, but I never imagined just how much I love you.*

Me too! Lori laughed and cried.

Hi, Lor-lie.

Turning at the new voice in her head, Lori looked through the dark waters and saw Coral floating next to Caspian.

Coral! She called. Reluctant to break her physical contact with Caspian, Lori finally swam over to the second whale. *It's so good to meet you, too! I know Miri is going to be thrilled. She hasn't stopped talking about you since my Trial.*

Leaving Coral, Lori swam back to Caspian's eye. *Everyone is up there waiting to meet you! Come up and say hi to my dad!*

The moment the whales broke the surface again, the air erupted with excited shouts and calls from the yacht. On the top deck, Jeremy was directing a spotlight down into the water, illuminating the grey-white skin of the whales until they seemed to glow.

"Hello lads!" he yelled as he climbed down the ladder to the main deck and leaned over the side. "We've got some people here anxious to meet you!"

At the surface, Lori was stunned by the excited sounds coming from the whales. In her head, she could clearly hear Caspian and Coral's voices calling back welcome, but in the open air of the surface, she could also hear the most beautiful singing sounds of their actual voices.

"Are you all right, Lori?" her father called down.

"Perfect!" she shouted back. "Dad, you've got to get down here, Caspian and Coral are wonderful!"

Lori felt Caspian gently nudging her. She then heard his joyous laughter as he suddenly ducked beneath her and was lifting her out of the water to rest on the top of his huge head.

"Cool!" Danny called. "Can I come down?"

"Sure!" Lori felt the happiest she'd ever been in her entire life. "Eddie, you've got to get down here too. There's room for everyone!"

Before long, everyone who could survive the cold seawater was in it and splashing around with the whales. Miranda and Aaron were on Coral's back and fighting to push each other off, while Jeremy carried his mother gently down to the lowermost platform at the rear of the boat. It was resting just above the waterline and allowed her to slide easily into the water. It wasn't long before she too was contentedly seated on Caspian's back with a beaming smile never leaving her face.

Unable to survive the biting cold of the water, Lori's father and Anne had to content themselves with meeting the whales from the dry safety of the boat.

The loud celebrations carried on late into the night. It took the arrival of dawn to finally tell everyone to break up the party and get some sleep before they started the long journey to the cavern.

Lori was already besotted with Caspian and couldn't bear the thought of tearing herself away from him. Even if it was just to get some sleep on the boat.

"Why can't I stay in the water with Caspian?" she argued with her father. "He's here, I'll be fine."

"I'm sorry Lori," he said back. "But you don't have enough experience with the sea just yet. I'd feel much better if you came back up into the boat. You can see Caspian again later."

"But Dad –"

Finally Caspian broke in. *I'll be right here, Lor-lie,* he promised, *right beside the boat. Go to bed and get some sleep. We can play all day on the way to Colleen's cavern.*

Lori reluctantly surrendered the argument and let her father lift her out of the water and back onto the lower platform. She was then handed up into Jeremy's arms on the main deck, where he carried her into the cabin she was sharing with Miranda and Anne.

When Jeremy lowered her onto her bunk, he smiled. "Don't worry lass, I know it's hard right now. But your dad doesn't understand about you and Caspian yet. He's worried about you. I'm sure he'll relax in time."

"Yeah, when we're back on land and Caspian is only in my head," Lori said bitterly.

"It won't be that bad," he promised. "I'll have a chat with him later and let him know Caspian would never let anything happen to you."

Several hours later, Lori woke to the hum of the boat engines. Sitting up in bed, she looked over and saw that Anne had already arisen and was out of the cabin, while Miranda was sleeping soundly in the bunk across from her.

Climbing quietly out of her bed, Lori softly whispered, "Caspian, you still out there?"

Where else would I be, silly? He started to laugh, *picking flowers?*

"Ha-ha, very funny," Lori responded dryly. She smiled as she recalled all the events of the previous night. It shocked her to realise that despite never having seen a whale before, she swam up to Caspian as if she'd known him all her life.

Are you coming for a swim?

"Just as soon as I can," she replied.

Lori dressed and left Miranda sleeping. She passed into the boat's spacious salon and walked the length of the long yacht, then exited onto the deck and saw that though it wasn't raining, the skies were dark and threatening.

"Morning, Bug," Eddie called from the top captain's deck.

Lori looked up and saw Eddie, Anne and Jeremy at the controls of the yacht. "Morning, all," she replied.

From the side there was a blast of air and water as the whales surfaced. Lori got her first daylight look at Caspian and Coral.

"Hey there, beautiful," she said as she leaned over the side of the boat and strained to touch Caspian's arching back as he moved alongside. Watching him, she realised he was much bigger than she remembered from the previous night. Gliding gracefully beside the boat, he and Coral were just over half of its seventy-two foot length. They were both a greyish white, and to most people she thought they might look identical, but already she knew how to tell them apart.

Sighing heavily, Lori ached to jump into the water and join them.

Then do it, Caspian called. *Undine is riding with Coral. I've got plenty of room for you.*

Lori looked over to Coral's back and didn't see her grandmother sitting there. "Where is Gran?"

She's riding in his mouth, Caspian explained.

"Really?"

In answer to her question, Coral slowed down until his head was parallel with Lori and opened his baleen mouth. She was stunned to see her grandmother resting comfortably on the whale's big tongue.

"Good morning, darling," her grandmother called.

"Morning, Gran," Lori said, waving back. "How are you feeling today?"

"Absolutely wonderful. How I have missed these sweet boys. Seeing them again reminds me of what I've lost. After we free Colleen, I just might let Anne take me to the hospital and try to fix me if it means I can return to the open sea again."

"I know she'll do her best," Lori said.

Lori heard her father approaching. She was over her anger with him and realised he might have been right. She had very little experience being a mermaid and the sea was very big. She turned and saw him carrying a tray with several steaming cups of tea.

"Amazing, isn't it," he said as he offered her a cup and nodded towards her grandmother in Coral's mouth. "I would never have believed it if I hadn't seen it for myself."

"I still don't," Lori admitted as she accepted the drink.

When he started to move away, he called back, "Why don't you grab yourself something to eat, then you can join our friends in the water."

116

"Really?" Lori said excitedly. "I can swim with Caspian as we go?"

"Beyond the fact that I don't think I could keep you two apart if I tried, Jeremy said you could still use the practice." He leaned over the side and spoke directly to the whales. "You'll take good care of Lori, won't you Caspian?"

Caspian lifted his massive head out of the water and bobbed it up and down.

"He says yes," Lori said.

"I don't think I need you to translate that time. I got it perfectly."

Lori raced through her breakfast. When she finished, she returned to her cabin and changed into her long swimming T-shirt. By the time she got back, Jeremy and Anne were down on deck with her father, while Eddie was piloting the large yacht and showing the controls to Danny.

"Just don't stray away from the boat," Jeremy warned as he sat on the bench beside Anne, sipping his tea.

"I won't," Lori promised.

"One more thing," her father said. "If you hear anything at all, like another boat or something in the air, I want you to duck down beneath Caspian. Let him cover you. We don't want to risk anyone catching sight of that tail of yours. Will you do that for me?"

Lori nodded and climbed down onto the lower platform. "I'll stay with Caspian and won't wander off."

This was the first time Lori had been in the open sea in full daylight. When she jumped in and changed, she saw how the colours streaming through the water were more intense than she could ever have imagined and, in all the excitement of the previous night, she hadn't been aware of the sounds around her. But now, she almost had to plug her ears until she could get used to the din.

Is it always this noisy? She called out to Caspian.

You'll get used to it, he assured her, as he drew back to catch up with her. *We'd better keep moving. The boat is already quite far ahead.*

Lori looked up and could see the boat's trail on the surface of the water. It was quickly drawing away from them.

Here, he offered, as he lightly flicked his long pectoral flipper. *Grab hold and I'll catch us up with the boat.*

117

Lori was once again struck by the difference between the pictures of whales she'd seen on television and the reality. On television, they always seemed to be moving in slow motion. But as she clung to Caspian's long flipper where it joined his body, she was amazed by how fast he could actually move.

They travelled together this way until Lori's arms started to get tired. Then as he had done the previous night, Caspian scooped Lori up onto his back and suggested she hold onto his small dorsal fin.

It took time to get used to staying on his back, as Lori's tail always seemed to slip off whenever Caspian dove deeper into the water. Countless times she found herself tumbling into the water. But after a few suggestions from her grandmother, she found her rhythm and was soon enjoying every moment of the ride.

"How long do you think it will take us to dig Mom out?" Lori asked as she sat comfortably curled against his dorsal fin.

I really don't know, Caspian mused. *Every time we tried to shove rocks away, more seemed to fall. I'm hoping that with your hands, you can move them without causing more rockslides.*

"And if we can't?" Lori asked darkly.

You will.

"I sure hope so." Looking over to the yacht, Lori watched Aaron expertly piloting the boat while everyone else was on the deck, busily preparing the equipment they would use for the rescue. Jeremy was once again taking Danny and Eddie through the process of checking gauges as well as the actual diving procedures.

"What if they get the bends?" Anne asked.

"That's not a problem for us," Jeremy responded. "Lori can dive all the way to the bottom without needing any assistance at all. We need the diving gear. But apart from that, we haven't yet found a depth we can't reach. Finding equipment that can survive the pressure has been our only problem so far."

Lor-lie, please tell everyone that your mother is quite deep, they have got to be prepared.

When Lori passed on Caspian's message, Jeremy nodded. "Well, we've got a lot of back-up hosing for the hydraulic drills, lights and enough back up scuba equipment that we should be able to get through this without too much problem. Hopefully, this rescue will go quite smoothly."

Chapter 22

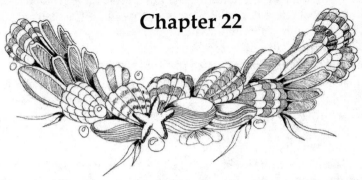

Despite how much Lori loved spending time with Caspian, the days seemed long and the journey endless. The weather worsened and large swells seemed to be doing everything possible to slow them down. Freezing rain came with rough, driving winds. Though Lori didn't feel the cold, the foul weather kept most of the family off the open deck.

Caspian told her to warn Jeremy that an even bigger storm was brewing at the cavern. When Jeremy emerged on the deck, she passed along the message.

"I've been watching the barometer and it is dropping. Fast. It looks like we're heading into a big blow. We can't waste a moment with this rescue. If it gets as bad as I think it's going to, we could be in trouble."

With the warning hanging heavily in the air, everyone on the boat and in the sea felt a twinge of fear. On their fourth morning at sea, Lori woke heavy-eyed, having had very little sleep. Climbing from her bunk, she found Miranda and Anne were already up and out of the cabin.

"Morning, Caspian," she yawned tiredly, as she reached for a clean swimming T-shirt.

Good morning, Lor-lie, it's about time you woke up! Isn't this a wonderful day!

Lori peered out of the small porthole to the dark, stormy skies. "You're awfully cheery today, what's up?"

Come on deck and find out for yourself.

There was something in Caspian's voice that instantly renewed her energy. But when she approached the deck, her heart sank at the sight of the heavy rain. The long striped canopy was pulled out over the open deck, but it offered very little protection from the foul weather. As she had done the previous rainy days, Lori took several steps back into the salon before racing out onto the deck.

By the time she ran across the open area and made it to the cushioned benches, she was soaking wet and her legs were already tingling and changing. Falling to the bench, even before she was able to sit up, she had transformed into her sea form. Around her, the rest of the family were wearing their heavy rain gear and leaning over the side of the yacht.

"Dad, what is it?" she called.

"Listen," her father said as he helped her move closer to the side and sit up on her tail. "They've been like this since dawn, what are they saying?"

Moments later, Lori heard the sound of Caspian and Coral's voices singing in the water. As she listened, she understood the words as Caspian called to his father. When the haunting song ended, she suddenly heard a response.

"Caspian, is that Zephyr?" she cried. "Are we there?"

Almost! Caspian cheered.

"He says we're almost there," Lori explained to her family. "Gran," she called over to Coral's open mouth. "I can hear Zephyr. They know we're coming!"

Lori looked from her grandmother's beaming smile to the faces of her family on the deck. Her father and Anne were shivering from the cold rain, but their smiles were as big as ever.

"Hey Jeremy," Aaron called from the upper deck.

Lori looked up and saw Danny standing confidently at the yacht's controls. Aaron was beside him and holding a large pair of binoculars.

"I can see the oil platform," he called. "It's still a long way away, but it's there all right!"

Cheers exploded from the deck as everyone excitedly embraced.

"Fantastic!" Lori's father called back up. "Full steam ahead, Danny!"

"Aye-aye, Captain!" Danny called back down.

"Well, we can't waste a moment," Eddie said clapping and rubbing his hands eagerly together. "Lori, why don't you get back into the water with the whales? Then Jeremy, Miri and I can go over the equipment for our final check." He then looked over to his father and Anne. "Dad, I really think you and Anne should get under cover. You both look half frozen."

"I'm not half frozen," Anne said through chattering teeth. "I'm completely frozen." She turned to Jeremy and smiled. "How you can stay out in this is beyond me!"

"It's our sea blood," he explained. "We can go out in much worse and not feel it."

"I wish I had some of that," she admitted.

"That makes two of us," Lori's father agreed. Despite his shivers, he reached out and lifted Lori into his arms. Carrying her to the back of the boat, he handed her down to Jeremy who was waiting on the lower platform to help her get down into the sea.

"Listen, lass," Jeremy said. "A lot of this is resting on your shoulders. You are going to have to guide us down to your mum but with that platform out there, it'll be tricky. Make sure you keep well hidden. If we have powerful binoculars, there's no reason why they shouldn't as well."

"I agree," her father added. "I really don't think they're going to be too pleased with us hanging around the area. We've got to be prepared for visits. You must be extra careful so they don't get a look at you."

Taking in the warning, Lori nodded. "I'll be careful."

Time seemed to slow down as they made their way towards the oil rig. Beside them, the yacht was bouncing through the large waves, but managing to plough ahead. As the afternoon wore on, Lori suddenly heard a soft new voice in her head. A voice she hadn't heard for so long that hearing it made her skin prickle with excitement.

"Mom?" she cried aloud. "Mom, is that you?"

Lori? Lori can you hear me? The faint voice answered.

"Mom!" Lori shouted, "Yes, I can hear you!" Lori excitedly slapped the warm skin of Caspian's back. "Caspian, I can hear Mom!" She then called up to the yacht. "Everyone, I can hear Mom! I really can!"

"It's Mom!" Eddie cried, rushing to the side of the boat.

Her father appeared on deck. "Lori, is it true?"

She nodded, unable to speak.

Oh, Lori, her mother cried. *How I have ached to hear your voice. My beautiful little girl.*

Tears rushed to Lori's eyes as she heard the pain and grief in her mother's words. Turning to her father, she sniffed. "Dad, it's really her."

"Tell her we're coming," he called back as his voice constricted with emotion. "She won't be trapped much longer!"

"We're coming Mom. Just hold on, we'll be there soon."

I'll wait forever, her mother replied.

As they drew closer to the oil platform, Jeremy returned to the side of the boat. "Lori, you'd better get off Caspian now," he warned. "And don't surface again until we tell Caspian it's all right."

Lori felt excited butterflies enter her stomach as she slid off Caspian's back and returned to the water. "It's really happening, Caspian," she said excitedly, pressing herself to his side.

It is, he agreed. Then he slowed down so that Lori could keep up with him.

Stay beneath me, Lor-lie, let me block you from their vision.

Lori struggled to keep up with the speed of the whales. Yet despite her best efforts, Caspian had to slow further to keep pace with her.

Go on ahead, she finally suggested. *I'll catch up in a moment.*

No, Lor-lie, Caspian said gently, *we're in this together. I'm not leaving you alone in the sea. We'll move at your pace, not mine.*

Touched by his words, Lori tried to swim faster, but her tail was still too new and she was far too inexperienced. Finally Caspian suggested that she travel in his mouth as her grandmother was doing with Coral.

Lori had seen her grandmother sitting comfortably on Coral's tongue for the entire journey and knew it was the only way she could avoid slowing down their progress. *Do you mind?* She asked him.

Not at all, Caspian answered. *Climb in.*

As she had watched her grandmother do, Lori swam into the whale's huge open mouth and settled down on his soft, pale tongue. It wasn't as gross as she'd expected it to be. In fact, she found sitting on his tongue with the water washing over her felt great.

I just hope I don't sneeze and accidentally swallow you.

"What!" Lori cried.

122

Just kidding, Caspian teased as he wiggled his tongue and sent her rolling around in his mouth. *That's for thinking that being in my mouth would be gross!*

Lori punched down on the thick tongue beneath her and then started to laugh. "I'm warning you, Caspian. You might be a million times bigger than me, but I can still make you pay for that!"

Go ahead and try it! He challenged, wiggling his tongue again.

Travelling in Caspian's mouth was fun but there wasn't a lot to see. He tried his best to keep his mouth open to give her some light, but it wasn't enough to let her see what was happening at the surface.

We're moving around the oil rig now, Caspian offered. *And we'll be meeting up with the rest of the family in just a moment.*

"Can you see anyone on the platform?" Lori asked, leaning forward on her tail and straining to peer out.

Of course, people are always on it. But they're used to seeing us here so they usually ignore us. We were here with Colleen before they built the thing and have been here ever since. In the beginning people used to come out to look at us, but we never let them get close. Now they leave us alone.

"Well, I hope they leave the yacht alone while we're here."

Me too, Caspian agreed.

A short while later, Lori heard the excited voices of other whales. Caspian opened his mouth. As water flooded in Lori swam forward. Soon she found herself completely surrounded by the family.

My sweet little Lor-lie, the closest whale said.

Lori opened her mouth in shock when she saw the size of whale that had spoken. He was massive. Easily double the size of Caspian or Coral. Along his side, she saw the deep scar from the harpoon that had nearly killed him. Suddenly the memories of the hunt came flooding back and she knew this was Caspian's father.

Zephyr! She cried.

Somehow, he was smiling. It didn't show on his face in the human sense because whales couldn't smile, but Lori knew it was there all the same. *Hello my love,* he said softly. *Welcome home.*

As Lori was introduced to all the members of the family, she was overwhelmed by the warmth and love that flowed between them. Floating amongst the pod of huge humpback whales, she knew she had come home.

Above them, she looked up and saw the anxious faces of her family staring down into the water. Flicking her tail, she broke the surface and called excitedly to her father, "Dad, this is amazing! This here is Zephyr! And that's Coral's dad, Zenith there and beside him is his mother, Markane. Well, you've just got to meet everyone. Eddie, Danny, come on into the water, it is fantastic!"

"We'd love to, kiddo," her father said nervously. "And we will, but now isn't the time."

Lori couldn't understand her father's sudden change of mood, or the odd expression on his face. Did the whales frighten him? Glancing over to Danny and her cousins, their expressions were the same.

"Is something wrong?" she finally asked.

He nodded and turned in the direction of the oil rig. Lori followed his gaze and saw that Eddie had turned the boat so that she was hidden at the rear. But they were still uncomfortably close to it. As she stared up, she saw that a few of the workers were gathered on the top and staring down at them.

"Might be a good idea for you to stay hidden beneath the surface until after sundown," Jeremy suggested.

"Do you think they can see me?" asked Lori nervously, as she pressed herself closer to the back of the boat.

124

"We don't know just how much they can see from up there," her father answered.

"Or have already seen," Anne added as she stole another look back up at the platform.

"I didn't think the rig would be so close," Miranda said. "How are we going to dive and bring Aunt Colleen up if they are watching all the time?"

Her father combed his fingers through his wet hair. "We're just going to have to be careful. The canopy hides most of the back of the yacht. If we angle it right, we might be able to block their view entirely."

Jeremy nodded his head. "Whether they see us or not, we can't give up. Not now. We will work night and day and with luck, get Colleen out of there fairly quickly."

"What are we waiting for then?" her father said excitedly. "Let's get going!"

While everyone started to get the diving equipment set up, Jeremy called to Lori, "I want you to have Caspian take you down to where your mum is trapped. Take a look at the area and see how much rubble we have to move. For the moment, you and your Gran will have to be our eyes. So take in as much as you can and let us know what you find."

Lori nodded and ducked down in the water.

It's this way, Zephyr said, taking the lead. *Follow me.*

With Caspian and Coral close at her side, Lori dove deeper into the sea. She watched the colours changing and growing darker as she went.

We're coming, Col, she heard Zephyr call, *and I've got two special people with me. Before long you'll be out of that wretched prison and we can all be free. Such joy there will be when the seas are ours again.*

I can't wait! Her mother cried. *I've missed you all so much!*

Lori listened to the exchange between her mother and Zephyr and smiled at how much is was like her and Caspian. It also made her realise that being a mermaid and speaking as they did meant that no conversation was ever private.

Not yet, Caspian said, answering her thoughts. *But my father tells me that in time, we will find a way.*

A way for what? Her mother asked.

Nothing, Lori said innocently.

I think our kids might be talking about us, Zephyr teased.

I think you might be right, her mother chuckled.

Lori glanced around and noticed that there wasn't much light coming from above. But although it was dark, she could still see the details on the fish that swam out of the way as the entire family of whales continued on their long journey down.

Just ahead, Lori started to see the details of an undersea cliff. *Colleen is trapped in a cavern at the base of that rock wall,* Caspian explained. *If you look closely, you can see that it isn't very stable. The pounding of the oil diggers dislodged a lot of it.*

We are all going to have to be especially careful, Zephyr said. *It won't take much to bring the whole thing down.*

His brother, Zenith, added, *we'll keep at least two of us posted here all the time. They'll warn us at the first sign of collapse.*

The closer they got to the rock face, the more details Lori could make out. It wasn't as smooth as it had first appeared. Rocks and boulders jutted out at odd angles while sea grasses grew from small cracks as the long tendrils waved in the current.

Deeper and deeper they moved. Around them darkness pressed heavily in and the temperature dropped. Lori wasn't cold, but she could feel the change. Gazing around, despite her mermaid vision, she couldn't see very far at all. In fact, even if she strained her eyes, she couldn't see all the members of the pod. The ones she could see were like images on a black and white television. There were just varying shades of grey.

I don't like it down here, Lori said nervously, keeping close to Caspian.

It's only because you're not used to it, he answered. *Give it time and you'll find that it won't bother you at all.*

I don't know about that, Lori continued as she strained to see around her. *Lord only knows what kind of monsters could be coming at us from all that darkness.*

Scaredy cat! Caspian teased. *Look at the size of us. Do you really think there is anything or anyone out there who is bigger than us who might try to cause trouble?*

But look at the size of me, Lori countered. *I'm a shrimp! I'd be a tasty meal for any number of unspeakable creatures hovering at the bottom.*

You read too many horror stories, Caspian teased. *Besides, whenever you're in the sea, I'll be right beside you. So you're perfectly safe.*

Here we are, Zephyr cut in. *Lor-lie come up here with me. I want you and Undine to get a good look so you can tell the others what you've seen.*

Lori flicked her tale and moved away from Caspian and up to Zephyr's head. Before her, she finally saw the sandy bottom of the seabed. To her left, she saw how the rocky wall ended in a huge pile of boulders and rubble.

Mom's in there? She asked incredulously.

Lori? I'm here. Follow my voice and you'll find exactly where I am.

Lori followed her mother's instructions and started to swim around the area. When her grandmother emerged from Coral's mouth, she joined Lori looking at the mess before them. Silt had collected on the boulders and made them look as though they hadn't been disturbed in years.

Mom?

I'm right here, baby.

Lori found the spot and motioned to her grandmother. Mouthing the words, 'She's right here, behind these rocks.'

Together they looked at the huge pile of rocks and boulders blocking the entrance of the cavern. The pile rose a good ten to fifteen metres up and spanned an equal distance along the natural, rocky wall.

Mom, how high up can you swim in there?

Not far, her mother answered. *No more than two or three metres from the bottom. I've tried digging away the smaller rocks at the top to see if I can squeeze through, but the wall is solid. You've got to move the big rocks away from out there, first.*

Lori's heart sank as she studied the tall blockade of rubble keeping her mother trapped in the cavern. Even if everyone worked night and day, she imagined it would take ages to clear it all away. She turned and looked back at the entire pod of whales anxiously waiting, counting on her to tell them that they could dig her mother out.

But could they?

You will, Caspian said, moving as close to the wall as he dared. *We'll all work together, and soon Colleen will be free.*

Caspian, Zephyr called. *Take Lor-lie back up to the surface and tell the others what you've seen.*

Lori gazed up into the oppressive darkness above her and thought of the long journey back to the surface. She reached for her grandmother's hand and motioned that she was going up. She asked if she wanted to go up as well.

In answer, her grandmother shook her head and then settled down on one of the larger boulders.

Mom, I'll be right back, Lori said. *Gran is staying down here with you.*

Be careful, her mother called back. *And Lori, please tell Jeremy that we are deep, very, very deep. This might be a problem for them.*

"I will," Lori promised. She pressed a webbed hand to a rock, as if touching it was like touching her mother. Then with a flick of her long tail, swam back over to Caspian. *Let's go.*

Chapter 23

"What are they doing out there?" Luc asked, holding the binoculars to his eyes. He, Arthur and Andre Robichaud stood on the observation deck watching the yacht moving in the high swells of the stormy sea. It had been there a while and was hovering in the area where the whales normally gathered.

"I haven't a clue," Arthur finally answered. "But this is really weird. The two missing whales are back. If I didn't know any better, I'd swear they'd been leading that boat."

"That's crazy," Luc said.

"Not necessarily," Robichaud said mysteriously.

Luc lowered his binoculars and looked at his father. "But Papa, if the whales were leading the boat, why did all the others leave the area? I can't see any of them any more. I think the boat must have scared them away."

"Not these whales, they don't scare that easily," Robichaud answered softly. "There is some other explanation. Something is definitely going on down there."

"Monsieur Robichaud," a voice called breathlessly. One of the technicians from the monitor room ran towards them. He wasn't wearing a coat or any protection against the freezing weather. When he arrived, he leaned on the railing, panting heavily. "Please Monsieur, you must come," he cried excitedly. "You must see this! It's simply amazing."

"What is it?" Robichaud demanded irritably. "Can't you see I'm busy here?"

The technician shook his head, still not believing what he had to report. "Mermaids, sir!" he panted. "There are two mermaids at the bottom and they're surrounded by all the whales!"

Chapter 24

Before Lori broke the surface, she let Caspian go ahead. Blowing out his air in a spray of water told everyone they were back. Keeping close to the back of the boat, Lori slowly surfaced.

"Is it safe to come up?" she called.

"Sure, lass," Jeremy answered, as he and the rest of the family crowded in at the back of the boat. "We're all clear."

"Well, did you find Mom?" Eddie asked.

Lori nodded. "But there's a big problem. She said to tell you that it's very, very deep. Much deeper than any of you have ever gone before. She's worried about the pressure."

Anne moved closer to the edge and peered down into Lori's face. "How did your feel down there? Did the pressure bother you? Did you have any trouble breathing, or were you dizzy at all?"

"I was fine," Lori answered truthfully. "Apart from being dark and really scary, it's just a little bit cooler. It felt just like being in Gran's cavern under the cottage.

"I'm glad to hear that," Anne said. "We can't risk anyone's life."

"Risk or no risk, we're not leaving Colleen trapped," Lori's father said firmly. "Now that we're finally here, we have got to find a way."

"We will," agreed Jeremy. "The question is, how many of us can make it down there?"

He stepped away from the back of the boat and crossed to where the scuba equipment was kept. Aaron was right behind him and started to reach for his gear.

"I think we should all try going down," Aaron said. "Maybe some of us can handle the pressure more than others."

Jeremy nodded. "We will, but I want me and Miri to go first."

"Why does Miranda get to go first?" Danny challenged. He then looked over at his cousin. "I don't mean that you shouldn't go, but I thought we should go first."

"Why? Because you're boys?" Miranda snapped back, "and they're stronger than girls?"

Danny started to nod his head when Anne stepped in to stop the brewing fight. "I would imagine Jeremy wants Miranda to go first because she is going to be a full mermaid soon. If Lori can handle the pressure, it stands to reason that Miranda can too."

"But she's not a mermaid yet," Danny continued.

"Sorry, lad," Jeremy put in. "But she is. She may not have her tail and gills, but our Miri is as much a mermaid as your sister is. I suspect that she won't have any troubles at all, while I'm not so sure about me or you boys."

Any further arguments were cut off when Zephyr impatiently slapped the water with his large flipper and caused a huge wash to hit the side of the boat.

Lori heard his message and turned back to Danny. "Zephyr says we've got to get to work freeing Mom before the big storm arrives. He says we don't have time to argue."

"Zephyr's right," Lori's father agreed. He then looked at Jeremy. "It is getting rough out here. Do you think this yacht can handle it?"

"It's going to have to," Jeremy said. "Miri, gear up, let's get moving."

When they both had their scuba gear on, Jeremy climbed onto the lower platform. Before he lowered his headpiece, he called down to Lori.

"Miri and I will have to go down slower that you. So I want you to stay with us. We've got microphones built into these masks. With your sea-hearing, you shouldn't have a problem hearing us. We'll keep talking," Jeremy paused and his expression darkened. "Lori, this is very important. If either of us start to speak or act strangely or disorientated, I need you to bring us up. There is always the slight chance we may suffer rapture of the deep. If that happens we may actually fight you, but you must bring us back up slowly. No faster than an air bubble can travel. Do you understand?"

Lori nodded as Caspian started to speak in her head.

Lor-lie, please tell Jeremy that we'll help. We've seen divers with rapture, so we know what to look for.

When Lori passed along Caspian's message, Jeremy looked over to the whale. "Thanks, lad, I feel safer knowing you are all with us." He then turned back to Miranda. "You ready to go?"

Nodding her head, Miranda gave her breathing equipment one last check before she awkwardly climbed down onto the lower platform beside her uncle. "This sure would be a lot easier if I had my tail!"

"It'll come soon enough," Jeremy said.

Once they entered the water, all of the whales moved in closer to act as escorts down to the bottom. Lori saw Coral so close to Miranda she was actually brushing against his side. She could hear the strange distorted sound of Miranda's giggles floating through the water as she stroked the whale's face.

With Caspian at her left and Jeremy and Miranda on her right, Lori felt a strange sense of peace wash over her, as if this was how it was meant to be.

It is, said Caspian softly. *Remember, your ancestors came from the sea. What you are feeling are the echoes of lost memories.*

But where did we come from? Lori asked, *and why aren't there any others like us around today?*

When your mum is free, ask her to tell you all the stories we know. There's not a lot of history, but there is a record of the first mermaid coming out of the sea and arriving on Herm.

There is? Lori asked, as she checked that Miranda and Jeremy were all right with their descent.

Yes, answered Caspian. *With everything happening to you and then with the plans for your mother's rescue, there wasn't time to tell the history. But we will once this is over.*

"Lori, can you hear us all right?" Jeremy asked as he reached over to touch her arm.

Turning to her uncle, Lori nodded. *Can you hear me?*

But even before Jeremy shook his head, she realised he couldn't hear her. She couldn't even hear her own voice in the water.

He won't hear you, Lori's mother called from below. *You can't use human speech beneath the surface, only our sea-speech. And unfortunately the men can't hear it. But Miranda might. Try talking to her.*

Miri, can you hear me and Mom? Lori asked.

132

"Yes I can!" Miranda called excitedly through her mask. "I can't hear your mother yet, but I can hear you." Lori then heard Miranda explain to Jeremy through the microphone that she and Lori could communicate.

Jeremy then turned back to Lori and nodded. "Good, we'll use you two to keep the lines of communication open when we're down there."

How are you feeling? Lori asked her cousin.

"So far so good," Miranda answered brightly. She asked Jeremy the same question.

"Not too bad," he responded. "Though I must admit I am starting to feel a bit of pressure on my chest. But it's not enough to stop me, so let's keep moving."

They continued down until all the light was gone and they were travelling only in darkness. Beside Lori, Jeremy suddenly held up his hand to stop the downward progress.

When Lori looked closer into her uncle's mask, she saw his face was starting to turn red and he was sweating.

What's wrong?

Miranda repeated the question.

"I can't go any further," Jeremy panted. And even though the microphone distorted his voice, Lori could hear his laboured breathing and the difficulty he had in speaking. "The bullet," he panted. "I forgot about the bullet in my chest. Lori, you're going to have to help me back up. I won't make it on my own."

Lori heard the effort it took him to say that much. Filled with concern, she moved closer to her uncle. She turned around and offered him her back as she looked over to Miranda.

Miri, tell Jeremy to put his hands on my shoulders, I'll take him back up.

Don't move him too fast, Lor-lie! Zephyr warned. *If we're not careful, he'll get the bends.*

The bends? Her mother urgently called from below. *Lori, what's wrong? What's happening up there?*

It's Jeremy, Lori quickly explained. *I don't know what's wrong. He said he'd forgotten about the bullet in his chest and can't make it down. He really doesn't look good at all. His face is turning bright red and he's sweating. We're taking him back up to the surface.*

133

I thought he'd had it removed, Lori's mother cried. *He told the whales who visited Herm that everything was fine with the family!*

When Lori repeated her mother's message to Miranda, she said back; "Tell Aunt Colleen he was fine. But we couldn't take him to the hospital to have it removed. He got better with the bullet still in him."

When Lori repeated the message, she heard her mother moaning. *If he knew the bullet was still there, he shouldn't have tried coming down here! It's too deep for him.*

I don't think we could have stopped him, Lori added. *Mom, you should have seen him. He's as desperate to get you out of there as we are.*

This is just too dangerous, her mother continued. *Listen to me Lori, tell your father to leave me here and go back to Herm. I don't want anyone else hurt –*

Stop it, Col, Zephyr cut in sharply. *We're all worried sick about Jeremy, but we're not leaving you there. Miri is all right. She is breathing well and not feeling any pressure at all. I know the boys will be fine too. We'll get you out, one way or another.*

But –

No buts, Col. We've waited long enough. We're all here and we're going to set you free.

Yes we will, Mom, Lori agreed. *We're not giving up. Not now.*

Holding on to Jeremy, Lori used only her tail to propel them slowly back up to the surface. Through his fingers resting on her shoulders, she could feel him trembling and fighting for each breath.

"We're almost there," Miranda said with fear in her voice. "Please hold on Jeremy, it isn't far now."

"I'm all right," he weakly called. "Just get me back to the yacht and I'll be fine."

Lori ached to kick out her tail and swim faster. She knew she could cross the distance to the surface in no time at all, but she had to restrain herself. Jeremy's life was at stake. She forced herself to keep to the pace that the whales set.

After what seemed an eternity, they were entering lighter waters. Soon Lori could see the outline of the yacht on the surface. *We're almost there;* she called, forgetting her uncle could not hear her.

Lori, Zephyr said, *tell Miranda to swim ahead. Warn the family that Jeremy is coming back up and he's in trouble.*

Lori repeated the message to her cousin and watched Miranda and Coral dart forward in the water to the surface.

By the time she arrived, her father and Eddie were standing on the lower deck, waiting to receive him.

"How is he?" her father asked, as he reached to take hold of one of Jeremy's hands.

"His breathing is terrible," said Lori. "I just don't know."

"I'll be fine," Jeremy said weakly once his mask was removed. "I just need a moment to catch my breath." Lori's father and Eddie hauled Jeremy onto the deck of the yacht. After his diving equipment was removed, Lori explained to Anne about the bullet still resting in his chest.

Anne retrieved her medical bag as everyone stood back to give her room to work. In the water, Lori floated at the surface, clinging to the lower ramp. "Well?" she called up, unable to see her uncle. "How is he?"

Sitting back on her heels, Anne pulled off her stethoscope and let out a worried sigh. "His heart is racing dangerously fast and his lungs sound like they might be filling with fluid. We're going to have to watch him very closely and then consider getting him to a hospital."

"No hospitals," Jeremy rasped as he struggled to sit up. "I'm all right. Just let me rest for a bit and we'll be ready to start again."

"You're not going anywhere!" Anne ordered. "Your rescue days are over. You should count yourself lucky to be alive. It's just too deep for you. Too deep for all of you."

"No way!" Danny said, jumping up from the bench. "Maybe Jeremy can't handle it, but I can. I'm going next."

"Wait a minute," Lori's father said. "Danny, if Jeremy can't handle the depth, what makes you think I'm going to let you try?"

"You've got to," Jeremy coughed. "The bullet stopped me, not the depth. Miranda was fine. I see no reason why the boys can't try."

"Miranda, you didn't go all the way, did you?" Anne asked.

"No, I came back up with Lori and Jeremy," Miranda said from the platform. "But I was okay."

"But you didn't go all the way. And we have no way of knowing what that will do to you."

Lor-lie, tell them they've all come too far to give up now, Zephyr said. *Your father and aunt must let everyone try. We can't leave Colleen trapped down there.*

After she passed along Zephyr's message, Lori added, "Dad, he's right. We can't leave Mom down there. You don't know what it's like. I can hear her voice, talk to her. Even if I have to do this alone, I'm not leaving her."

"Listen to Zephyr," said Jeremy. "I failed because of my old wound. It kills me to risk your lives, but we've got to. Miranda and the boys must try."

"You can't stop us anyway," Danny challenged. "Dad, I am going to do this whether you say yes or no."

Eddie stood beside his brother, "I'm with Danny. I'm not leaving here until Mom is free. So you might just as well let us do this."

Lori's father stood, put his arms around his sons and pulled them into a tight embrace. "I know you have to try. It just kills me that I can't go with you. Promise me you'll be careful. Don't take any foolish risks."

"We won't," Eddie promised. He looked at Danny and Aaron, "Come on, let's suit up. We want to see if we can do this before it gets dark."

Chapter 25

"Run it again," Robichaud excitedly demanded.

Luc stood beside his father, speechless. They'd watched the same images time and time again and yet he still couldn't believe what he was seeing. Due to the strange, distorted colours of the infrared camera, it wasn't overly clear. But one thing was certain. There was no mistaking the sight of the two long-tailed mermaids arriving at the area where the scarred whale always lay.

After the recording ended, they went back to the live image. It showed a very elderly mermaid sitting on one of the boulders. She was pulling away small rocks from the pile and casting them aside.

Suddenly the old mermaid looked up. Moments later, the whales were back in frame. Luc strained to see around the many large animals as he caught glimpses of more than just whales.

"Divers?" Arthur cried. "But that's impossible! They're too deep. No one can survive the pressure at that depth, let alone the temperatures."

"No human can survive," Robichaud corrected, excitedly. "But as you can see by that lovely little mermaid with them, these divers are so much more than human."

Arthur stood beside Luc staring at the monitor and shaking his head. "I can't believe this. It's completely insane. Mermaids don't exist, they're just folklore."

"And yet you bear witness to the contrary," Robichaud remarked.

As they watched the monitors, the infrared camera showed four divers, two mermaids and the whales, starting to explore the area. The young mermaid was pointing at a specific area of the rubble and motioning to the others to look at it.

"I wonder what they're looking at?" Luc asked. "They seem very interested in that one spot."

"No, it can't be –" Robichaud suddenly said.

"Papa, what is it?" Luc asked.

"Of course, it's her!" he cried. "She's been here all this time, trapped behind that wall." He excitedly slapped his palm to his forehead. "What a fool I've been! I could have had her ages ago. How stupid of me! I should have known he would never leave her, no matter what."

"Papa, who is trapped?" Luc asked. "Who would never leave her? I don't understand. What are you talking about?"

"My dreams coming true," Robichaud said, without drawing his eyes from the screen. "There is another mermaid down at the base of that mountain."

"Really?" Luc said, straining his eyes to see what his father must be seeing. "I don't see her."

"You can't see her," his father said. "She's trapped. But that scarred whale knows she is there, which is why he has remained here all this time. He and his mermaid are inseparable. Now they've brought the others here to try to dig her out!"

"Papa, I don't understand. How do you know this?"

Robichaud turned to Luc, "Do you remember when I told you of my time as a young man working on my father's fishing boats? And of the day we first came upon the pod of special white whales?"

When Luc nodded, he continued. "What I did not mention was that this was the first time I saw her; the most beautiful mermaid imaginable. She was magnificent. Seated on the back of that scarred male. Everyone on my father's boat was instantly enchanted by her. But she never left her whale, even after we started to chase them. All day we pursued them, until they finally slipped away from me in the night. I've been searching for her ever since. Many times I've almost had them both, but they always managed to get away. But not now. Oh no, not now."

Luc felt his blood run cold as he watched his father approach the large screen. Robichaud reached up and traced the outline of the young mermaid amongst the divers. "I've got you too now, my beautiful siren. I will have all of you. You're mine. Soon my collection will be complete!"

Chapter 26

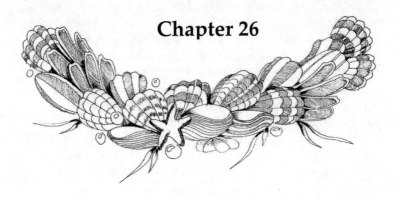

As Lori and the family searched for the best way to get started, she heard another whale urgently calling her name. It was Coral's sister, Sargasso.

Lor-lie, Sargasso urgently called as she drew near, *you must come back to the surface immediately. Jeremy is in trouble.*

What's wrong with Jeremy? Lori's mother called.

I don't know, Sargasso replied. *Lor-lie's father just told me to get her up there immediately. His voice sounded very frightened.*

Go, Lori, don't worry about me, her mother cried. *Tell your gran what's happening and take her up with you.*

Lori explained what she knew to Miranda and while she told the boys, Lori motioned to her grandmother that they needed to go up immediately.

"We're coming up too!" Aaron said. "We can come back later to start work."

Tell them that's fine, Zephyr said to Lori, *but also tell them they have to go up slowly. I can't have these kids hurting themselves, either.* The huge whale moved in the water to face Lori; *Lor-lie, you and Caspian start up now. Coral will be right behind you with Undine. The rest of us will follow at a safe pace. Get going!*

Lori, her mother called. *Tell me what's happening the moment you know.*

I will, Lori promised, as she gave a mighty flick of her tail.

As they journeyed to the yacht, the memories of Jeremy's laboured breathing flooded Lori's mind. Finally breaking the surface at the back of the boat, she swam up to the lower platform.

"Dad?" she called.

"Lori!" He clambered down onto the lower platform. "We've got a big problem. Jeremy is coughing up blood. Anne thinks the bullet may have shifted and ruptured something in his lungs."

Fear gripped Lori's heart. It was worse than she imagined. "What are we going to do?"

"I don't know. He refuses to let us take him to the oil rig for help or to a hospital. He says it will betray the family secret."

From behind her, Lori heard Coral breaking the surface. When he opened his mouth, Undine carefully moved off his tongue and slowly entered the water.

"Where's my son?" she called as she reached for the bottom platform.

"He's here Undine," Brian said. Lifting her into his arms, he awkwardly carried her up onto the boat.

Lori also climbed up onto the lower platform and stood as best she could on the end of her tail. Peering over the railings, she saw Jeremy was still lying on the deck. He had rolled onto his side and was coughing. Each spasm brought with it a spray of blood.

What's happening with Jeremy? Her mother called from below.

He's coughing up blood. Anne thinks the bullet shifted and has ruptured something in his lungs, Lori explained. *He doesn't look good.*

When her father lowered Undine onto the deck beside Jeremy, she immediately reached for him. She placed her hand on his forehead and checked his eyes.

Finally she looked up to Lori's father and Anne. "He needs healing moss."

"With all due respect, Undine," Anne said, "what he urgently needs is surgery."

"No hospitals!" Jeremy rasped between bouts of coughing.

"There can be no hospitals for us," Undine said defiantly. "Not unless you are the only doctor there. Any tests they run will expose us."

"We can't just let him die!" Anne argued. "No secret in the world is worth a man's life!"

"This is!" Jeremy coughed out. "Consider Lori and Miranda, and what would happen to them if the world knew the truth –"

"But there has got to be another way!" Anne said desperately.

140

"There is," Undine insisted. "The healing moss! Believe me, it will save him."

Anne was about to protest further when Lori's father held up his hand. He looked to Undine. "How will we find some in time? The whole reason Colleen is trapped down there is because this was the only cavern in the area with the moss."

Hearing the argument on deck, Lori called to Caspian, "Have you been able to hear what they're saying? Do you know of any other caverns where healing moss grows?"

Caspian excitedly answered, *Yes I do! It's only about a day's swim from here. If we leave now, we could be back tomorrow. Tell them Lor-lie, so that you and I can get started.*

With the heaving waves rocking the yacht, Lori was having great difficulty, trying to stay upright on the end of her tail. "Dad, bring me up!" she anxiously called.

Her father reached the back of the yacht and gently hauled her on board. Lori slid over to Jeremy.

"Caspian just told me there is another cavern of healing moss not too far away. He says if we leave now, we can be back with it tomorrow."

"Are you talking about spending the entire night in the open sea?" her father asked.

Lori nodded. "Dad, it's the only way. Jeremy saved my life during the Trial. Please let me do this for him now."

"Lori is right," said Undine. "Caspian won't let anything happen to her; she'll be perfectly safe." She took hold of Lori's webbed hand. "I wish I could go too, but I would only hold you back. Time is not an ally right now. Every moment counts." Undine turned to Lori's father. "Brian, you must trust Lori and Caspian, they will be all right."

Lor-lie, we've got to get moving, Caspian called from the water.

"Dad, please, I've got to go," Lori begged. "Look at him, he needs our help."

"Brian, if it's the only way, we've got to let her try," Anne added, as she gently stroked Jeremy's forehead.

"Of course," her father said. "Just please, please be careful."

"I will," Lori promised. She leaned over and kissed Jeremy's cheek. "Please hold on Jeremy, just like you told me to in the helicopter. Hold on and I'll be back soon."

"I'll try, lass," Jeremy said weakly. "I'll try."

Lori was soon returned to the water. Anne placed a sharp knife in a pillowcase and handed it down to her. "Here, Undine said you'll need this for the moss. Bring back as much as you can, I'm not sure how much it will take. And please for heaven's sake, watch yourself out there!"

"We will," Lori promised as she received the pillowcase. "Take good care of Jeremy. Don't let anything happen to him."

Lori and Caspian started out on their long journey. She was holding on to his flipper and pressed close to his side. *Caspian, he looks so pale, he won't die, will he?*

No, Jeremy is strong. He'll be fine.

Heading into deeper water Lori found it difficult holding on. Caspian was moving faster than she'd ever imagined and the strain was making her arms ache. Finally she gave up and accepted his offer of a ride. Climbing into his mouth, she settled down on his tongue.

This was supposed to be a happy time, she said miserably. *We were going to free Mom and be a family again.*

You will, Caspian assured her. *And Jeremy will be there for the celebration. This is just a minor set back. Once Jeremy has the healing moss in him, he'll be back on his feet in no time.*

But what if he dies?

He won't.

But if he does?

You can't think that way. You have to be strong, for Jeremy. He needs you to believe in him.

I do, it's just that –

I know, Lor-lie, Caspian said gently. *I'm frightened too. But we have to have faith. Without that, none of us could go on.*

Lori nodded, but said nothing. Caspian was right. She had to believe that everything would be all right. There was no other choice.

Chapter 27

"Something is definitely wrong," Robichaud said as he paced before the monitors. All the deep sea camera was showing was the pile of rubble. Even the elderly mermaid was gone.

Luc had witnessed the mermaid and divers' quick departure from the seabed. When it happened, he'd followed his father out on deck to watch the yacht. The whales gathered around it. But as they watched and counted, they realised that the young male had disappeared again.

"What do you think happened?" Luc asked, holding the binoculars to his eyes.

"I don't know," Robichaud answered. "But by the looks of our friends down there, it's got to be serious."

"What are we going to do?"

Robichaud glanced at his son. "We'll give them a few hours. If we don't see my little mermaid again, we will go over there and learn for ourselves what has happened to her."

Luc had been aching to ask his father this question from the moment he learned of the mermaid's existence. "Papa, that tank at the estate? It's for her isn't it? You want to put the mermaid and her whale in it, don't you?"

His father remained silent for a long time. Finally, he nodded. "That had been my plan, my dream. But now, seeing the others, that the tank will soon be holding more than one mermaid."

"And the whales?"

"It was never about the whales," Robichaud said. "Once I have what I want, I don't need them any more. I have ordered a whaling ship to come and capture the scarred one for my collection and destroy the rest."

"Destroy?" Luc repeated. "You don't mean that you're going to have the other whales killed?"

"Of course," his father replied. "I told you Luc, the point of any collection lies in possessing something no one else can have. There isn't room for more than one whale in the tank so I need to ensure that no one else could ever have one like him. To do that, the rest must be removed from the equation."

"But Papa, that's murder!"

His father's dark eyes sparkled threateningly. "It is not murder. They are mindless animals. All I am doing is protecting my collection. If you are going to have a problem with that, tell me now and I'll arrange your transport back to school."

"No, Papa," Luc said softly. "I want to stay."

Robichaud studied him as if he was an insect. "Fine, but be warned. I have been after that mermaid and whale longer than you have been alive. Do not get in my way. I will not let anyone, even you, try to stop me."

Luc sucked in his breath. The threat was crystal clear. His father was so obsessed with this collection that he wouldn't hesitate to kill to complete it.

Chapter 28

Several hours later, Lori sat up on Caspian's tongue. *Is it much further?*

Not too far now, Caspian responded.

What does the moss look like? How will I find it?

To be truthful, Caspian admitted, *I'm not sure. Whenever we've needed it, there has always been someone to ask to get it for us.*

You mean like Mom or Gran?

No, Caspian said hesitantly. *Actually, Lor-lie, sharks usually collect it for us. And I know how frightened you are of them, but we're going to need their help now. There is no way I could ever fit into any of the caverns where the moss grows. They will have to show you the way.*

You mean I'm going to have to meet a real, live shark? Lori asked fearfully. *And trust them not to eat me?*

I keep telling you, Lor-lie, there is nothing in this sea that would hurt you. Most of what you've been taught about sea-creatures simply doesn't apply to us. I promise you'll be perfectly safe.

Lori wasn't convinced. But Jeremy's life was at stake and everyone was counting on them. Sitting on Caspian's tongue, unable to see anything outside his mouth, she could only wait and hope.

After a long while, Caspian started to sing. But it wasn't a song she'd heard before. Lori kept getting strange flashes in her mind. It reminded her of some kind of weird music video with flashing images that were only on screen for the briefest moment. As she concentrated, she thought she saw images of Jeremy, but she couldn't be certain. Then there were other flashes, like pictures of her mother, and grandmother and the yacht. But nothing was very clear.

When he finished, she asked, *what was that you were singing?*

I was calling out to the sea. It was kind of a distress signal, Caspian explained. *I've sent out the message that we need help, and that Jeremy is ill. Anyone in the area who could help will be at the cavern of the healing moss waiting for us.*

Really?

Really, Caspian continued. *That is one of the languages you have yet to learn. It is how you will be able to communicate with the other creatures of the sea. When Jeremy is well and your mother free, she will teach it to you. After that, you will be able to communicate with all the animals of the world.*

Despite her fears for Jeremy, Lori couldn't help but be a bit excited. *There are a lot of things I've got to learn,* she admitted. *Will you teach me?*

Caspian chuckled and then gently wrapped his tongue around her. *Of course, it would be my honour.*

Thank you, Caspian, Lori said, stroking his tongue lightly. *Thank you.*

Travelling through the night, Lori wondered if the journey would ever end. Finally Caspian announced that they had arrived. He opened his mouth and water flooded in, carrying Lori smoothly out again. Around her the sea was dark and filled with sound.

Lor-lie, we're not far from the caverns. There are several sharks waiting for us there. They know about Jeremy and want to help. Please don't be frightened of them. They won't hurt you, I promise. But they won't understand your fear and might be offended by it. Sharks are thinking creatures, but they aren't like you or me. There is only like and dislike for them. If they think you dislike them, they may leave. And we need them to show you the moss.

How can I talk to them? Let them know that I want to be their friend? Lori asked.

For now, just talk to me and I'll pass along your message. Oh, and when you greet them, they will open their mouths to you. This is not aggression. They are offering you their tongue as a gesture of peace. It is the softest most vulnerable part of their body and is their way of saying they won't hurt you.

147

"What do I do when they do that?"

It's simple. You stroke their tongue. That's all you need to do and they will serve you forever. Oh, and remember, you can't stroke a shark's skin. It is very rough and could cut your hand. That's why they offer you their mouth.

It's for Jeremy, Lori said, bracing herself. *I'm ready, let's go.*

She stayed beside Caspian as they moved steadily down towards the seabed. Though she could see fairly well, everything appeared in shadow and muted colours. Gazing around, she was amazed by all the sea-life she saw. Large schools of fish darted out of their way as they swam.

We're almost there, Caspian said. *Are you ready?*

Almost immediately, Lori heard and saw images flashing through her mind. But she couldn't understand what they meant. Straining to see in the darkness, she caught sight of movement coming towards her. Before she had time to react, three great white sharks came up to Caspian's side. Moving slowly towards her, as Caspian had said they would, they all opened their terrifying mouths in greeting.

Swallowing her fear, Lori followed Caspian's instructions and offered her own greeting. Reaching past their sharp teeth, she gently stroked all of their soft, smooth tongues and felt her own tension slipping away.

Now that wasn't so bad, was it? Caspian asked, as they all continued together towards the bottom of the sea.

No, it wasn't, she admitted, still hardly believing what she had just done.

The sea is full of wonders like this. You'll soon get used to it, Caspian said. They reached the bottom, and were facing a dark, wide crack in the sea floor. *This is as far as I can go,* he said. *The others will lead you into the cavern and show you which moss to collect. Are you ready?*

Reaching back into Caspian's mouth, Lori retrieved her pillowcase and started to follow the sharks. *How much should I take?*

As much as you can, Caspian answered. *It grows very quickly, so don't worry about others if they need some.*

Lori felt the first powerful twinges of fear as she reluctantly moved away from Caspian and towards the dark entrance of the cavern. Her mind was spinning at the thought of getting separated from her escorts, or even another cave-in that would leave her as trapped as her mother.

Lor-lie, don't be frightened, Caspian called. *The sharks know where they are going and you are safe. In fact, one of them has offered her dorsal fin for you to hold onto if you want.*

Lori gratefully reached out a webbed hand to catch hold of the shark's fin. *This is for Jeremy,* she said to herself over and over again. *He needs this.*

Soon they were entering the crack in the seafloor that led to the deep cavern. Barely able to see anything at all, she discovered they were in a tight tunnel with sharp rocks that cut into her back and the scales along her tail, and caught in her hair painfully.

At times the passage became so narrow that she had to release the shark in order to squeeze through. But just as she began to fear that they weren't going to make it, the walls suddenly opened out again and an amazing sight struck her.

Swimming to the very centre of the massive cavern, Lori looked around in wonder. The walls were covered in a moss that shimmered and glowed, filling the entire cavern with an eerie, greenish light.

Oh Caspian, I wish you were here; it's so beautiful! I've never seen anything like it before. The walls look like they're alive and the whole cavern is glowing!

I wish I could see it too, Caspian said wistfully. *I've heard Colleen and Undine describe them before, but I've never been able to see one for myself.*

A shark gently nudged Lori in the back. It turned in the water and started to swim towards one of the walls.

She wants you to follow her, Caspian said. *She says there is an area with especially potent moss. She wants you to take it to Jeremy.*

Lori kicked out her tail and started to follow. Around her, she saw smaller fish picking at the moss around the cavern.

Caspian, there are lots of small glowing fish in here. They're so cute! They look just like little gardeners tending their gardens.

That's exactly what they are, Caspian answered. *Those fish spend their entire lives in there, keeping the moss groomed and alive.*

Lori looked at the tiny fish darting around the moss and was grateful to them. Moss just like this had been keeping her mother alive, and would hopefully save the life of her uncle. Pulling the pillowcase along with her, she reached inside and caught hold of the knife. She approached a rocky outcropping that was completely covered in the glowing moss. She started to cut and scrape large pieces away from the rock. Close beside her, the female shark moved forward and seemed to be pointing out other areas for her to start cutting.

After a while, she stole a glance over her shoulder and saw the two other sharks hovering closely behind her. When she smiled at them, her mind was suddenly filled with images again.

Can you understand what they are saying? She called to Caspian.

Yes. They are asking if you would like them to come back to your mother's cavern to help with the rescue.

Would they really do that?

Of course. I told you Lor-le; all your fears about sharks have been unfounded. They can be very helpful when you need them.

Would you please tell them yes for me, and thank them.

A moment later, Lori heard and felt Caspian's response to the sharks. She watched them, and although she couldn't see any visible

150

reaction, once again her head was filled with images she couldn't understand.

They'll come, Caspian called. *Just as soon as you fill your bag, we'll head back to Jeremy.*

Lori worked quickly to gather moss. When the pillowcase was full, she followed her escorts out of the cavern and back through the opening in the sea floor.

Caspian, who was waiting just ahead, opened his huge mouth and invited her in.

Try to get some rest, he suggested. *It's been a very long night, and we have an even longer day ahead of us.*

Lori was exhausted. She settled down, and it wasn't long before she was deeply asleep.

Chapter 29

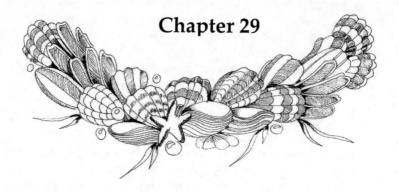

Several hours later, Caspian's voice was calling to her. *Lor-lie, wake up! We're almost back at the yacht. Something is very wrong.*

Instantly awake, Lori heard loud singing and immediately recognised Zephyr's urgent voice.

Caspian, what's happening? She asked.

Lori? Her mother called.

Mom, what's wrong? Is Jeremy all right?

He's unconscious. Anne thinks he's fallen into a coma, her mother said with a voice filled with fear. *Lori, he desperately needs the moss. But there's a bigger problem. Two launches from the rig are at the yacht, and there is a lot of shouting.*

What do they want?

I don't know. Zephyr couldn't hear properly. Now he's down at the bottom with Zenith and the others. They can't risk letting anyone know they can communicate with the family.

Where's Gran?

She's still on the yacht! Her mother replied. *There wasn't time to get her into the water without being seen. So your father carried her into the back. But we don't know what the strangers want.*

Caspian, let me out, Lori said. *I'm going up there to see if I can hear what's going on.*

No, Lori, you can't, her mother cried. *It's too dangerous. They might see you.*

Mom, I've got to go, Lori said as she swam out of Caspian's mouth and started towards the surface. *How else will we know what's happening? I'll be able to hear and tell you. I promise I'll be careful.*

I'm coming with you, Caspian said.

No son, you're not, said Zephyr. *We can't be seen too near the boat or let them know that we can communicate with each other. Stay here with us. Lori is a smart girl. She won't do anything silly. Besides, she's got the sharks with her.*

Lori came back to Caspian and stroked his side. *I'll be all right. I've got to hear what they are saying. I promise I'll be careful.*

You'd better be! Caspian warned.

I will, Lori assured him. She kicked out her tail and started up again. Immediately the sharks took up their position on either side of her. Grateful for their presence, she entered the lighter waters closer to the surface and saw the outline of the three boats. The rig's launches had completely blocked the rear of the yacht.

Unable to go to the back, Lori swam under the dark belly of the boat. Touching the smooth keel, she could feel the vibrations of the voices from her family. Her father's was loudest, then Anne's.

Lor-lie, be careful! Caspian warned. *Don't get too close.*

It's all right, Caspian, I'm fine.

Despite her best attempts, Lori still couldn't make out what they were saying. Checking the position of the two launches, she figured they wouldn't be able to see her from the far side of the yacht. Passing beneath the keel, she quietly came to the surface and could finally hear the argument between her family and the people from the oil rig.

They were arguing about Jeremy. The men from the rig wanted to take him back to their medical centre for treatment, but her father refused. Anne also added that she was a doctor and that Jeremy was already receiving treatment. But the more Lori listened the more she realised they were losing the fight.

What's happening, Lori? Her mother urgently called from below.

Quickly repeating what had been said, Lori heard her mother's groan.

How many men are there? Zephyr asked. *Can you count the voices? Are they still on their boats, or have they boarded the yacht?*

I'm not sure how many there are, Lori answered. *They're still on their boats, but I don't know for how long. It sounds like they want to come on board to take Jeremy.*

They can't! Her mother cried. *We've got to get the healing moss into him. He'll die on their rig.*

I know, Lori cried. *But what can we do?*

We can attack their boat! Caspian cried, and Coral joined in with agreement.

No, we can't, Zephyr said. *We do that, and it will be an all-out war with the rig. We haven't got Colleen out of the cavern yet. We need more time.*

Lori listened to the exchange coming from below. What she heard was terrifying. But what she heard from above was worse. Her father was shouting for the men to stop. They were boarding the yacht!

Unable to see anything from the water line, Lori used the upward swell of a large wave to reach up and catch hold of one of the side portholes. Holding on to it, she hauled herself out of the water and was able to peer over the railing. She could see her brothers and cousins standing back, while her father and Anne were kneeling on the deck guarding Jeremy. As she watched, the men on the rig's launches climbed onto the lower deck of the yacht.

Her brothers and cousins raced forward to fight them off.

"Get off our boat!" Danny shouted. "Leave us alone!"

Eddie caught hold of one of the men. Hoisting him easily into the air, he threw him over the side and into the cold sea. When a second man from the rig was shoved overboard by Aaron, Lori saw a tall, dark haired man hold up a large gun. He fired a shot in the air.

"One more move, and the next bullet will be aimed at one of you."

Lor-lie, Caspian called. *What was that sound? What's happening?*

They've got guns! Lori cried. Drawing herself further up, she saw the tall man pointing the gun at Eddie. While she watched, she explained to the whales what she was seeing.

"You are very strong for someone so young," Robichaud said casually. "You all are. But you are not stronger than this gun or my men's weapons. So please don't move. I should hate to have to kill one of you." He looked down at Jeremy and all the blood on the deck. "This man is going to die unless we take him back to my rig for treatment."

"This is a private yacht," Lori's father challenged, fearlessly approaching the stranger. "You have no right to be here. Now get off and leave us alone!"

154

The man looked her father up and down. Suddenly he whipped him across the face with his gun barrel. "One more word from you and you'll need a doctor more than he does."

As her father fell to the deck, Robichaud looked back as his other men. "Search the yacht, I want them found!"

Lori had to fight not to scream as three men pushed past her family and entered the salon. Her brothers, cousins and aunt were driven to the back corner of the open deck by the other armed men. As her father climbed to his hands and knees, the stranger bent down to speak with him.

"Where are the two mermaids?"

"Mermaids?" Lori's father repeated. "What are you talking about? There's no such thing. I've brought my family here to see some whales. That's all!"

"There is no point in lying to me," Robichaud said casually. "That is not an oil rig you see over there. It is a research platform. Research dedicated solely to these whales and the mermaid who travelled with them. We have had our deep sea camera on you the whole time. I've seen you all working down below in depths and pressures no human could survive. And I've seen the two mermaids, the young one and the old one. Now tell me, where are they?"

He knows about us! Lori cried. *He's had a camera on us the whole time. He's looking for Gran and me!*

Lor-Lie, get away from the yacht! Caspian ordered. *It's too dangerous.*

They can't see me. I've got to hear what they're saying.

Her father stood before the man with the gun. "Just leave us alone," he said. "You have no right to be here."

The stranger shook his head slowly. "I don't think you quite understand the situation," he paused and pointed at the rig with the barrel of his gun. "I am Andre Robichaud. That is my research platform. Out there, those are all my whales and my mermaids. I want them. Now tell me, where are they?"

"They don't belong to you!" Miranda challenged, stepping forward. "So leave us alone!"

Robichaud looked at Miranda. He slowly walked over to her. Lori could no longer see his face, but she could see the fear on Miranda's as he approached. "You may not be a mermaid in the traditional sense but I've seen you and the boys diving to depths no human could survive. So yes, dear girl, you belong to me too. Make no mistake."

Suddenly screams from the back of the salon caught everyone's attention. Soon the three men emerged, struggling to carry Undine in their arms.

"Gran!" Miranda cried. "Leave her alone!"

"Put me back in the sea!" Undine shouted as she fought them. "Release me!"

"Please leave her alone, she's hurt!" Anne cried, trying to push past Robichaud. "She's very fragile. Her tail bones have been broken."

Robichaud shoved Anne brutally aside and turned to his men. "Did you find the young one?" When they shook their heads, he continued, "Bring her here. I have waited a long time to meet this very special lady."

Lori watched in terror as her grandmother was carried to Robichaud. She called down to the whales, *they've got Gran!*

"Madam," Robichaud said, as he bowed elegantly before her. "It is my great honour to meet you. Now, if you will please tell me where the young mermaid is, we can get back to my rig."

"Please put me back in the water," Undine said. "I've been out too long. I'm going to die."

Robichaud frowned. "Of what?"

"Please," Anne called, "she's telling the truth. She is from the sea. Mermaids can't stay out of the water long or they'll suffocate. Look at her neck if you don't believe me. She's got gills, she needs to breathe water."

Robichaud leaned closer to her grandmother. He inspected her neck and saw the large gill flaps. "Of course, she will be returned to the water immediately; there is plenty on my rig."

"No!" Undine cried. "I must go back to the sea!"

As Lori watched Robichaud with her grandmother, she felt one of the sharks urgently nudging her tail. When she turned to look down into the water, she suddenly became aware of a boy on one of the rig's launches watching her intently. He was about Aaron's age and had the same colouring as Andre Robichaud. His mouth was hanging open in surprise.

Frozen with fear, Lori didn't know what to do. She looked down at herself and realised her T-shirt ended well above where her tail

156

started. What was worse, in the heaving waves, at times most of her tail was out of the water. He could see everything. And yet, as she watched him, he said nothing to the others and just stood staring at her.

Unable to think of anything else to do, Lori shook her head and pleaded softly, "Please, please don't tell them –"

"Luc, what are you looking at?" Robichaud demanded.

"Nothing, Papa," he said. "I just thought I saw a shark."

"Don't be ridiculous. Sharks wouldn't come anywhere near the whales. Now come on board and help me. We've got a lot to do."

Lori watched the boy climb out of the launch and onto the yacht. She saw him take occasional glances her way, but he didn't mention anything to the others.

Suddenly Caspian surfaced. *Get down, Lor-Lie. Move away from the boat. We are not going to let them take Undine away.*

Lori released her hold on the porthole and slipped back into the water just as the entire whale family came to the surface. Staying behind Caspian, she could no longer see what was happening on board, but she could hear.

"Please put me back in the water," Undine begged. "Look around, you are surrounded. They won't let you take me away. I belong with them."

Lori strained to see round Caspian, but every time she moved, he moved to block her. "Caspian, please, I want to see what's happening. What are they doing to Gran?"

You can't let him see you, Lor-lie. Caspian said. "It's too dangerous."

Blocked from view, all Lori could do was listen and what she heard terrified her more than anything had before in her life.

"I am sorry, dear lady, but I will not release you. You belong to me now," Robichaud said. "You all do. And before this day is over, I will know all your secrets."

Lori heard him raise his voice. "All of you out there listen to me! Should any of you try to stop us, I swear I will kill a member of this family. And if you think I won't –"

Suddenly there was the sound of a gunshot. Her brothers screamed and Anne shouted, "Brian! No!"

"Dad!" Lori cried. "Caspian, what did he do to Dad?"

Get Lor-lie away from here! Zephyr ordered. *Caspian, take her below.*

Before Lori could see what had happened to her father, Caspian scooped her up in his mouth and slipped beneath the surface.

"Let me out!" Lori shouted, struggling to get Caspian to open his mouth. "Please, Caspian, please, I need to know what happened!"

Forgive me, Lor-lie, Caspian said sadly. *But I think that man just shot your father.*

Chapter 30

Luc lay on his bed. He could hardly believe the events of the day. He had been so excited when he'd first arrived on the rig and seen the whales; so filled with hope that his father might actually care for at least one species. But then he discovered the truth.

Andre Robichaud's collection.

That obsession was all the mattered. It was one thing owning a Spix Macaw or any of the other unfortunate species in his private collection. But now, his father had what no one else on earth believed existed. He had a mermaid.

But was he content? No. He didn't just want one mermaid he wanted all of them and he was prepared to kill to get them.

Luc was certain his father hadn't heard the anguished cry that had followed the gunshot. Maybe Luc had heard it because he knew the mermaid was there. He knew she believed her father had been shot. He ached to call to her, and let her know it had only been a warning shot, fired into the side of the boat. But fear of his father kept him silent. He doubted he would ever get over the look of terror on her face when she realised he'd seen her. Or the heartbreaking sound of her cries right before the whale took her below.

How could he let her know he would never betray her, and that he too was a victim of his father? Instead, he had to stand back and watch his father abuse an innocent family.

Part of him wished the whales had attacked the yacht. Luc was sure the members of the family would have survived. And if he and his father had died? Well, the world would be a better place without Andre Robichaud.

But the attack had been stopped before it started. By showing the whales he was prepared to kill, Andre Robichaud had won. And although they surrounded the yacht, bumping it and following it as it was piloted back to the rig, they did nothing, nothing but slap their flippers on the water in rage as they watched the family being forcibly taken on board the rig.

Unable to rest, Luc climbed from his bunk and started to pace his room. His mind kept replaying the interrogations over and over again. The way the family had fought to keep silent until finally, Andre Robichaud used violence against the woman doctor to break them. He tortured her to get the others to talk, tearing from them the truth that there was indeed another mermaid trapped at the bottom of the sea, and they had come to rescue her. When they finally went into details, his father nodded his head in approval.

"Very good," Robichaud said. "You will find I can be quite generous when you cooperate. Now, here is the new plan. Anne and Miranda, you will remain here on the rig to care for Jeremy and Undine. The rest of you will be returned to your yacht and continue with the rescue. You will have some of my men and all the equipment of this rig available to you. You will open that cavern and free my mermaid."

Luc had seen the defiance in Brian's face, and how his sister held him back, so that he'd stood in silent fury as Robichaud went on. "Brian, you and your sister are human. That makes you completely disposable." He'd moved over to Eddie, Danny and Aaron. "If you three try anything against us, it will be your father and aunt who pay for your disobedience."

Eddie had been ready to fight, but Robichaud raised a warning finger. "Think very carefully before you do or say anything. I won't hesitate to punish your father."

When Eddie lowered his head and stepped back without speaking, Robichaud continued. "Finally, you will tell your sister she is to come to me on the sea platform below this rig. I want her here as well."

This time Eddie did not back down. "Lori stays with us if you want our mother free," he said. "She's the only one who can communicate with the whales. Without her, the rescue will fail."

Robichaud stood staring at Eddie for a long while. Luc was certain his father had been about to strike him. Instead, he nodded.

160

"Very well, your sister stays free for the moment. But these are my terms –"

Now, Luc continued to pace his quarters as he recalled the expression of complete despair on everyone's faces. He hated his family name more than anything in the world and couldn't remain in his cabin a moment longer. Entering the corridor, he turned left and went down to the medical centre.

Two armed guards were posted outside the door. They watched him approach, but did not block him from entering. The lights in the room had been dimmed. He saw the bed containing Jeremy. Miranda was seated in a chair beside the giant, while Anne checked on her patient.

"What do you want," Miranda angrily challenged, as she stood and faced him. "Get out of here!"

"Miri, calm down," Anne said, walking away from the bed. She came to Luc. "It's late. My patient needs his rest. I suggest you leave."

Luc saw the dark bruises on her arms and swelling around her blackened eye. The way she moved showed the pain she was in from her brutal encounter with his father. He was reminded of the days when his mother was still alive. Luc dropped his head. "I'm so sorry for everything. I just wanted to know how you are."

"It's none of your business!" Miranda snapped, shoving him towards the door. "You hurt my aunt and Gran. Why couldn't you just leave us alone?"

Luc was cut by her words because they were true. It was his father's fault they were here. "I wish more than anything my father had left you alone," he said sadly. "I know it doesn't matter to you, but I swear I never knew what he was planning. I thought we were here to watch whales, not hunt mermaids."

Anne sighed. "Whether you knew or not doesn't change anything. We're trapped here and my patient is going to die because we can't get the medicine he desperately needs. I've taken the bullet from his chest, but he's lost too much blood. Because of his physiology, there isn't any more to give him. The kids have donated all they can. But it's still not enough."

"Jeremy will be the lucky one if he does die," Miranda said miserably. "At least he'll be free. What about the rest of us? What is

161

your father going to do to us? Sell us to some laboratory? Put us in a zoo?"

Luc shrugged. "I don't know. He's got this big sea tank at his estate. I always thought he was going to put dolphins in it. But –"

"He's going to put us in it instead," Miranda answered.

Saying nothing, Luc nodded. Finally he looked back at Miranda. "You look a lot like Lori."

"You've seen Lori?" Anne asked.

"Yes, I first saw her on the monitors. But then I saw her today when we first arrived at the yacht. I was on the launch and saw her hanging onto a porthole to see what was happening." Luc dropped his head in shame. "She looked terrified when she caught me watching her. I wish I could have told her I didn't want to hurt her. I don't want to hurt any of you. I would help if I could."

Anne raised her hands to Luc's shoulders. "Do you mean that? Would you help us if you could? Because there is something you could do for us –"

"Anne no," Miranda shot. "He won't help. He's the enemy! He's going to catch Lori and put her in a fish tank like he did Gran."

"I'm not your enemy," Luc insisted. "I hate what my father is doing and where he's put your grandmother. If I could stop him, believe me, I would. But when it comes to his collection, he's completely obsessed. I mean nothing to him. He'd kill me if I stood in his way."

Anne shook her head. "I'm not asking you to betray you father or risk your life. But Lori has some medicine that can save Jeremy. If we could get it to him, he might survive."

"What can I do?" Luc asked. "I'm not allowed to leave the rig. Some of my father's men are with the Brian and the boys on your yacht. But most are here guarding you. I have no way of reaching Lori. And even if I did, she wouldn't trust me." Luc turned to Miranda. "You don't trust me, why should she?"

"Because we have no choice," Anne said. She looked at Miranda, "Miri, think about it. How can we reach Lori?"

"Take me down to the sea platform where we moored the yacht today," Miranda said. "I could reach her."

"No," Luc said, shaking his head. "There are too many guards. My father would never allow you anywhere near the water. He knows you'll get away."

162

"But I'm not a mermaid," Miranda argued. "Look at me, I've got legs."

"I know," Luc agreed. "But you're not human either, and everyone knows it. They tested your blood and we've seen you at the bottom. You could jump in the water and get away."

"See!" Miranda challenged, "He won't help us. All he sees in us is freaks." She looked furiously at Luc. "Now get out of here before I show you just how different I really am!"

Chapter 31

Please don't be mad at me.

I'm not mad at you, Lori said to Caspian, as she worked to clear away rubble from the cavern entrance. *I'm just upset.*

That means you're mad, Caspian said.

Lori stopped and looked over at the large whale. In truth, she was mad at him. He shouldn't have taken her away from the yacht. She'd needed to see what had happened to her father. Finding out later that he hadn't been shot wasn't the same as seeing for herself.

It's just that – she said, trying to think of the right words.

Lori, her mother called, *Caspian wasn't wrong in what he did. If Robichaud had seen you in the water, he would have used the threat of violence against the rest of the family to get you on board. Then you'd be stuck on that rig too.*

But we're going to end up there anyway, Lori moaned. *Mom, the only reason I'm still free is because he needs me to talk to the whales to free you. The moment we get you out of there, Robichaud wants us to surrender to the rig, or he'll kill Dad and Anne. They've got cameras on us. We're trapped.*

Zephyr joined the conversation. *What Robichaud wants and what he gets are two different things. This is far from over. We will slow down the rescue, give Jeremy time to heal. When he is sufficiently recovered, we will get Colleen free and make our move against the others. Just make sure you tell the boys not to work too fast.*

Lori stopped working and looked around. Eddie and Aaron were drilling holes in the large boulders blocking the entrance to the cavern. When they finished one, Danny slowly screwed in the hooks.

Watching her brothers and cousin work, she could see they all felt the same. They were slaves to Andre Robichaud.

When Danny finished screwing in the hook, he waved at her. Lori swam over to him and she heard him call through his mask. "We're ready with this one, bring Caspian over."

Caspian, we're ready with another one, Lori said. As she watched his hesitation and felt his emotions, she dropped her head in shame. *I'm so sorry Caspian,* she said softly, as she swam over to his side and rested her forehead against him. *I've been unfair. I know you were trying to protect me. It's just that* – she paused as the pain of the situation overwhelmed her. *Oh I wish I could cry underwater.*

Me too, he sadly agreed. *I'm sorry Lor-lie; I shouldn't have listened to my father. I should have let you see that your father was unhurt.*

No. Zephyr was right. I was just panicking when you said Robichaud had shot Dad. But he's fine and on the yacht. So it's over. C'mon, she finally said. *Let's get back to work.*

Caspian coasted over the large boulder. Lori reached out and attached the harness he wore to the hook in the boulder.

Okay, it's attached, she said. *Nice and easy, see if you can lift it.*

Everyone at the base of the cavern moved away for safety as Caspian strained to shift the boulder. Finally, the strength of the whale proved greater than the weight of the boulder. He drew it up and carefully away from the area. Lori stayed at his side as the huge rock moved over the top of what they now knew was the camera watching their every move.

Lori ached to have Caspian drop the boulder on the spying equipment. But that was one of the rules set by Robichaud. She was to remain in constant view of the camera. Even when they weren't working, she was to sleep on the sea bed in front of the equipment so they could see her. Lori had never spent more than a single night away from home but now, because of Robichaud, she had to sleep in the open sea away from her family.

The only time she was allowed to leave the camera's prying eye was when she signalled that she had to go to the toilet. Even that was timed. If she took too long, she knew Anne and her father would pay for her defiance.

Moving with Caspian to the area where they deposited the rubble from the entrance, Lori unhooked the boulder from the harness and together, the two made their way back to the work area.

While Lori waited for the next boulder to be prepared, she heard a lot of activity from the whales outside the camera's range. Finally Zephyr called to both Lori and her mother.

We've got a situation.

What's happening? Lori's mother called.

Zephyr moved closer, but tried to look as though he was struggling to move rubble away. *Coral has been to the rig, keeping watch. It seems there is a boy on the rig's lower platform. He is calling for Lori and asking to speak with her.*

What does he want? Lori asked.

We don't know. But Coral says the boy sounds very frightened.

It's a trap, Caspian called. *They want to get Lori to the rig.*

This whole thing was a trap and we're in it, Lori said. *But if Robichaud wanted me at the rig, he only needs to say so. I'd have no choice but to go.*

Then what does he want? Caspian wondered aloud.

I don't know, Lori said. *But I think I should go. I could let the camera know that I have to go to the toilet. Then we could sneak over there and see what he wants.*

Chapter 32

Luc stood on the rig's waterline platform shivering from the terrible, wet cold. He was worrying and wondering whether his message had made it to Lori. His frightened eyes kept darting up to the roof of the rig's underside and the web-like maintenance scaffold that ran around the entire area almost fifty metres above him. From there, he checked the heavy metal stairs that led down to the floating waterline platform. He was terrified that his father would miss him and have people start to look for him. It wouldn't take them long to find him on the sea platform.

The only thing that eased his tension was his father's obsession with watching the rescue work being shown on the monitors. He hardly ever left the monitor room. When he did, it was only to check on Undine in her prison tank. After that, a quick trip to the medical centre for Jeremy, then back to the monitors. Luc doubted his father even slept any more.

When the idea of helping the family had first come to him, Luc had hoped to get Arthur to join him. But when he approached the young marine biologist, he'd changed his mind. Arthur was as obsessed with the mermaids as his father was. But there was a big difference. Where his father was interested in possessing the family to complete his exotic collection, Arthur's interests were much more sinister and dangerous to the family.

Arthur had excitedly gone into details of how he would love to get his hands on Undine to dissect her. He desperately wanted to find out how she could possibly exist. When Luc asked about the mermaid's right to life, Arthur laughed in his face and said freaks of nature didn't have the same rights humans did – that if he could, he would love to get all of the mermaids into a lab to run experiments on them.

Hearing this chilled Luc to the bone. He suddenly realised what life must be like for the family and the deep fear they must be suffering right now.

So when Arthur was on deck watching the whales, Luc managed to sneak into his quarters to take the keys to the lower platform. This added to his worry about being caught should Arthur miss them and raise the alarm.

As he waited, Luc also began to worry that he'd been wrong about the whales. Maybe they couldn't understand him when he'd said he needed to reach Lori. He was already taking a big risk in coming down here. If he was gone much longer, someone would miss him and start to ask questions.

He was turning to leave when he heard the loud whoosh of air as a whale broke the surface just a few feet from the platform. Behind him, a second whale suddenly surfaced and then a third.

"I need to reach Lori," Luc said. "Please, I really must speak with her."

"I'm here," called a voice from behind the whales. "What do you want?"

Luc's feet felt like lead as he stepped closer to the edge of the platform. He no longer felt the cold sea water that rushed over the platform and soaked his shoes and bottom of his jeans. "I'm Luc," he said awkwardly, "and I need to speak with you about the healing moss for Jeremy."

There was short pause and then Luc heard the whales start to sing. Moments later, Lori called. "Are there any cameras down here?"

Luc strained to see where the voice was coming from. "No," he answered. "They're all pointed at the yacht or where you are working at the cavern. I promise we're alone down here."

After another pause, the mermaid he'd seen at the yacht surfaced at the edge of the platform.

"I don't have a lot of time," Lori said. "If I'm gone too long, your father will punish Anne. What do you want?"

Luc felt awkward and foolish. He could see the hate and suspicion on her pretty face and would have given anything to make

168

it go away. "I'm so sorry for what my father is doing to you and your family. I know you all hate me, but I swear I want to help you."

"How is Jeremy?" Lori asked.

"Anne told me he's lost too much blood. Even after the surgery he's not getting any better. She's asked for the healing moss – says it's the only chance he's got and hopes you were able to get some."

Luc watched the indecision on Lori's face. He could see part of her wanted to believe him, but another part of her also knew he was a Robichaud.

"Please, Lori," he continued. "Let me help. I swear I'm not like my father. He's an evil man. He murdered my mother and wouldn't hesitate to kill me if he knew I was helping you. He's been obsessed with your mother for years. Now that he's seen you, he wants all of you for his own private collection. He has ordered a large whaling ship to come here and capture the big, scarred whale. Then they are going to kill the rest."

"What?" Lori cried. "You father is going to kill the family?" She turned to the whale beside her. "Caspian, did you hear that?"

Luc watched all the whales in the water react violently to his words as the water erupted with noise and song. "Can they really understand me?"

Lori nodded. "Luc, I can't expect you to understand. But these whales are my family, my blood. If your father kills them, he'll kill all of us. We've got to stop him!"

"I know," Luc agreed. "We will. But the first step is saving Jeremy. To do that, I need the healing moss."

"You'll get it," Lori promised. She turned back to Caspian. "Please ask the sharks to get the moss. They saw where I dropped it. They must bring it back here as quickly as possible."

Luc heard the large whale start to sing again. "He can talk to sharks too?"

Lori nodded. "They can talk to all the creatures in the sea."

"What about you? Can't you talk to sharks? I saw you with them at the yacht."

Lori shook her head. "Not yet, I've still got to learn."

Beside them, the second whale started to sing. When he finished, Lori said, "Coral wants to know why you father plans to kill everyone except Zephyr."

169

When Luc heard the whales' names, he looked at Lori in amazement, "Have they all got names?"

"Of course," Lori said. "This is Caspian and back there is Coral and his sister Sargasso. Luc, they're just like you and me. Doesn't you father understand that? They're family. He can't kill them, it would be murder."

"I know. But my father doesn't care. His collection is all that matters to him. More than his business and more than me."

"But why kill the whales?" Lori asked. "I just don't understand."

Luc moved to the very edge and bent down to speak with Lori as she clung to the side of the floating platform. "Because being part of my father's collection means there are no others anywhere else in the world. Since he can't keep all the whales, he'll take one and get rid of the rest so no one else can have them."

"So does that mean he's going to catch my mother and kill the rest of us?"

Luc shook his head. "I don't think so. He's making plans to have you all taken back to his estate on the whaling ship."

"Then what?" Lori asked. "Keep us in an aquarium? Feed us goldfish food and show us off to all his friends?"

"My father doesn't have any friends," Luc answered. "Even if he did, he would never show his collection to them. I'm barely allowed in to see it." Luc paused and considered. "But I'm not sure what he's planning for Miranda and those of you without tails. Maybe he'll put

170

them in cages. I don't know. But whatever he does, it won't be good for any of you."

Luc watched fear return to Lori's face. He reached out and touched her arm. When he did, he was shocked by how cold it was. "You're freezing!"

"I don't feel the cold," Lori said softly. Finally she looked up at Luc. "Luc, we've got to stop him."

"I know," he agreed. "I'm just not sure what we can do. My father's men have weapons and will do whatever he tells them to. But it's not over yet. I'm sure we'll think of something."

Beside her, Caspian nudged Lori and sang beautiful notes.

"What did he say?"

"That we've got to get back. Coral will stay here until the sharks come with the moss. Get it to Anne as fast as you can. Before we can do anything, we need to know Jeremy is all right."

"I will," Luc promised. He watched Lori turn in the water. Once again, he marvelled at the amazing green tail she flashed at him as she ducked down in the water.

Not long after she left, Luc was holding the pillowcase full of healing moss. He hid the cold wet bag under his shirt and climbed the metal stairs to the scaffold and exit door. As he ran through the corridors, he was terrified that he would round a bend and run straight into his father.

When he arrived at the medical centre and walked past the guards on the door, he breathed his first sigh of relief.

"I told you to leave us alone!" Miranda said angrily. "Now get out of here."

Luc knew this wasn't going to be easy. They had no reason to trust him. Finally, he held up his hands in surrender. "Wait, please. I said I wanted to help and I do." He pulled out the wet bag of moss and carried it over to Anne. "You said you needed this for Jeremy."

When Anne received the pillowcase and peered inside, she looked at him in disbelief. "Is this what I think it is?"

"Healing moss," Luc said. "Lori gave it to me," then he paused and corrected himself. "Actually a really big, scary shark gave it to me. But Lori told Caspian and he told the shark."

171

"Caspian?" Miranda said. "You've seen Caspian?"

"And Coral and Sargasso," Luc added. "I went below and told them I wanted to help. I think they believed me."

"I think I'm beginning to also," Anne said, as she pulled chunks of the dark green moss from the bag. She went back to Jeremy and started to work.

"Why would you do that?" Miranda asked.

"I told you," Luc said. "I'm not like my father. I hate what he's doing to you. I want to help you get out of here."

"But he's your father," Miranda said, still not understanding. "How can you go against him?"

Luc sighed heavily. "I've lived my whole life watching him ruin people's lives. All he cares about is himself and no one else. He doesn't even like me very much. He sends me away to private school and rarely lets me come home for holidays."

"Why?"

Luc looked away, unable to meet her stare. "He's disappointed that I'm not like him. He's always telling me I'm too much like my mother. He murdered her when I was a young. He tried to kill me too, but somehow I survived. Now he treats me like he doesn't care what happens to me."

"How awful!" Miranda cried.

Luc nodded. "I've only just started to remember. I can't believe I'd forgotten her, or what my father did. He used to beat her all the time. When she finally wanted to leave, he killed her."

Both he and Miranda looked over to where Anne was crushing up moss and preparing it for Jeremy. They both saw the dark bruises on her face and arms.

"If it happened when you were young, maybe you forgot because it was too painful."

"Maybe," Luc agreed. "But I forgot everything about her. It was like she didn't exist for me. Like my father had somehow erased her from my life."

"But now that you know, what are you going to do?"

Luc shrugged. "The first thing is to get you all away from here. After that, I'm going to the police. I can't wait till I'm older. My father must be made to pay for what he did to my mother."

172

Chapter 33

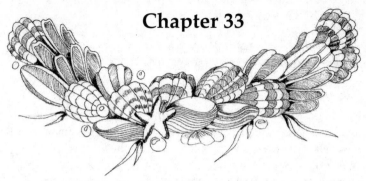

Lori returned to the cavern and told her mother and the whales about her meeting with Luc. She also told them about Robichaud's plan to kill all the whales except Zephyr.

It will never happen! Zephyr said fiercely, as shock spread amongst the whales. *We will stop them and then finally get away from this wretched place.*

How? Her mother called. *They've got guns, we don't. How can we hope to fight them and still get away?*

I don't know, Zephyr answered. *But we've got to try.*

We will, agreed Zenith, as he joined the others outside the camera's range. *They won't take the family from us.*

We do have Jeremy, Caspian offered. *When Anne gets the healing moss into him, he'll recover quickly and then we can make our plans.*

"*I just wish I could tell the boys,* Lori added, as she got back to work and reached for a rock that would have been too heavy for an adult man. Lifting it easily, she flicked her tail and carried it away from the area. She looked over at her brothers as they worked to remove rubble, oblivious to Robichaud's murderous plans.

Perhaps later when you surface for your supper, Zephyr said. *You have got to find a way to let your father and the boys know we have a friend on the rig.*

Because of the pressure and depth, her brothers and cousins couldn't stay under for more than two hours at a time as their equipment started to fail. Rising to the surface with them, Lori and Caspian slowly made their way back to the yacht.

She was always grateful to see her father, safe and unharmed. But there were four other men from the rig with him. They'd been assigned to help out with the running of the yacht and the equipment. They were also there to keep watch over everyone and to report back to the rig.

After a couple of days, the men became accustomed to the whales, and to seeing the mermaid with them. So whenever Lori surfaced, she was ordered to remain on the platform while an armed guard sat on a bench above her, keeping watch over her.

"How's it going, kiddo," her father said softly as he handed down her supper.

Lori first glared at the guard and then looked back to her father. "So far, so good, but it's slow. There is a lot of rubble down there."

"It would go faster if you didn't keep stopping," the guard said irritably. "Then we could all get out of this foul, cold, wet weather and back to the rig where it's warmer."

Lori looked at him and felt nothing but anger, "Well, I'd like to see you try working down there! It's not our fault that the equipment can't take the depth."

"Lori," her father warned. "Don't start."

But Lori's nerves were already frayed to the point of breaking. She knew she needed to reach her father to tell him what was happening, but with the guards there, she wasn't given a single moment alone.

"No Dad," she said angrily, "if he wants to complain, why doesn't he come in the water and try. We'd show him what it was like to work down below!"

"Are you threatening me?" the guard said, reaching for his weapon and looking nervously at the whales in the water around the yacht.

"No, I'm not. But I'd like to know what you are complaining about. All you ever do is sit around pointing guns at us. If you really wanted to get out of the cold, you'd shoot Robichaud then we could all go home."

"Watch your mouth, little girl," the guard warned. "Andre Robichaud would hit you if he heard you say that. Don't think being a fish will protect you from him. He will not tolerate disobedience!"

174

"I'm not a fish!" Lori shouted, finally losing her temper. Throwing down her plate of food, she curled the fluke at the end of her tail into a bowl shape. Filling it with cold sea water, she furiously kicked it up at the guard.

The guard screamed and cursed as the freezing water soaked through his clothing. "You little brat!" he shouted. "Don't you dare move a muscle. I'm going to change my clothes and you'd better be there when I get back or they'll be hell to pay!"

When he was gone, her father moved closer. "My God, Lori, are you crazy? He could have killed the both of us!"

"Dad, please," Lori urgently said. "I need to tell you something. It was the only way to make him go."

Lori moved closer and explained to her father the latest revelations and how Jeremy now had the healing moss.

"Does Caspian have any idea how long it will take to work?" her father asked.

"No," Lori answered. "Anne told Luc it may already be too late."

"Jeremy is strong," her father said. "I'm sure he'll be fine. We just have to hope he recovers quickly. From what I hear from the boys, it won't be long before you get the cavern open. After that, we've got to make some kind of move."

"Luc said he wanted to help."

"Do you trust him?"

Lori shrugged. "I don't know. What if it's all a trick?"

Her father sighed and ran his wet hands through his hair. "We'll find out soon enough –"

A different guard appeared on deck and came over to them. Lori recognized him as the radio operator. "A launch from the rig is coming." He looked directly at Lori. "You, stay there. Robichaud is coming to see you."

"Why?" her father demanded.

"I wouldn't ask questions if I were you," he responded. "Just do as you are told and hope he's in a good mood."

Soon they heard the sound of the launch engines. This was going to be Lori's first meeting with Andre Robichaud. The thought of it made her stomach turn.

Maybe we should sink his boat, Caspian offered. *Then we could end this right now.*

We can't, Zenith called. *He's got Anne with him and is holding a weapon to her head. I think he may have had the same thought you did. He's letting us know not to move against him.*

Caspian, we must be patient, Lori's mother called. *We can't endanger Anne. Just see what he wants.*

He wants you, Col, Zephyr answered angrily. *That's what he wants. But he's not going to get you.*

Lori heard the conversation between the whales and her mother, but said nothing. She couldn't let the guards on the boat know what the family was thinking. Instead she sat on the lower platform fighting every instinct she had to dive under the surface and stay away until he left.

Soon bow lines were tossed and the launch was moored beside the yacht. From her position on the lower platform, Lori couldn't see anything, but she could hear the sound of voices, and men climbing on board their boat.

"Brian, bring your daughter up," the deep voice said. "I would like to finally meet her face to face."

Lori's heart raced as her father climbed down onto the platform. As he reached for her, he whispered in her ear. "Don't antagonise him. He's very dangerous and we need to keep you away from that rig. Play along for the moment,"

I'm here, Lor-Lie, Caspian said reassuringly. *Please don't be frightened. I won't let him hurt you. Just do as your father says. We'll figure something out.*

Lori looked over to Caspian floating behind the yacht and knew he was trying to help. But it wasn't working. As her father carried her up to the main deck, she thought she was going to be sick.

"At last," Andre Robichaud sighed, as he stroked the length of her green tail. "Lorelie, you are simply magnificent! Just look at you, a real sea princess. No harpoon scars, all your scales intact and such a pretty young tail."

Lori felt bile rise in her throat as Andre Robichaud inspected every detail of her tail. When his eyes trailed up to her waist, he lifted the edge of her T-shirt and marvelled at the point where her tail became skin.

"Look at those tiny scales, aren't they perfect." Finally his predatory eyes made it up to her face. "You are such a rare beauty. I have dreamt of this day for a very long time. It is wonderful to

176

finally meet you in person. I have watched you on the monitors and feel that we are already very good friends."

"My name is Lori," she corrected, as she tried to shy away from his dark, piercing eyes. "And if you really wanted to be my friend, you wouldn't be doing this to us."

"Lori," her father warned, giving her a light squeeze. "Don't start."

Robichaud looked at her father and then chuckled as he leaned in closer to her. "I prefer to call you Lorelie." Then his expression changed to one of complete innocence. "And tell me, my dear child, what have I done that is so awful? We are treating Jeremy on the rig, and we both know he would have died had he stayed here. My men are helping you with the rescue of your mother. We haven't hurt anyone. I think perhaps you have the wrong idea about me. I just want to help your family, not harm them."

Lori ached to kick out her tail and knock him off the yacht. She knew full well what he wanted. He was planning to capture Zephyr and murder the rest of the whales. Instead of speaking, she looked over to her aunt who was being held by a guard. Lori was shocked the see the swollen, dark bruises on her face. Everyone knew who had done that to her and why.

"You're lying," she challenged. "You tortured Anne so you could learn why we're here. Your men have guns and are always threatening us. You are an evil, horrible man and I hate you!"

Robichaud burst out laughing. "Oh my, but you are delightful. Such spirit! I shall enjoy spending a lot of time with you when we get back to my estate."

While they had been speaking, Lori felt her father trembling. As first she thought he was frightened, but she soon realised it was contained fury.

"What do you want, Robichaud?" he demanded. "Why have you come? You've got cameras on us and your spies here on the yacht. You know we are working. There is no reason for you to come here and torment my daughter."

"Temper, temper, Brian," warned Robichaud as his face became dark and threatening. "I should hate for your children to see what happens to people who displease me."

"Dad, please," Danny called from the salon. "Don't."

"Listen to your son," Robichaud continued. "Of all the people here, you are the least important. Watch yourself or your children will lose their father."

Lori looked at her father and knew he wanted to say and do more. Then she looked back to Robichaud. She could tell by the sickening way he regarded her that he would not harm her, but he

178

wouldn't hesitate to kill her father. "Why are you here?" she demanded.

Robichaud's challenging stare lingered on her father a moment more. Finally the sparkle returned to his eyes and he concentrated on her. "I came because I wanted to meet you for myself and to warn you, a large storm is coming this way. The winds and swells will be much greater than this yacht can withstand. It will not survive. I'm told we've only got two or three days at best before it arrives. You must have Colleen free before then. Then you will all join me on the rig to ride out the storm."

Eddie came out of the salon and approached Robichaud. "That's impossible! You've got your cameras down there. You've seen the mess. We need more time."

"You don't have it," Robichaud said. "This isn't my decision, it is nature. Even under the protection of the rig, there's a strong chance your yacht will be destroyed. We can pull the launches out of the water and suspend them in the rigging, but not this boat. If we don't get Colleen out before then, the rescue will fail. So I suggest you gear up and get back to work. I want your mother out of that cavern, and soon."

As Robichaud turned and ordered his men to get Anne back on the launch, there was a sudden commotion in the water. The whales were singing loudly and becoming agitated.

"No!" Lori suddenly cried. "No it can't be!" Her eyes darted from the whales, up to the rig, and back to the whales again. "It's too fast!"

"What is it?" Robichaud demanded. He looked at the whales and saw the growing activity in the water. "What is wrong with them? What is happening?"

Lori was only half paying attention as she looked out over the water. Caspian was moving away from the boat and over to Coral. Soon all the whales were gathered around him.

"Lorelie," Robichaud repeated as he grasped her webbed hand. "What is happening in the water? What is wrong with the whales?"

Don't tell him, Lor-Lie, Caspian urgently warned. *He can't know.*

Turning back to Robichaud, Lori felt herself starting to tremble. She finally she shook her head. "I – I don't know. Something is wrong. I think something might have happened to Jeremy. The whales feel something but they don't know what it is."

179

"Then I must take the doctor back to him." Robichaud boarded the launch. "All of you get back to work. I want Colleen out of there before that storm hits."

Lori's terror increased as the bow lines were freed and the launch pulled away. When it was gone, her brothers came forward to ask what was wrong, but the guards ordered them back to work. While they put their diving gear on, her father carried her down to the platform.

"What is it? What's wrong with Jeremy?"

Lori put her arms around his neck and hugged him tightly. "Dad, it's not Jeremy. It's Miranda. Her Trial has started!"

Chapter 34

The moment his father left for the yacht, Luc had arrived at the medical centre to spend time with Miranda. Talking to her was so easy. Before long, he was sharing things with her he'd never shared with anyone else in his life. They talked of their families, and compared childhoods. Luc had listened with envy to the stories Miranda told of the closeness of her family and the adventures she'd had growing up with the whales.

He told her of his loneliness, being shuttled from one boarding school to another. How he never had any friends and the horror he felt knowing his father made his fortune from selling weapons to anyone who had the money to pay for them.

They even managed to laugh together on more than one occasion. But suddenly everything had changed. Not long after Anne left, Miranda started to pace the confines of the room. Her eyes became wild and frightened.

"Miranda, please talk to me."

Miranda said nothing but continued to pace and rub at her legs.

Finally, Luc caught hold of her arm. "I know something is wrong. Please tell me. You know you can trust me."

"Luc, something awful is going to happen tonight and there's nothing anyone can do to stop it."

"What is it?" he begged. "Is something going to happen on the yacht?"

Miranda shook her head. "No, it's not the yacht. Tonight Coral and I are going to die."

"What?" Luc cried. "No you're not."

"Yes we are," she insisted. "We are going to die." Miranda left him and crossed over to the bed. She reached for Jeremy's arm. "Please wake up, Jeremy. I don't want to go through this alone."

"What do you mean?" Luc demanded. "Go through what? My father won't hurt you. I swear I won't let him."

"You don't understand," Miranda cried. "It's not your father. It's me! Luc, I can hear Coral! Really loudly. It's only a matter of time now. I'm going to change and we're both going to die."

"What are you talking about?" Luc demanded. "Please, Miranda, you're scaring me. Change into what?"

Miranda turned tear-filled eyes to him. "It's my Trial."

"What trial? You're just not making sense."

"Luc, I lied to you," Miranda admitted. "I am a mermaid, just like Lori and just like Gran. And tonight I'm going to change from legs to my tail. But out here on the rig, it's going to kill me."

Luc saw the genuine terror shining brightly in her sea green eyes. "Please Miranda, please sit down and talk to me. I don't understand any of this." He drew her over to a chair and listened in horror to the details of her upcoming Trial.

"Lori and Caspian nearly died," Miranda finished, as she rocked back and forth. "It was only because she was in our home waters that she lived. Don't you see? I'm away from Herm. When I change to my tail, it will kill me and Coral. We're both going to die horribly."

"No," Luc said. "It won't happen. It can't. Maybe if we take the helicopter we can get you back to Herm in time."

"No!" Miranda cried. "Your father must never know about Herm. It's the only home we have. Besides, it's too late. The Trial has started, there's no stopping it."

"This is our fault," Luc said angrily as he rose and started to pace. "I bet the stress and fear of my father brought it on. If we hadn't been here, this probably wouldn't have happened."

"Coral agrees with you," Mirada said miserably

"How about if we try to sneak you down to the platform and get you into the sea? Will that help?"

Miranda shook her head sadly. "It must be Herm waters. As it is, the Trial kills girls even when they are on Herm. My aunt died and my gran's sister too. Luc, more mermaids die by the Trial than survive it. Lori was lucky, she lived. But out here, I don't stand a chance."

"Then we must tell my father," Luc finally decided.

"No!" Miranda shouted. "I'd rather die than tell him!"

Luc came back to Miranda and knelt before her chair. "Listen to me please. You're the first friend I've ever had. I don't want anything to happen to you. If we tell my father, maybe he can help. I know how bad he is, and I know we've got to get you all away from him. But the most important thing right now is your survival. We can deal with the rest later."

Miranda shook her head. "You're father can't help me. No one can."

"We don't know that for sure. Miranda, he's going to find out anyway when you start to change. Isn't it better that we control when he knows? Maybe we can turn things around on him."

"I don't know," Miranda said, wringing her hands.

"Trust me, please," Luc begged. "I know what I'm doing."

Suddenly the door to the medical centre flew open. Robichaud stormed in and raced over to the side of the bed. "Doctor, come, check on your patient."

Luc stayed with Miranda as Anne examined Jeremy. Finally she stepped away from the bed. "Nothing has changed, he's fine."

"But Miranda isn't," Luc said.

Anne looked over at Miranda. Only then did she see the tears shining in her frightened eyes and trailing down her cheeks. "Miri, what's wrong? What's happened?"

"Luc, what is going on here?" Robichaud furiously demanded. "What did you do to her? I let you spend time with her because you are both young and I hoped you would get along. But if you have done something –"

"No Papa, I have done nothing," Luc said as he faced his father. He turned to Anne. "It is her Trial, Miranda is changing."

"Oh my God!" Anne cried, "Miri no! When did it start?" She raced over to Miranda and caught hold of her hands. "Tell me, sweetheart, when did it start? What's happening right now?"

"It started a while ago," Miranda said miserably "Now my legs are really starting to burn."

"Luc, what is happening here?" Robichaud demanded. "What is wrong with Miranda?"

A sudden fury overcame Luc. "You've killed her! That's what is happening. Your obsession with Colleen has blinded you to everything else. They are mermaids, Papa, they aren't like us. Miranda is changing into her sea form. Because of what you've done to these people, that change is going to kill her. Right here, right now on this rig. In your obsession to capture one mermaid, you've killed another!"

Chapter 35

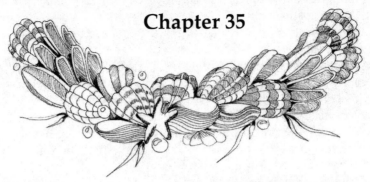

As the evening progressed, Lori worked with her brothers and cousin to remove the big boulders. She felt so guilty for not telling Aaron what was happening to his sister.

This is awful, Caspian moaned. *I feel so bad. We should all be with Miranda and Coral, not working here as if nothing was wrong.*

If we tell the others, Zephyr sadly said, *they would try to get to the rig. Robichaud would surely kill them and take Lor-lie and Undine away to his estate.*

You can't tell them what's happening, Coral agreed. *There is nothing they can do for us now. Miri agrees with me. This way, if they continue to work, they may finally free Colleen.*

Then what? Lori's mother called miserably. *Do you really think I'll ever be free, knowing what happened to you two because of me?*

Although Lori never told her brothers or Aaron what was happening, the boys sensed it. When the time came to surface and change equipment again, they rose up to the yacht and immediately turned on her.

"All right, Lori, what's going on," Aaron demanded, as he climbed on board and removed his diving mask. "Coral doesn't look well. All the whales are upset. Something is very wrong, I can feel it!"

"Aaron," Lori started, "I – I…"

"Lori, tell us," Danny insisted. He pointed to the water where the spotlight shone brightly on the whales. "Look at them. They all know something is wrong. Is it Jeremy?"

Two guards approached the family. "What's going on here?" One of them pointed at Danny. "You there, change your equipment and get back in the water."

Aaron dismissed the guards and focused on Lori's father. "What is it? What's happening?"

Furious at being ignored, the guard stepped closer. "I said get back to work!"

Lori recognized him as the one she had splashed with freezing water. He was the most dangerous of all the guards on their boat, and the quickest to draw his weapon. "Wait, please," she cried. "We just need a moment."

He turned vicious eyes to her. "Shut up, you freaking fish, this is none of your business." He drew his gun and pointed it at the boys. "You heard me. All of you, back to work!"

Coral suddenly rose to the surface, screaming. The other whales gathered around him in the water and pressed in closer.

"Wait, it's not Jeremy," Aaron cried. He ran to the side of the yacht and pointed at Coral. "It's Miranda! It's her Trial, isn't it?" He turned to look at the rig, and then back to Coral. "Miranda is up there going through the Trial, isn't she?"

Lori nodded her head sadly. "It started a few hours ago. Zephyr thinks stress brought it on. Anne is with her and trying her best, but..."

"She's going to die," Aaron panicked. "My sister is going to die!"

Lori's father stepped forward. "Aaron, calm down! You don't know that. Anne is a great doctor she'll do everything she can to help."

"No, Uncle Brian, Miri's going to die. Look where we are, she can't survive the Trial this far from home!"

Aaron turned his full fury on the guards. "You've killed my sister!"

The first guard raised his weapon. "Stay back or I swear I'll shoot!"

If Aaron heard the warning, he gave no clue. He charged the guard, shouting, "You killed Miranda!"

Lori screamed at the sound of the gunshot. But she couldn't see if Aaron had been hit. Instead she saw him wrestling the guard to the deck. The other guards ran forward and raised their weapons to shoot. But her father, Eddie and Danny launched themselves at the remaining guards. Immediately, everyone on the yacht was fighting.

186

Sea strength proved greater than human strength. Guns were knocked out of hands as they fought within the tight confines of the open deck. Aaron easily hoisted a guard into the air and threw him into the freezing salt water. After that, Eddie did the same. A third guard followed the first two.

From her place on the platform, Lori watched the sharks she had been so friendly with rush over. She remembered what Caspian had said about them; there was only like and dislike, with no shades of grey and no mercy. With the spotlight shining brightly in the water, she saw them catch hold of the screaming men and haul them beneath the surface. Moments later, the water turned crimson.

That's for my brother, Coral! Sargasso shouted furiously.

As Lori's father fought with the final guard, Eddie joined in and quickly overpowered the man.

"Throw him overboard," Aaron howled furiously. "It's because of him and the others that Miri is going to die. Let the sharks have him!"

"We can't!" panted Lori's father. He saw the spreading bloodstain on Aaron's shoulder. "My God, Aaron, you've been shot!"

"It's not bad," Aaron said, ignoring his wound. He reached forward. "Now, let me have him."

"Aaron, listen to me," Lori's father said. "This is the radio operator. We need him alive to keep in touch with the rig. I've got an idea that may save all of us. Please, you're bleeding. Let Eddie take care of that shoulder. You're going to need all your strength for what is coming. Do this for me, will you?"

Lori watched the rage and grief on Aaron's face. Finally, he nodded and Eddie went into the back to get the medical supplies.

Her father turned his attention to the radio operator. "If you want to live another day, you'll do exactly what I say or I swear I'll kill you myself!"

Chapter 36

Luc sat in the medical centre with Miranda and Anne as a large, steel bathtub was carried in and filled with sea water. On the floor lay Undine, who had been brought in to help Miranda through the Trial. She was wrapped in a soaking blanket and clinging to Miranda's hand. The men filling the tub stared at the old mermaid curiously, but said nothing as Robichaud personally supervised the task.

"I can't believe we're going through this again," Anne muttered softly as she squeezed Miranda's other hand. "But don't you worry, sweetheart, everything will be all right."

"No it won't," Miranda said miserably, tears streaming down her cheeks. She pulled her hands free of her grandmother and Anne, and balled them into fists to try to ease the growing pain.

Luc looked to the old mermaid, hoping that Undine would contradict her. Instead she lowered her head in grief, confirming to Luc that it was true. He felt such a deep sense of shame. His father had caused this. Beautiful Miranda was going to die, and all his father cared about was his wretched collection.

In that instant, Luc hated his father more than ever before. He would never forgive him for what he had done to his mother, but now he was responsible for Miranda's death as well.

"All right," Robichaud said when his men finished. He walked over to where Undine lay. "The tub is filled with sea water. Do we put her in it now?"

"No!" Miranda shrieked. "No, please don't put me in the water yet. It will kill me!"

For the first time in his life, Luc saw fear rise in his father's eyes. But it wasn't concern for Miranda. It was the threat of losing a mermaid for his collection.

"You are a doctor," Robichaud barked to Anne. "Surely there is something you can do to save your niece's life?"

Anne put her arm protectively around Miranda's shoulders. "I am going to try. But their physiology is something I just don't understand." She turned from Robichaud and looked into Miranda's frightened face. "Listen to me, you know I'll do all I can. But you've got to try to save yourself. Remember what Lori told you from her Trial. You will leave your body and go to a very strange and peaceful place. Please, Miri, don't stay there. Come back to us."

Miranda turned a pain-filled face to Anne. "I'll try. It's just that…"

Suddenly a wave of pain struck and Luc watched Miranda howl and fall to the floor writhing in agony.

"Coral!" she screamed.

Robichaud was the first at Miranda's side. He turned and barked at his men, "Get out of here. Wait outside until I call you." He then looked at Luc. "You go too!"

Luc sprang from his chair and went to Miranda, "No Papa. I won't!" He turned pleading eyes to Anne. "Help her please!" he begged. "Do something!"

Anne shoved Robichaud aside and knelt on the floor beside Miranda. "Miri, breathe," she ordered. "Keep breathing!" She placed her stethoscope on Miranda's chest. "Her heart is racing. It's going to explode!"

Luc watched the pain on Miranda's face and became aware of red stains forming on her jeans. "Anne, look at her legs. What's happening?"

"Oh my God!" Anne cried. She reached for the belt of Miranda's jeans. "It's happening so fast! Luc, her tail is coming. We've got to get her out of these jeans."

Luc did everything he was told to and helped get Miranda down to her underwear. He sucked in his breath as he saw the skin on her legs starting to open and bleed. Soon, silver green scales pushed out.

Miranda howled as the scales cut through her skin. Convulsions followed as her legs came together and her feet flattened.

Luc clung to his friend and tried to calm her down, "Hold on Miranda. Please don't die!" But nothing he tried worked. As he watched her face contort in pain, he knew she couldn't hear him.

189

"It's happening too fast!" Anne cried. She looked to Undine. "This isn't like Lori's Trial, it's just too fast. How can we slow it down?"

"We can't," Undine wept. "She is just like my daughter, Serena. The change was fast for her also. We will lose her soon."

"No we won't!" Anne shouted. She looked at Luc, "It's time! Grab her arms. Help me get Miranda into the water."

Chapter 37

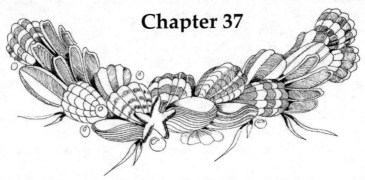

Lori was in the sea with Caspian as the entire whale family gathered around Coral. She ached to swim up to his head and to do whatever she could to comfort him. But Caspian warned her away. Coral was thrashing in the water and smashing his flippers down on the surface. One hit from a flipper could kill her.

"What can I do?" Lori cried, as she helplessly watched Coral's agony.

All we can do is pray, her mother called from below. *Hold on Coral, we are all with you!*

The water around her was filled with the sounds of Coral's pain-filled cries mixing with the song of the whales. They were singing to him to try to ease his pain as they struggled to keep his head at the surface so he could breathe.

"Was it like this for you?" Lori fearfully asked Caspian.

I don't remember, Caspian answered softly.

Yes, Lor-lie, it was, Zenith grieved, as he stayed with his dying son. *Only by now, Jeremy had you in Herm waters to complete the Trial. Miri is too far from home.*

The pain in Zenith's voice brought tears to Lori's eyes. Looking up to the oil rig, she could see its lights shining brightly in the dark night, looking like some kind of terrifying, multi-limbed insect hovering above the dark sea. Somewhere up there in the middle of that insect, Miranda was suffering the Trial, a very, very long way from the healing waters of Herm.

The family gathered at the back of the yacht, watching and waiting.

"Come on, Miri," Aaron called, as he watched the whale suffering. "Please, live. Please…"

Suddenly there was a terrible and final scream from Coral. He flipped over on his back and became still.

"Miri, no!" Aaron howled. Heedless of the dangers to himself, he leapt off the back of the yacht and entered the water. "Miri!"

Lori was over to him in an instant. "Wait, Aaron," she called. Catching him by the arm, she held him back. "They're going to turn him over, stay here with me a moment."

Floating together, Lori and Aaron watched as the whales struggled to flip Coral back on to his stomach so his air hole was out of the water. Once he was righted, Lori and Aaron swam up to his head.

"Miri, don't stay in that place," Lori cried as she searched for signs of life from the large, still whale. "Please, don't stay. Do what Coral tells you, go back to the pain. It's the only way. Please Miri, hear me! We'll get out of this somehow, but to do it, you've got to live. Please, don't die!"

"Miri!" Aaron howled. "I love you. Please come back. Don't leave me!"

Around her, Lori could hear the whales starting to howl and sing in grief.

Lor-lie, it's over, Caspian said sadly. *They're both gone.*

"No, Caspian, you're wrong!" Lori cried. "I warned Miranda about that place. She knows not to stay. She'll come back to us. I know she will."

But she's not in Herm waters, Caspian said sadly. *She couldn't possibly survive.*

"Yes she can! She has to!" Lori reached up and started to pound Coral's side. "She has to."

Caspian approached Lori and gently nudged her and Aaron away. *Coral is dead. They're both dead.*

Chapter 38

"No!" Anne cried, clinging to Miranda.

Luc watched Miranda's new green tail became still in the blood-filled water. Her eyes closed and her body became limp. Tears trailed down his cheeks as he watched Anne cradling his dead friend.

Behind him, the old mermaid held her hands up to her face and wept openly.

"No!" Anne howled again. Suddenly angry, she reached into the water, hauled Miranda's body out and laid her on the floor. "No, I *won't* lose you!"

She ran over to the medicine cabinet and searched through the many bottles of drugs. When she found the right one, she rummaged through drawers, pulled out a large syringe and filled it.

Without pausing, she forced the long needle into Miranda's chest and directly into her heart.

"Come on!" she cried, as she pressed down on the plunger. "Come on, Miri, come back to me!"

"Doctor, your patient is dead," Robichaud said quietly. "Leave her be."

"No!" Anne shouted. "She can't die. I won't let her!" Removing the empty syringe, she filled it a second time and injected Miranda again.

Just as though Anne had switched on a light, Miranda inhaled deeply. She opened her bright green eyes, sat up and started to cough. Luc heard her make the loudest, pain-filled cry he had ever heard in his life.

Just as quickly, Miranda crumpled back to the floor, unconscious, her chest rising and falling steadily.

Anne leaned forward and used her stethoscope. She sat back on her heels and started to weep. "Miri's heart rate is back to normal," she finally said. "She's going to live."

"Anne?" Undine called as she struggled to drag her broken body closer. "Is it true? Is Miranda really alive?"

Unable to speak, Anne nodded.

"How? We are not in home waters. How is this possible?"

Anne slid over to Undine and hugged the frail old mermaid. Finally she sniffed, "I'm not sure. But Miri is alive. She survived her Trial."

As the two women clung to each other, Luc saw his father reach for Miranda.

"Don't you dare touch her!" He angrily swatted his father's hands away.

Shock rose on his father's face, but he withdrew his hands. "She must be put back in the water."

"I'll do it," Luc shot. He gently picked Miranda up and placed her back in the seawater. He looked over to Undine. "Do I put her all the way under?"

"No," the old mermaid warned. "Her gills aren't ready. She needs a few days yet. But she must be kept in seawater at all times. Miranda is of the sea now, like me, she can't survive out of it."

"I understand," Luc said. He settled Miranda in the tub so her tail was completely submerged, but her head remained above the surface. When he'd finished, he looked at his father. The expression in Robichaud's eyes chilled him. There was fury at his open defiance but also, barely contained excitement. His father now had everything he'd ever wanted. Andre Robichaud had won again.

"Luc," his father said as he straightened. "Later you and I will discuss your behaviour."

"Don't ask me to apologize, Papa," Luc finally said, "because I won't. Miranda is my friend and I had to help her."

"Friend?" Robichaud repeated. "This mermaid is your friend?"

"Yes, Papa," he said defiantly. "She is my friend."

"Then we shall be discussing your friendship with her as well." When he finished, Robichaud stepped over to Anne. "Doctor, you did a remarkable job with Miranda this evening. I think it's only fair to tell you, you saved your own life tonight. I now see that my mermaids need you as their personal physician. When we return to my estate, you shall be joining us to continue their care."

Robichaud stepped casually to the door. He ordered his men to carry Undine back to her tank. As an afterthought, he took a few steps back to where Luc knelt beside Miranda. He looked at the unconscious mermaid in the tub. Finally his eyes settled on Luc. "Friends?"

When Luc nodded, Robichaud returned to the door. Before leaving, he ordered the guards to be doubled.

Chapter 39

Both Lori and Aaron had felt the sudden change in Coral. They didn't know how to describe it, but it was there. One moment he was dead, then suddenly there was a spark of life, and he came back to himself.

When Coral weakly opened his eyes, cries of joy echoed amongst the whales. The family slapped their flippers on the surface of the water and leaped for joy.

"He's alive!" Lori cried as she embraced Aaron. "Aaron, Miri's alive!"

"Lori, are you sure?" her father called.

"Yes Dad! Somehow, Miri survived the Trial!"

Lori helped Aaron swim back to the boat. She could hear the cheering, and cries of joy rising from her mother. Somehow, Miranda's survival gave them all the strength and encouragement they needed to face whatever lay ahead.

Lor-lie, Zephyr called. *Tell the boys to suit up. We've got to get Colleen free so we can get everyone off that rig and finally go home!*

Chapter 40

Luc remained at Miranda's side throughout the long night. He was terrified her head would slip beneath the surface and she would drown. The old mermaid had said her gills weren't ready for water breathing yet so he stayed awake to keep her safe.

Anne remained awake with him, splitting her time between her two patients. Just before dawn, Jeremy started to stir.

"Anne," Jeremy roughly said. "Where am I?"

"Thank God you're awake," Anne said, racing to his side. "We're on the rig. I've removed the bullet from your chest and everything went fine. But I need you to relax and rest. You've lost a lot of blood and are seriously ill."

Luc left Miranda and crossed over to the bed.

Jeremy was weakly lifting his head and looking around. Soon his eyes came to rest on him. "Who are you?"

"I'm Luc," he answered quietly. He turned to the door and held up his hand. "Please, you must be very quiet. We don't want the guards to know you are awake or they will tell my father."

Jeremy frowned at Anne. "Guards? What guards?" It was only then he noticed the dark bruises on her face and arms. "What – what happened to you?"

Anne sighed, "It's a long story."

"Tell me."

Luc and Anne quietly explained the events of the past few days. Including Robichaud's violent interrogation and how he had learned most of the family's precious secrets. He knew about the mermaids but not Herm. He knew Colleen was trapped in the cavern and that the family was trying to rescue her. They ended by telling him about

Miranda and how just a few hours ago she had suffered the Trial and survived.

Jeremy looked over to the tub. Despite their strong protests, he climbed painfully from his bed and crossed over to the tub. He knelt down and gently stroked Miranda's face. "I – I don't understand," he said. "Her Trial? So soon? How could she survive? We're not on Herm."

"Please get back to bed and I'll tell you," Anne said as she reached for his arm. "You're still very weak and need rest. We don't want Robichaud to find out you're conscious. It's safer for everyone if he still thinks you're in a coma."

Jeremy considered for a moment and then nodded. He leaned forward and kissed Miranda on the forehead. Then let Luc and Anne help him back to bed. Once he was settled, Anne explained how she had saved Miranda's life by giving her a shot of adrenaline right in her heart.

"And that worked?" Jeremy quietly asked.

Anne nodded. "We were very lucky."

"So it was never Herm waters that saved the girls?" he mused. "Does that mean adrenaline could have saved my sister?"

"I don't know for sure," Anne said. "Possibly. All I do know is that Miri is alive and recovering."

"But you're still prisoners of my father," Luc added miserably.

"Not for long," Jeremy said. "This family has faced worse things than Andre Robichaud."

"You don't understand how dangerous he is," Luc said. "I know he's killed a lot of people and ordered the murder of many more. He's an arms dealer who doesn't care who he sells weapons to." Luc lowered his head, "And he murdered my mother."

Anne looked at him in shock. "Your mother?"

Luc nodded. "When I was very young. I was going to search for proof to take to the police. But then we came here and he went after all of you."

"I'm so sorry," Anne said, putting her arm around him.

Luc sighed and leaned into her. "My father is insane when it comes to his collection. He has a private zoo filled with endangered and extinct animals. Many years ago he saw Colleen in the sea and has been obsessed with capturing her ever since. But now he's seen Lori and Miranda, he wants all of you. When Colleen is finally free from the cavern, he's taking you all back to his estate. I know there's a big sea tank waiting for the mermaids of the family. I don't know what he plans for the rest of you."

"That tank will never hold mermaids," Jeremy said. "We will get out of this somehow."

Anne nodded. "Yes we will. But for now, you need your rest and more of this," she walked around the bed and retrieved the bag of healing moss. She handed him large chunk. "I want you to eat as much of it as you can. Undine was right. Whatever is in this stuff has got more healing power than I do."

Jeremy looked at the moss and frowned. "Lori got this for me?"

Anne nodded. "She and Caspian collected it and Luc risked his life to smuggle it in here. It's what has saved you."

Jeremy looked at Luc and nodded his head. "Thank you, lad. This family owes you a lot."

"Don't thank me yet. I told you, my father is obsessed with your family. He has guards with weapons. They're prepared to kill to keep you. Getting away will be much harder than you think."

Chapter 41

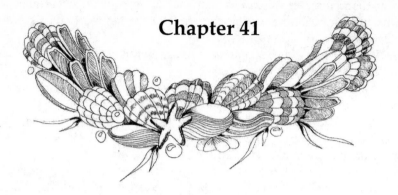

Throughout the endless night of working, Lori split her time between removing rubble from the cavern and going to the surface to check on Coral. The large whale was being supported by Zenith, Sargasso and his mother, Markane. He was deeply asleep, but his breathing had returned to normal.

As dawn started to break in the eastern sky, tired and aching from the long night of heavy work, Lori called Zephyr and hooked his harness to a huge boulder.

You're connected, she said tiredly, patting the whale's side. *Take it away.*

As Zephyr slowly shifted the boulder, it caused several smaller rocks to collapse from the pile of rubble. Those rocks caused others to shift. This made even more tumble and knock out the lights, casting the seabed back into darkness. Everyone heard loud, angry cracking sounds as a rumbling started deep within the rock face.

Get the boys away from there! Zephyr cried. *The entire side is breaking free!"*

Lori could barely see three whales move in and snatch the boys away, just as rocks started to fall from above.

Everyone, get away! Warned a panicked whale from above. *It's all coming down!*

Mom! Lori shouted.

Lori, get back! Her mother cried in terror. *Zephyr, keep Lori away! Keep everyone away, the cavern is collapsing –*

They all backed off, watching in horror as the entire rock face came crashing down. Thick, choking sediment and silt was churned up, leaving them unable to see their hands in front of their faces, let alone the damage to the cavern entrance.

Everyone get back! Zephyr warned. *Move further away!*

No! Lori insisted. *I've got to stay with Mom!*

Lor-lie, please come, Caspian cried. *You'll be killed!*

"Mom!" her brothers desperately called through their microphones. "What's happening to Mom?"

Suddenly her mother screamed in terror.

Colleen! Zephyr shouted, as he charged through the murky water back towards the crumbling rock face. *Colleen, speak to me!*

Chapter 42

Lori huddled with her brothers and the whales as the sickening sound of the collapse vibrated throughout the sea. It seemed it was never going to end. But as more and more sediment was churned up from the seabed, Lori found it increasingly difficult to breathe.

Your gills are clogging up, Caspian warned. *Lor-lie, you must get away from here and back to clear water or you'll suffocate.*

No, Caspian, she choked, *I'm not leaving Mom.*

Go Lor-Lie, Zephyr ordered from deep within the murky waters. *You can't do your mother any good if you choke. You'll hear the moment I know she is alive. Please, my child, go back to the surface. Tell your father what's happened.*

Lori did her best to clear away the sediment that settled heavily in her gills. But shaking her head did little to remove the bits of sand and debris. When breathing became too difficult she let Caspian carry her away from the dark depths.

Mom! She constantly called, as Caspian drew her up to the surface. *Mom, talk to me!*

When they made it to back to the yacht, Lori took a breath of fresh air and started to cough violently. Caspian carried her to the platform.

"Dad," she choked, "Dad!"

"Lori's what's wrong?" her father cried, as he climbed down to the lower platform. He helped her out of Caspian's mouth and saw the dark sediment pouring down her throat from her gill flaps. "My God, Lori what happened down there?"

"It collapsed," Lori gasped, between coughs. "Dad, it all collapsed; the rock face, the cavern, all of it. Zephyr and I moved a boulder and it collapsed!"

"Collapsed? What about your mother? Is she alive? The boys, are they all right?"

"The whales got the boys away just before the wall fell," Lori explained in a rushed panic. "But I can't reach Mom! Zephyr is calling and calling, but we can't hear anything. Now the water down there is so thick with sediment, I can't breathe."

Lori suddenly started coughing again as more sediment poured from her gills. As she fought for each breath, her father climbed back up onto the yacht and disappeared. He returned with two large bottles of water.

"Here, take this. We've got to flush out your gills."

With trembling hands, Lori lifted the first bottle to her lips. She immediately felt the cool fresh water sliding down her throat and through her clogged gills. By the time she'd drained the second bottle, she found she could breathe again. Only then did she realize her mother was probably dead.

Tears rushed to her eyes. "Mom!" she cried. "Mom, can you hear me? Please answer!"

Silence

"Mom!" Lori screamed in anguish.

Lori, I'm here! Her mother called unsteadily. *I'm with Zephyr. We're all right!*

Suddenly the water exploded with excited surfacing whales as Lori's mother rose up from the depths being carried by Zephyr. Blood ran down her face from a deep cut on her forehead.

"Dad!" Lori shouted. "Over there, look, it's Mom!"

Lori slid off the platform and entered the water. Kicking her tail with all her strength, she crossed the distance to her mother in an instant. Lori wrapped her arms around her and held her as tightly as she could while all the whales started to sing their songs of joy.

Moments later her father entered the freezing water and joined in the noisy reunion. Lori felt her throat constrict as she watched her parents embrace. All the hurt and pain disappeared as they held each other tightly.

"Dad," she finally said with tears in her eyes. "You've got to get out of the water. It's too cold for you."

Her mother helped him back to the yacht. When he climbed out of the water, he reached back to draw his mermaid wife up onto the platform. While he treated the gash on her forehead, Zephyr was at the back of the boat pressing in to be close. Lori felt his joy as he touched the end of Lori's mother's tail.

It's so wonderful, Caspian said softly. *I don't think I've ever seen my father so happy.*

"Mine too," Lori agreed as she watched her shivering father treat her mother's wounds. When he finished with the bandage, her parents kissed.

More whales surfaced, drawing Eddie, Danny and Aaron with them. When they saw their mother on the platform, the excited reunion continued.

While the weak light of dawn tried to glow in the stormy skies above them, everyone gathered on the covered deck. Lori clung to her mother's hand as they sat on the wet bench and listened to how Colleen had managed to slip through a hole just as the whole mountain collapsed.

"It's a miracle," her mother finished. "Simply a miracle."

"For all of us," her father said. He looked at everyone else on the boat. "We were all very lucky none of you were hurt."

"It wasn't us," Eddie explained, walking to the side of the yacht. He pointed at the water. "It was them. The whales got us out of there just as the whole thing came down. It they hadn't, we'd have been crushed. We owe them our lives."

Lori watched her mother gaze lovingly over the side of the yacht to Zephyr. Caspian was beside him, staying as close as he could get to the yacht to be near Lori while behind them, the other whales supported Coral, who was still sleeping peacefully after the Trial.

"Now all we have to do is free everyone from the rig and we can leave this place for good," her mother finished.

"Amen to that!" Her father stood and looked at the rig. "Actually, I've been thinking a lot about how to do it. I've got a few ideas, but we need help from the others on the rig. Once Miranda wakes up, I pray we can reach her. Otherwise we don't stand much chance."

"She'd better wake up soon, we're running out of time," Eddie said. He was looking out over the large swells of the approaching storm. "Look, there's the whaling ship Luc told us about. It's here to capture Zephyr and kill the rest of the whales."

Everyone shivered at the sight of the huge whaler cutting through the tall waves. Its arrival was the final confirmation that they were in for the fight of their lives.

Chapter 43

Andre Robichaud had summoned Luc to the monitor room. He made his way there, knowing this was the conversation he'd been dreading. His father was going to punish him for his angry defiance during Miranda's Trial. He might even try to forbid him from seeing her again. After everything they'd been through, Luc wouldn't let that happen. Miranda was now part of his life. If this was going to be the final showdown with his father, then so be it.

When he arrived, he found his father already in a fury. He was standing by the wall of large screens and cursing loudly.

"Again I said!" his father shouted. "Run it again!"

Luc approached the screen and started to watch. At first everything seemed normal. Lori was working with the large scarred whale. He saw her connect the harness to the hook in a huge boulder. She started to direct him away. But then something changed. The waters around the camera started to fill with sediment. Suddenly the lights shook and went out. The vibrating camera reverted back to infrared, but then stopped completely with a flash of static on screen and then nothing. "Papa, what just happened?"

"She's dead!" Andre Robichaud fumed. "After all these years of searching, I finally find her and now this! My beautiful mermaid is dead." He turned a vicious face to the technician. "Run it again!"

Luc concentrated on the screen. On the second viewing, he understood what he was seeing. Once the large boulder had been removed, it had caused a chain reaction of falling rocks until the entire side of the mountain collapsed and crashed down on the underwater camera. What he'd seen before the image went blank was the total destruction of the cavern.

"What about the others?" Luc panicked. "Were they hurt? Are they all right?"

His father shook his head. "You saw as much as I did. They were right under the rock face when it collapsed. Are they alive? Was my Lorelie crushed? I do not know. But I've got to find out."

"How?" Luc called as his father stormed away from the monitors.

Andre Robichaud paused at the door long enough to shout; "My men on the yacht will tell me. If there is no Colleen and no Lorelie, there is no point remaining here a moment longer. I've still got Miranda and the old woman. I'll have the whaling ship start filling its holding tank. Then we'll capture one of the whales, kill the rest and we can finally go. It's time to complete my collection!"

Just before he left, he popped his head back round the door. "Luc, I don't want you telling any of this to you new friend. Miranda is not to be distressed by the death of her family or the slaughter that is to come. Do you understand me?"

"Yes, Papa," Luc said. "I understand."

"Do you?" his father challenged. "Because I don't want your loyalties tested."

Luc stood unmoving for a full minute after his father's departure. Finally he looked over to the technician. "Did you see anyone moving before we lost the camera? Are they alive?"

"I saw no one," the technician answered. "And because of the storm and rain, the surface cameras can't clearly see the yacht. My guess is that they were killed instantly when the wall came down."

Luc returned to the screen and asked to watch the collapse a final time. He desperately searched for any signs of survival. There were none. He inhaled deeply, grieving the loss of Lori and her family. And though his father had forbidden him to speak to Miranda, he was going to tell her anyway. She deserved to know what had happened to her family.

Making his way to the medical centre, Luc tried to think of the gentlest way he could to tell them. But when the guard opened the door to the room and he saw Anne's face, he realised there would be no easy way to do it.

Luc waited for the guard to close the door behind him before crossing to where Anne stood at Jeremy's bedside. Halfway there, Miranda's voice stopped him.

"Luc!" she excitedly called from the tub. "There's wonderful news."

Luc was stunned to see Miranda not just conscious, but actually smiling and reaching for him.

"Miranda, you're awake. How are you feeling?"

"Really awful, I hurt all over!" she laughed.

"Then why are you laughing?"

"Because I'm alive!" Miranda cheered, "And my Aunt Colleen is finally free!"

It broke Luc's heart to have to tell her the truth. He shook his head sadly. "No, Miranda. I'm so sorry, she's not." He reached for her hand and held it tightly. Inhaling deeply, he started to break the news. "My father told me not to tell you. But I won't lie to you. I just saw what happened on the monitor. It was terrible. The whole rock face collapsed. I've watched it time and time again and can't see that anyone escaped. I'm afraid everyone is dead."

Miranda laughed harder and then winced as she moved her tail. "No, silly, they're not! I can hear my Aunt Colleen and Lori right now. They're on the yacht with everyone else."

Luc could hardly believe what he was hearing. "But – but I saw the collapse. No one could survive that."

"Believe me, they did!" Miranda insisted. "Just as it started to come down, the whales got the boys and Lori away. And right before the cavern collapsed completely, the roof split open and Colleen got out. She's a little cut up and her head's bruised, but they're all safe."

"You mean she's really free, and Lori is alive?"

When Miranda nodded, Luc lunged forward and hugged her tightly. "This is wonderful news! I'm so happy –" Then he remembered the last thing his father said. "Wait, this is awful. We've got to warn them."

"About what?" Anne asked.

"The whaling ship is here. Because of the storm it's circling out there, but my father has ordered them to fill their holding tank and prepare to kill the whales. The moment the weather clears a bit, the slaughter will begin."

When he finished, Jeremy looked over to Miranda and whispered softly. "This is perfect! Miri, tell Colleen that Robichaud thinks they're all dead. Have her tell Brian to force the radio man to

208

convince Robichaud they haven't heard from anyone. But have him say they'll report back if there are any survivors."

"But if we do that," Miranda said, "he might order Uncle Brian to bring the yacht to the rig."

Luc shook his head. "No, he won't. Brian is human. My father has no interest in him. He was planning to kill him after Colleen was freed. If I know my father, he'll leave the yacht to sink in the storm."

"He was going to kill my brother?" Anne asked in shock.

"Yes, and you, too. That is until you saved Miranda's life. This is why you must all get away.

Miranda repeated the conversation back to Lori and her mother.

"But I still don't understand how," Luc continued. "With the storm and the whalers here, everything is against you. How can you hope to get away when the seas will be too rough for your yacht?"

"Because we have to," Jeremy said seriously. "The alternative is just too terrible to consider."

Chapter 44

As the morning progressed, the skies became darker with more thick storm clouds moving in. Rain was falling heavily and the sea was getting rougher. It was tossing the yacht around as if it was a plastic toy in a bathtub. Despite the bilge pumps working full out, they were taking on a lot of water.

In the distance, the whaling ship was bounced around by the waves and staying well away from the rig. But it was there, a silent reminder of the fight yet to come.

Lori and her mother were carried into a cabin where they dried off and regained their legs. As they changed, Lori's mother worried that after having her tail for so long, she wouldn't be able to walk. But soon she and Lori were both on their feet and pulling on clothes.

"I really like being in the sea with Caspian," Lori said, as she did up her jeans. "But sometimes, it's just as nice being dry and having legs again."

"It sure is," her mother agreed as she took her first unsteady steps and walked over to Lori. Putting her arms around her, she gave Lori a fierce hug. "I have missed you so much. Every day I prayed for the moment when I would be free. Now it's finally here."

"I've missed you, too," Lori said, as she held her mother tighter.

The sudden knocking on the door stopped further conversation. "Are my girls decent?" her father asked.

Lori looked at her mother and they both nodded. "As decent as we'll ever be."

She watched her father's reaction when he saw her mother with legs. He stood speechless in the doorway, trying to stay upright with the rocking of the yacht.

"I think I'll go into the salon for a while," Lori said, giving her parents time alone together.

"I wish you could see my dad's face," Lori said softly to Caspian, as she closed the door behind her. "He's so happy."

We all are, Caspian responded. *But we're also worried about the whaling ship and getting the others off the rig in time. The storm is really picking up. We'll stay with the yacht to keep it upright, but the waves are getting very high even for us.*

Lori looked through a porthole and saw the sea splashing against the glass. She felt her nerves growing. "Do you think you can keep us from sinking?"

I don't know, Caspian admitted. *But we're going to try.*

Lori chatted with Caspian and walked down the hall and into the salon. Her brothers and cousin were seated on the sofa. On the table before them was a huge stack of sandwiches, large enough to feed more than double their number.

Their prisoner had been untied and was also sitting in a corner quietly eating his own stack of sandwiches. When she entered, he looked up and his eyes flew wide at seeing her with legs.

Lori tried to ignore his shocked stare as she crossed over to her brothers and reached for some food.

"Hey Bug," Eddie said. "How's Mom?"

Lori stole a final look at the guard before answering. "She's a little stiff and unsteady on her feet, but she's fine."

"It has been three years," Aaron said. "I'm actually surprised she could change at all."

"So is she," Lori admitted.

"What about Miri?" Aaron continued. "Is she feeling any better?"

Lori passed along Aaron's question to his sister on the rig. She waited for the response and then looked back to Aaron. "She's really sore, just like I was after the Trial. But says it's getting better. She also said that Jeremy is feeling much better –" Lori paused. "Wait, Miri says that Robichaud has just entered the medical centre. He's coming over to her...."

Everyone on the sofa fell silent as they waited to hear what was happening at the rig. The minutes ticked by. Lori was anxious to call out to her cousin, but Caspian warned her not to. Miri might accidentally reveal to Robichaud that they were actually alive. Then all their plans for the rescue would be ruined.

Instead she sat in silence with her family, waiting and worrying.

Before long, her parents emerged and joined them in the lounge. Once again, their prisoner's eyes went wide at the sight of the mermaid with legs. Colleen crossed over to where he sat.

"I see your surprise at these," she said as she pointed down to her legs. "There is more to us than you or your boss could ever imagine. It was a grave mistake taking my family to the rig. Your boss will pay for that. But if you continue to behave yourself, I assure you, the sea with give you its full protection. The choice is yours."

Everyone could see the terror in the man's eyes. "I – I won't do anything, I swear. I never liked Robichaud but couldn't leave. No one who works for him can ever leave. If we try, he has us killed."

"He can't kill someone he believes is already dead," Brian added. "If my plan works, Robichaud will think you died with me when the yacht sinks. Then you will be free of him for good. But to earn that freedom, you will continue to report to him everything I tell you to."

"Of course," the radio operator said, nodding. "Just don't throw me in the sea with the whales and sharks."

"If you do as we ask," Colleen continued, "we won't. In fact, I will personally ensure your safety. Then when this is over, we will drop you off wherever you like and make you a very wealthy man. The treasures of the seas are mine. I will share them with you."

"I don't care about any treasure," the man said earnestly. "All I want to do is get as far away from all of this as I can!"

"Agreed," Colleen said, as she crossed over to the sofa and sat down.

When her parents were settled, Lori and the boys explained what was happening at the rig. Falling silent, they waited for a message from Miranda.

After what seemed ages, Lori and her mother both nodded. "He's gone," Lori said.

"What did he want?" Aaron asked. "Did he do anything? Say anything?"

Lori shook her head. "From what Miri says, he just came in and checked on her. He asked how she was feeling, and if she was hungry. Then he asked Anne how Miri was recovering from the Trial and if she was fit to travel."

"Did he mention us?" Brian asked.

"No," Colleen answered. "Perhaps he still believes we all died in the collapse."

"Then why hasn't he called the yacht back to the rig?" Eddie asked.

"Luc told Miranda that Robichaud was planning to kill Dad," Lori answered. "Maybe he's hoping the yacht will sink and the sea will do it for him."

"But what about his men?" Danny added. "He still thinks they're here on the yacht too."

It was the radio man who answered. "I told you. Everyone around Andre Robichaud is disposable. Even if the others were still here, he would just as happily see us all go down with the ship. We have seen what you are. He won't want any of his people to know he's captured mermaids. I'm sure he's already ordered the death of every man on the rig. Those men on that whaler will do more than slaughter the whales. They will eliminate the rig's men. Then when everyone arrives at the estate, Robichaud will arrange for the disposal of the whaling ship's men well, so that any traces of your capture will be erased. Only he will know of your existence."

"But that's so evil," Lori said.

"That is Andre Robichaud," said the radio operator.

"Well, if he wants this yacht to sink, that's what he's going to get," Brian said. "Just after dark, we're going to send out a brief distress signal. Right after that, he will believe this yacht is going down."

Chapter 45

Luc remained in the medical centre as the family discussed the plans for the escape. Keeping their voices low, they passed messages back and forth via Miranda. When the idea of letting Robichaud think the yacht had sunk was proposed, Luc held up a hand.

"I'm sorry, Jeremy, but that won't work. I know the camera at the bottom has been destroyed, but all the other cameras on the rig are working fine. My father has them all over the outside and pointing at the yacht. They've all got night vision lenses. My father would see that the yacht hasn't really sunk and know you were planning something."

"Then we've got to break all those cameras too," Miranda offered.

Luc shook his head, "We can't easily reach them. It would be dangerous to try in clear weather. At night, in the middle of this gale, it would be suicide."

"But we've got to do something," Anne said. "We can't let Robichaud kill the whales and everybody here on the rig."

"We won't," Jeremy said. "I'm feeling much better. Just after sundown, we'll break out of here and fight our way off."

"Now that's really suicide!" Anne said. She turned to Luc, "I've lost track of how many men there are here. But they wouldn't believe us if we tried to warn them of their own fate. They will follow their boss to the end. Luc, would you please tell Jeremy how many there are?"

Luc nodded apologetically, "Anne is right. My father's got at least twenty armed men here. You may be super-strong, Jeremy. But I don't think even you could beat all of them and still be able to carry

Miranda and Undine out of here." Luc paused and then added, "But I might have an idea that can help. It will be a little risky, but I'm willing to try."

"Luc, whatever it is, it's too dangerous," Miranda cut in. "Remember what your father did to your mother. He won't hesitate to kill you, too."

Luc knelt by Miranda's tub and took her webbed hand in his. "My whole life I've been frightened of my father. I've seen him do terrible things and never stood in his way. I can't do that any more."

"But I don't want you hurt," Miranda said.

"Miranda, I told you. You're the first friend I've ever had. I won't let my father do this to you. I'll be all right, I promise. Then maybe when this is over, you can introduce me to the whales and let me spend time in the sea with all of you."

"We will," Miranda promised. She reached out and put her arms around Luc's neck. "Just be careful."

As the daylight started to fade, Luc was walking through the rig trying to act as though nothing had changed. In fact, his heart was in his throat and his legs were turning to rubber. He was wearing a heavy-duty raincoat with his winter coat beneath it to protect his precious cargo. Even so, when he opened the door to the outside, he was shocked by the cold blast of wet winter wind.

The rain was coming down in heavy sheets and the wind was blowing it sideways. Luc put his head down and staggered to the railing. He lifted the binoculars to his eyes and peered out over the angry sea.

In the rough water, the yacht's lights could briefly be seen on the fall of every third wave. There were whales surrounding it and pressing close to help it stay afloat. Not far off he saw the whaling ship's lights as it bounced in the waves, waiting to carry out its deadly mission.

Luc realised there would only be one chance at the escape. As it was, he doubted whether the strength of the whales could keep the yacht from sinking.

He lowered his binoculars and tried to look casual as he turned around and inspected the rig's deck. There were no people about. Everyone had been driven inside by the foul weather.

He held onto the railing and trudged against the driving wind, towards a free-standing cabin at the far end of the rig. It seemed impossible that it alone held the difference between success or failure of the escape.

As he drew closer, Luc searched for any prying camera eyes. But out here on the deck, there were none that he could see. He inhaled deeply and pushed open the door to the generator cabin.

He flicked on the light and looked at the monster generator. This was the heart of the rig and the source of all its power. Beyond the lights and other electrical appliances, it also powered the cameras and monitors.

The smell of diesel fuel and exhaust fumes burned his throat and eyes and the roar of the monstrous motor nearly deafened him. But after a quick search, he found what he was seeking. The fuel tank for the generator was huge, but its cap was within easy reach. His hands started to tremble as he reached inside his clothing and pulled free the first of three large bags of sugar.

Luc was very careful to clear away any grains of sugar he spilled while pouring it into the huge fuel tank. There could be no traces of his sabotage left after things started to move later that night.

When the last bag was emptied and the mess was cleared away, Luc stashed the empty bags away in his coat. He turned off the light in the cabin and, seeing that the deck was still empty of people, exited back into the storm. From there it was a quick trip back into the protected area of the rig to await the failure of the generator and the ensuing blackout.

Chapter 46

Lori sat in the lounge with her family, feeling fear starting to build. The storm was increasing and their boat was being buffeted violently by the heavy sea. Her father was in the radio room with their prisoner, sending out the first bogus distress call.

"I sure hope this works," she said softly to Caspian.

It must. That whaling ship keeps getting closer. It looks just like the one that killed my mother. Only this one has several large harpoon guns on the deck. They are loaded and ready to kill us.

"It won't happen," Lori insisted, hearing the fear in his voice. "Dad's idea will work."

Moments later, her father reappeared with Eddie and their prisoner. "All done," he said. "They know the yacht's in trouble. But when Robichaud found out there were no survivors from the collapse, he lost interest in us. He said we had to ride out the storm on our own."

"He really does want you to die," Lori said, almost in a whisper.

Her father nodded. "Seems like."

"So what do we do now?" Colleen asked.

"We wait," said Eddie. "Just as the power starts to go out on the rig, we'll make a final call and tell them the yacht's going down. If Luc's sabotage works, their cameras won't be able to see us heading straight for them. And with luck, they won't be able to get the generator working again for several hours. We'll be gone by then."

While her mother explained the plan to Miranda, Lori stumbled her way to a porthole. She could no longer see the large waves that were thrashing them about on the sea, but she could feel them. She could also feel Caspian pressing close to the yacht to help keep them afloat. Coral was beside him. Though still sore from the Trial, he was much recovered, and anxious to help.

Lori knew she could easily survive the storm. So could her mother, Miranda and grandmother if they got off the rig. It was the other members of her family she worried about, especially her father and Anne, who couldn't possibly live if they were adrift in the freezing temperatures of the open sea.

We won't let that happen, Caspian said. *If the worse happens and your boat does sink, we can keep everyone safe in our mouths. It won't be comfortable or very warm, but it will keep everyone alive.*

Lori heard the murmurs of the other whales as they all offered to help. She glanced over to her mother. She smiled and nodded her head. *It will be all right, Lori,* her mother said silently. *They won't let anything bad happen to any of us.*

Even Luc? Lori asked.

Her mother nodded. *Especially Luc.*

It was easy to hear, but harder to believe. As the hours ticked by, Lori felt herself getting more and more frightened. Finally, her father stood and pointed out of the side porthole. "Look, the rig's lights are starting to flicker. We'll move in a few minutes." He nodded to their prisoner. "This is where you save your own life. Convince Robichaud we're going down and this will be over for you very quickly."

"Just as long as I don't end up in the water," the man said fearfully.

"You won't," Brian promised. "If all goes well, you will be a free man by morning."

"Dad, they're out!" Eddie called excitedly. "The rig's gone dark."

Brian hauled their prisoner to his feet. "This is it," he said. "Let's go."

Chapter 47

"They're making the final distress call," Miranda said.

Anne was lighting emergency candles. Luc knelt beside Miranda's tub. "Well, this is it. Soon you'll be free and away from here," he said.

"Soon we'll all be free," Miranda corrected. "You're coming with us. How else can we play in the sea with the whales?"

"You really want me to come with you?" Luc asked in shock. "Even after everything my father has done to you?"

"Of course, lad," Jeremy said. "You must come. It won't take them long to uncover your handiwork with the generator. Who do you think your father is going to blame? Do you really think he will forgive your betrayal?"

Luc sat back on his heels. "I hadn't really thought about it. All I wanted was to help you get away."

"We will," Miranda said. "But you've got to come with us."

"Wait," said Anne. "We've got to give Luc the choice. It wouldn't be fair to force him to come with us."

"But he must," Miranda pleaded. "His father will kill him."

Finally Luc nodded his head. "I'd like to come. I can't stay with my father. Not now."

Jeremy nodded. "Then it's settled. Lori will let us know when the yacht is approaching the rig. Until then, we've got to stay patient. We don't want to get found out early."

Luc stayed beside Miranda as the minutes ticked by and the rig remained in darkness. Just as the message arrived that the yacht was approaching the lower platform, they had a very unwelcome visitor.

"I thought I might find you in here," Robichaud said to Luc.

"Papa, what's happened?" Luc asked innocently. "What's wrong with the lights?"

"Nothing serious, it's just the storm," Robichaud approached the tub. "I see you have found the emergency candles. Very good." He knelt by the tub and reached for Miranda's hand. "I don't want you to be frightened. Out here on the rig, they are always experiencing such problems. I'm sure the power will be back on soon."

"Not soon enough for you!" Jeremy said, approaching Robichaud from behind. Before he could react, Jeremy smashed down with a crushing blow that instantly knocked him unconscious. As Robichaud crumpled to the floor, Jeremy looked at Luc. "I'm sorry, lad, it had to be done."

"I understand. Is he alive?"

Anne checked the pulse at Robichaud's neck. "Yes he is. But he's going to have a terrible headache when he wakes up." She looked at Jeremy. "That's a lethal talent you've got there."

"Trust me," Jeremy said gravely. "I just gave him a tap. He's very lucky I didn't lose my temper." He turned to Luc. "Help me get him into the bed, I've got an idea."

Luc helped carry his unconscious father to the bed. It scared him to realise he was so cool, as if he was carrying a stranger – not someone he loved and who should have loved him back. Nor did it bother him to help bind his father's arms behind his back, or watch Anne putting medical tape over his mouth. Luc realised that Andre Robichaud meant nothing to him.

"All right," Jeremy said. "That's one down." He turned to Miranda in the tub. "Let's get you out of there and changed. Then we can free Mum and get the hell out of here!"

He crossed to the tub and pulled Miranda out of it. Anne moved in with towels and a white lab coat.

As Anne started to wipe down Miranda's tail, Jeremy caught Luc by the arm. "Turn around, lad. Let's give Miri her privacy while she changes."

Behind him, Luc heard strange sounds.

"Lori was right," Miranda winced. "It sure does pinch! Gosh, look at me, I'm a mess!"

After another moment, Luc and Jeremy received the all clear and turned around again. Luc was stunned to see Miranda standing with two very badly bruised legs, and wearing the lab coat.

"You've got legs!" he said, coming forward to look at her. "How did you do that? I thought the coat was to cover your tail."

"Magic," Miranda answered. She started to sway on her feet.

Luc caught hold of her and supported her weight. "Are you all right?"

"My legs feel like they're going to explode," Miranda said, through gritted teeth.

"It's the swelling," Anne explained. "It took Lori a few days for the bruising to go down."

"But we don't have that kind of time," Luc said. He looked back at Miranda. "Let me help you."

Miranda blushed in his arms but nodded just as she received a message from the yacht. "They're moored beneath the rig. Lori says the water is really rough under there, so we've got to be quick."

"We're ready," Jeremy said. "Okay, lad, you know what to do."

Luc reluctantly released Miranda and crossed to the door. He knew the four guards were still at their post waiting for his father to come out. As Jeremy got into position behind the door, Luc cried "Please help me! My father has collapsed!"

It all happened very quickly after that. The guards rushed in. They were met with the giant, Jeremy. Luc stepped in to help, but by the time he did, Jeremy had the men down without even breaking into a sweat.

Once the guards were tied and gagged, Luc peered into the hall. Emergency lights were running on battery packs every few metres. Their weak light gave the hall an eerie, pale glow. Seeing it was empty of people, he looked back.

"It's all clear. The door to the sea platform is this way. Undine is down that way. But she also has guards on her door."

"Let's get the sea door open first," Jeremy said. "We'll need back-up before we move on Mum's quarters."

Luc helped support Miranda as they moved down the hall. "Before I came to you earlier," he said, "I saw most of the men working on the generator. If we can keep from being found out, we might get away before anyone notices."

Creeping through the halls of the rig, they didn't meet anyone. "There's the door," Luc said. Reaching into his pocket, he pulled out the keys.

"Where did you get those?" Miranda asked.

"I stole them from Arthur again," Luc explained. He inserted a key and opened the door. Behind it, the entire family was waiting for him. The greetings were brief but emotion-filled as Colleen finally saw her brother and niece after so many years apart. Aaron was gratefully united with Miranda.

As Colleen greeted her family, Luc watched in open-mouthed shock. The portrait! Colleen was the woman from the painting in his father's study. It hadn't been of his mother after all, but the two women were so close in appearance they could have been sisters. Suddenly he understood. His father had only married his mother because she resembled Colleen. But he'd killed her because she wasn't the one he wanted. His father had been in love with the mermaid all these years.

"All right, everyone," Jeremy finally said. "We don't have a lot of time. Anne, I want you to take Miri, Lori, Aaron and Danny back down below and disable all but one of the launches.

"Why can't we destroy all of them?" Aaron asked.

"Because when we leave here, I'll be driving one of them right into the whaler's rudder. We've got to disable it so it won't follow us. Now get going. We'll be down in a moment with your gran."

Chapter 48

Once the others had gone below, Luc led the group forward. While they walked, he kept stealing glances at Colleen. The resemblance to his mother was almost painful.

"Are you all right?" Colleen quietly asked. "You look like you've seen a ghost."

"I'm – I'm fine," Luc finally said. "It's just that you look so much like my mother. I think that's why my dad married her. But –" He stopped speaking, unable to say more to her.

Colleen smiled gently and put her arm around him. "I understand. I'm sure she would be very proud of you."

Falling silent, they moved deeper into the rig. Before long, Luc started to worry that they weren't seeing any other people. It was true a lot were working on the generator, but the halls were too empty.

When he voiced his fear, Jeremy stopped the group. "Luc is right. This place is too quiet. We must be extra careful. In fact –" he reached up and disconnected the nearest battery-powered lighting unit. "Let's give ourselves an advantage."

"But I can't see in the dark," Luc complained.

"We can," Eddie said. "Stay near me and I'll lead you."

Darkness filled the halls as Jeremy disabled every battery light unit they encountered.

"Stop," Luc whispered as they neared a T-junction. "Just around the corner to the right is where they are holding Undine. Wait here, I'll see if the guards are still there. If they are, I'll distract them so you can come and get them."

"Be careful, lad," Jeremy warned.

"I will," Luc promised. He moved cautiously round the corner. Up ahead were two guards, posted outside the door. "Hello," he loudly called. "Is my father in with the old mermaid?"

When the guards said no, Luc moved closer. His heart was pounding ferociously and he was starting to feel sick. "Well, if you see him will you tell him –" Luc suddenly clutched his abdomen as if he was in terrible pain. "Oh, my stomach!" he howled. He fell to the floor and started to writhe. "Oh, oh, it hurts, it hurts! Do something!"

When both guards approached, Luc kicked one of them in the stomach. He saw Jeremy charging down the hall. The giant was a terrifying sight and was upon them in an instant.

"Well done!" Jeremy said, as the last guard fell unconscious to the floor. He helped Luc to his feet. "I couldn't have done better."

This was the first time since his mother's death that anyone had ever praised Luc, or offered any kind of affection. He felt his face flushing under the compliment. "I – I just did my best and hoped it would work."

"It worked perfectly," Colleen added. "So let's drag these men in here and get Mum out."

When they pushed open the door to Undine's quarters, they saw the large metal tank of water in the middle of the room. Undine raised her head above the surface.

"Colleen? Jeremy?" she cried. "Thank heavens!"

There was no time for lengthy reunions. "We've come to get you out of here," Jeremy said. He reached into the water to pull his mother out.

Undine was once again wrapped in a wet blanket. She was handed over to Brian to carry, leaving the stronger members of the family free to fight.

Luc took the lead and checked the hall. "All clear, let's go."

Further and further they travelled through the darkened rig, never meeting anyone. As they approached the corridor leading to the lower platform, Luc started to hope they were going to make it.

Suddenly, high intensity floodlights blasted them and several armed men rushed forward. Everyone was temporarily blinded.

"Hands in the air!" one of the guards shouted. "Do it now or we'll open fire!"

Luc felt his stomach drop as he realised they'd been caught. He held his hands up against the blinding light and could see most of the men from the rig waiting for them. Then he saw the furious face of his father.

"I should have known you would betray me," Robichaud said coldly. "You are weak, just like your mother –" Suddenly his eyes found Colleen. "It's you," he cried breathlessly, "my beautiful mermaid! You didn't die in the collapse?" His eyes searched the rest of the family. "But where are the others? Where are Miranda and Lorelie?"

When he received no answer, he raised his weapon to Brian's head and faced Colleen. "I do not wish to make you suffer on our first meeting, but I will. Tell me where the children are now or, I promise you, I will kill him."

Luc watched Colleen hesitate. Finally she said, "They're waiting for us down below."

"Thank you," Robichaud said. He turned back to his second in command. "You and your men, go bring them back to me. Use your weapons on the boys if you must, but I want those girls unharmed. Do you understand? I want them alive!"

As more than half the men ran to follow his orders, Robichaud looked back at Colleen. A huge smile spread across his predatory face and his eyes sparkled. "I can hardly believe what I am seeing. My beautiful Sea Queen. But look at you. You have legs. How is this possible?"

He came forward and stood before her. "No matter, legs or tail, you are just as breathtaking as the day I first saw you. Do you remember? Just over twenty years ago. I was on my father's fishing boat. You were in the sea with the whales. Such a sight to behold, seeing you on that whale's back. We followed you all day, hoping to catch you. I have never forgotten that magical day."

"That was you?" Colleen breathed in shock. "You were the one chasing us?"

When Robichaud nodded, she continued. "Oh, yes, I remember that day very well. You hunted us as prey. It took us well into the night to finally get away. We were all terrified. We thought you were going to kill us."

"I would never have hurt you," Robichaud said, sounding wounded. "I just wanted to catch you. And now my love, after all this time, I have."

Luc watched his father with Colleen. He'd never seen him behave like this before. Andre Robichaud was like an unsure, lovesick puppy. This made him all the more dangerous. His father's mood could snap in an instant with disastrous results.

"You will release us now," Colleen softly challenged as her anger grew. "Or I swear you'll regret it. I won't let you have my family."

Luc expected his father's temper to rise. Instead he started to laugh. "Oh, my dear, precious mermaid, how wrong you are. You have been mine from the very first instant I saw you. And soon you will love me, and the home I am going to make for you. There is a tank all your own; where you and your girls will live out the rest of your lives in absolute luxury. I will spoil you all, you will never lack for anything."

Colleen shook her head in disgust. "We are not fish you can keep in a tank! And we aren't going anywhere with you. We are free and staying that way."

His father's deeply hurt expression terrified Luc. After so many years of loving her, his reaction to this kind of rejection could prove fatal for everyone.

"Listen to me very carefully, mermaid," Robichaud warned softly. "You will do as I say. Or I swear other members of your family will suffer –"

Suddenly Luc pushed himself between Colleen and his father. "No, Papa, please," he cried. "Don't do this. It isn't right. They are people, not part of a collection. You must release them."

"Step back, Luc," Robichaud spat as his temper flared. "This doesn't concern you."

"Yes it does," Luc challenged, standing his ground. "All my life I've watched you destroy people's lives. I remember what you did to my mother in the study. You always wanted her to be like Colleen and when she wasn't, you killed her. But you're not going to have Colleen, Lori or Miranda."

Robichaud looked at Luc in disgust. "I should have killed you that night. Say one more word, Luc, just one, and I will finish what I started."

In that moment, something in Luc snapped. He was no longer frightened of this man who had bullied and brutalised him all his life.

Now he felt calm and clear-headed. He slowly turned back to Jeremy. "Tell Miranda I'm sorry."

All the years of hurt and rage exploded as he lunged forward and unleashed himself on his father. "This ends now!"

Chapter 49

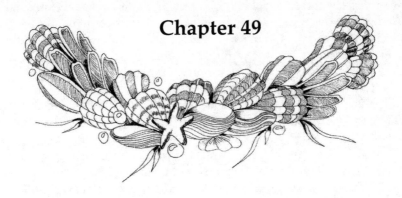

The launches had been pulled out of the water and were hanging from hoists on the rig's underside to ride out the vicious storm. Danny and Aaron found the controls and lowered the largest launch back into the water.

Danny called down to his sister, "Lori, tell the whales to push the launch out into the sea. We're going to use this one to ram the whaling ship."

While Lori passed along the instructions to the whales, Miranda and Anne stood together on the upper scaffold keeping watch. Danny and Aaron then went from launch to launch, to sabotage the remaining ships.

Suddenly Lori stopped as she and Miranda heard the warning call from above.

"It's a trap!" Lori cried. "They've got Mom and Dad!"

"And men are coming for us," Miranda added. "They've got guns!"

Beneath the platform, the water churned as Zephyr and Zenith rose to the surface. *All of you come back into the water. Hurry! They mustn't catch you!*

Everyone ran down the metal stairs to the water level platform. With the full force of the storm raging around them, beneath the rig the heavy swells washed over the platform, freezing sea water dragging at their legs.

Lor-lie hurry! Caspian cried.

Miranda and Anne were the first at the bottom and stepping into the freezing water. The moment Miranda's bare feet touched the seawater, she fell to the platform's deck and transformed. Danny and Aaron were quick to follow onto the swamped platform.

Lori hesitated at the base of the metal stairs. She was fully dressed. If she entered the water, she would be in terrible pain as her body tried to change.

"Lori, come on!" Danny shouted.

"Wait, I've got to get my shoes and jeans off!" she cried as she fumbled with the zipper of her jeans. "I don't want to get wet like this!"

Before she was half way finished, the door from above burst open. Men poured into the upper area of the scaffold.

"You there," the leader shouted over the side. "Stop! Stay where you are!"

"Lori c'mon," Danny cried.

With her jeans only half down her legs, Lori jumped off the final step and onto the flooded platform. She immediately felt her body start to change. Danny and Anne arrived and helped tear her jeans off.

"I said stop!" the leader shouted from above. He fired a warning shot in the air. "One more move and the next bullet will hit one of you! Just put your hands in the air and stay away from the edge of the platform."

While Lori and Miranda lay in the water, fully transformed, Danny, Aaron and Anne stood helpless beside them. Everyone raised their hands in the air.

Zephyr and Zenith slipped silently beneath the surface. *Stay where you are and keep closely together,* Zephyr called to the girls. *Don't let the boys try anything. We've got to lure all those men onto the platform.*

Lori stole a glance over to the water. None of the whales could be seen but she knew Caspian, Coral, Zephyr and Zenith and the three sharks were there. The others were waiting just outside the rig, at the launch.

Robichaud's men descended the metal stairs. The leader was in front, holding his weapon. "All right, nobody has to get hurt. Just stay where you are and don't make a move for the open water."

"Everyone," Lori quickly whispered. "Zephyr's got a plan. Don't move. We've got to stay together."

230

When the men reached the bottom of the stairs, they started to step down into the cold water on the platform.

"Nice and easy," the leader said, moving closer. "Now boys, please pick up the mermaids. You are going to carry them up the stairs."

"I can't," said Aaron. "I've been shot." He opened his shirt to show the thick bandages covering his shoulder wound. "I can't lift Miranda."

"Shot!" Anne cried. She looked back at Aaron. "Aaron, you were shot?"

When Aaron nodded, she angrily turned to the men. "Is this what you want? Hurting innocent children? How can you live with yourselves?"

"We do as we're told," the leader said. "And you are going to do the same." He lifted his weapon threateningly. "Now pick up the mermaids and let's go!"

Danny shook his head. "I'm not going to help you capture my sister. If you want her, come and get her yourself."

The leader took another step forward. Lori saw that all the men were now on the platform. "Listen boy, you will do as you are told or I will shoot you –"

They're all here, she called silently.

Then hold on! Zephyr cried.

"Everyone hold on!" Lori shouted to her family.

Suddenly the two oldest and largest whales leaped high out of the water. Arching their backs in the air, Zephyr and Zenith came crashing down on the end of the platform, right where Robichaud's men were standing. The sudden weight of the two massive whales landing on the platform caused its moorings to shatter. The ropes tying it to the yacht snapped and the yacht heaved in the rough water. The platform tipped and the men were plunged deep into the freezing sea.

At the platform's other end, Lori and her family were catapulted high into the air. Their screams mixed together as they were thrown off the top edge. Flying through the air, they soared high over the yacht and finally came crashing down into the seawater several metres away.

Lor-Lie, Caspian cried. *Are you all right?*

Lori righted herself in the water and shook her head, trying to clear the dizziness. She looked around. Not far away, Danny and Aaron were making their way to the surface. Miranda was struggling to swim with her new tail. But further below, she saw Anne's unconscious body sinking into the sea's dark depths.

Anne! Lori cried as she kicked out her tail and dove towards her aunt.

I've got her! Sargasso called as she approached from below and scooped Anne up in her mouth. *She's alive. Just had the wind knocked out of her.*

Lori! Miranda called. *I can't swim!*

Turning in the water, Lori saw Miranda was struggling to swim with her tail. Coral was beside her, offering what help he could, but she couldn't make it work.

Lori crossed the distance to her cousin and reached out to her. *Are you all right?*

I guess so, Miranda answered as together they slowly made their way to the surface. *But I wish Zephyr had warned us what he was planning.*

It would have been nice, Lori agreed.

There was no time, Caspian answered. *We had to move quickly before they took you away.*

Lori and Miranda broke the surface and saw the devastation beneath the rig. The platform was gone. Danny and Aaron were helping to draw Anne up the torn and bent end of the metal stairs.

"Where are all the men?" Lori inquired, as she searched the surface of the water for Robichaud's men.

Don't ask, Caspian answered darkly. *You don't want to know.*

In her head, Lori could hear Zephyr explaining everything to her mother up above. He let her know that everyone was safe and the men were gone.

"Are they dead?" Miranda asked.

They're gone, was all Coral would answer.

"Lori, Miri," Danny called from the stairs. "Are you okay?"

Lori caught hold of Miranda and helped her to swim over to the base of the stairs. She nodded. "How is Anne?"

"I'm fine," Anne answered shakily, from further up the stairs. "Though that's not something I want to do again any time soon."

"So what do we do now?" Lori asked.

"Dan and I go up and get the family," Aaron answered.

"What about us?" Lori asked.

Danny leaned down to his sister. "You've got your tails. There's no time to get dry clothing or to change. You're going to have to stay here with Anne while we go get Mom and Dad."

"No way!" Lori shouted. "You're not leaving us down here while you go play hero!"

"We have to," Aaron said. "You can't help us."

"What do you mean? We're just as strong as you are," Miranda challenged.

"Yes," Aaron said. "But you don't have legs! What are you going to do, drag yourselves down the halls and cut the men down with your scales?"

"If we have to," Lori answered.

Suddenly from above, they heard the sound of a gun shot.

"Mom!" Lori called. "What was that? What happened?"

As Lori and Miranda listened, Miranda howled, "Luc no!"

Lori screamed to Danny and Aaron, "Robichaud just shot Luc! There's no time to argue, just pick us up at take us above!"

Chapter 50

It felt as though someone had kicked him in the chest. Suddenly Luc had no strength. He fell to the floor and struggled to take a breath.

"I warned you!" Robichaud shouted, looming above him. "But you wouldn't listen. I told you not to betray me, but you did. You have disappointed me for the last time!" He raised the gun to fire a second time.

From somewhere behind him, Luc heard Jeremy howling, "Damn it man, he's your son! No!"

All at once the area erupted in fighting. Jeremy lunged at Robichaud while Colleen and Eddie attacked his men. Danny and Aaron arrived out of nowhere, carrying Lori and Miranda, who still had their tails.

Luc dragged himself away from the fighting and saw his father's men being cut down by the mermaid family. He was fading in and out of consciousness. One moment, there was terrible shouting and fighting as even Lori rose as high as she could on her tail and threw herself at his father's men.

The next, he awoke to find Miranda lying beside him on the floor. She was clutching his hand and begging him not to die. Anne was on the other side of him, applying pressure to his chest to stop the bleeding.

As his eyes weakly lifted, he saw the family anxiously gathered around him. Jeremy was next to Anne as she worked, while Eddie held Lori in his arms. Danny was holding Undine in her wet blanket. Brian and Colleen stood together.

"Wha – what happened?" he weakly asked.

"It's over, lad." Jeremy said gently. He reached out and stroked Luc's forehead. "We're all free."

"My father?" he weakly panted.

"He won't hurt you ever again," Jeremy answered. He reached forward and lifted Luc in his strong arms. "Now let's get you back to the yacht for treatment. Then we've got a whaling ship to stop."

Chapter 51

While the rest of the family struggled to get Luc aboard the yacht, Lori stayed with Jeremy. The whales carried them away from the rig and out to the launch bobbing on the open sea. Even with her mermaid vision, she couldn't see much through the inky-black sky and beating rain. If the whaler was still out there, she couldn't see it.

"You stay in the water with Caspian!" Jeremy ordered as he climbed on board the heaving launch. "You need to lead me to the whaling ship. I can't see it in this weather."

Lori struggled to stay at the surface. The storm was peaking and huge waves were driving her down. With every swell, they threatened to swamp the launch. "Jeremy, it's too rough. Come back to the yacht."

"I can't. We've got to disable that whaler. They can travel much faster than us. With their radar, it won't take them long to find the yacht."

He must do this, Lor-lie, Caspian agreed. *The ship isn't far away. Stay with me and I'll lead you in.*

Lori knew he was right, but watching her recovering uncle try to manoeuvre the launch in the fierce storm was terrifying. Even with whales at either side, the launch was taking a ferocious beating.

Progress was painfully slow as the waves buffeted them. Eventually they saw the lights of the whaler drawing nearer. Jeremy piloted the launch towards the huge ship's rudder at the rear.

"Lori, get ready!" he shouted. "I'm going to open the throttle and go full speed at them. With the waves against us, I have to stay with the launch."

"No Jeremy!" Lori howled. "You'll be killed!"

"We have no choice – they must be stopped. Find me in the water Lori, but be careful of the ship's propellers. They'll be right beside the rudder."

Lori shouted back to Jeremy, but he was concentrating fully on the controls and couldn't hear her. "Caspian, he'll be killed!"

You can't stop him, Caspian said. *He's determined to do it. He's got to protect the family.*

"By dying?"

"Jeremy won't die," her mother said as she surfaced with Zephyr. "We won't let him." She looked back at all the whales. "Is everyone ready? As soon as it hits, we move in and grab Jeremy."

Lori stayed with Caspian as the launch headed full speed at the whaling ship. She was shaking with fear as she watched her uncle standing at the controls. Even as the launch approached the massive rudder, Jeremy didn't flinch. He remained steady at the helm.

The collision was awful. The moment the launch struck the rudder, it was driven into the whaler's massive propeller. The

237

horrible sound of grinding metal and shattering wood filled the air as the whaling ship appeared to eat the launch. One moment it was there, the next, it was gone.

Suddenly, there was a massive explosion as the large ship's propellers bit into the launch's fuel tank. Everyone in the water felt the blast as the sky lit up with broiling flame.

"Jeremy!" Lori howled. She dove beneath the surface and swam. Whales surrounded her as she and her mother searched through the launch's burning debris for Jeremy.

There! Lori cried, as she saw Jeremy's unconscious body drifting down into the dark sea. Kicking her tail, she cut through the water to her uncle. With Caspian at her side, Lori carried him back up to the surface.

"Mom, over here!" she cried.

Jeremy's face was burned and bleeding and his clothes were in shreds. But as she cradled him in her arms, she heard him moan.

"He's alive!" her mother cried. "Everyone help us! We must get him to Anne on the yacht!"

Chapter 52

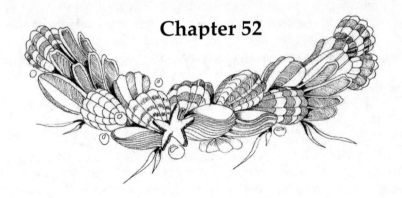

With the storm at its peak, huge waves washed over the top of the yacht and threatened to sink it. But with everyone safely on board and the entire family of whales pressed at the sides, they could fight the raging tempest.

Finally, on the third day, the storm blew itself out and the sun started to rise over a clear, calm sky. Soon the whales rose to the surface to sing their morning song.

Lori woke to the sound of the melody and smiled. True to his promise, Zephyr changed the song and gave it a joyous sound as they celebrated the rescue of her mother and the survival of the whole family.

As she left her cabin, Lori saw Anne carrying an empty tray out of Luc's room. Her aunt had split her time between Luc and Jeremy. She'd removed the bullet in Luc's chest and treated Jeremy's burns and broken bones. As days passed, both her patients were recovering.

"How is Luc?" Lori asked.

"Getting better. He keeps complaining about the taste of the healing moss, but it's saved his life. I do think we have a bigger problem with him though."

"What's wrong?" Lori asked, "Is it because Jeremy killed his father?"

Anne shook her head. "Nope. It's Miranda. I can't get her to leave him alone and he needs his rest."

Lori smiled as she and Anne walked towards the open deck of the yacht. "I think she's got a big crush on him," Lori said.

"I think he's got one for her too."

Outside, Lori looked up to the sun and felt its welcome warmth on her face. She watched Anne sit down beside Jeremy. His face was still bandaged and his left arm in a sling. But he smiled broadly at her approach and put his good arm around her.

"Miranda's not the only one," Lori teased as she winked at her aunt.

"Watch it young lady," her aunt warned, but then laughed.

Her father came to her side. "What's up?"

Lori hugged him and smiled. "Nothing."

Standing together, she and her father looked out at the whales swimming beside the yacht. She saw her beautiful mermaid mother seated on the back of Zephyr, while her grandmother rode Zenith. Her mother's face was beaming as she waved at her, "morning sweetheart!"

"Morning, Mom!"

"We've sure come a long way," her father sighed, as he kissed her on the top of her head.

"Yes we have," Lori said. She looked back in the direction of the rig and couldn't see any traces of the whaling ship following them. Jeremy had been right. Ramming the rudder had disabled it enough for them to slip away. "Do you think they'll come after us?"

Her father shook his head. "Not with Robichaud gone. His men are free to get back to their own lives."

"Yes, but they know about us. Dad, they know mermaids exist."

Caspian surfaced beside the boat. *Would you stop worrying!* He called. *We're all safe for now, let's just celebrate. Come into the water and let's play.*

"What did he say?" her father asked.

When Lori explained, he nodded. "That's a great idea. Go on, you've earned it!"

Not needing to be told twice, Lori stripped down to her nightshirt. Climbing on the bench, she excitedly jumped into the sea where Caspian was waiting for her. Kicking out her long, green tail, Lori swam up to his large eye and kissed him.

"We're free, Caspian!" she cried joyfully as she swam beside the large humpback whale. "Free."